P9-CAX-462

A Gathering of Gunmen

By Howard R. Simpson

A GATHERING OF GUNMEN
JUNIOR YEAR ABROAD
THE JUMPMASTER
RENDEZVOUS OF NEWPORT
THE THREE DAY ALLIANCE
ASSIGNMENT FOR A MERCENARY
TO A SILENT VALLEY

A Gathering of Gunmen

HOWARD R. SIMPSON

PUBLISHED FOR THE CRIME CLUB BY
DOUBLEDAY & COMPANY, INC.
GARDEN CITY, NEW YORK
1987

All of the characters in this book
are fictitious, and any resemblance
to actual persons, living or dead,
is purely coincidental.

Library of Congress Cataloging-in-Publication Data

Simpson, Howard R., 1925–
A gathering of gunmen.

I. Title.
PS3569.I49G38 1987 813'.54 86–29283
ISBN 0-385-24216-6

Printed in the United States of America
First Edition

To Lisa

French Argot

apéro—aperitif
bicot—Arab
bousiller—shoot, hit
détox—detoxification (narcotics)
dur—tough guy
flingueur—gunman, killer
flic—cop
fric—money
gonzesse—wench, broad
gueule de bois—hangover
je m'en fous!—I don't give a damn!
macchabée—corpse
ménesse—woman
mec—guy
motard—motorcycle policeman
nettoyage—cleanup
pétard—pistol
planque—hideout
poulets—policemen
putain—whore
règlement de comptes—settling of accounts, revenge
rouquin—redhead
salaud—scum
salope—slut
schnouff—narcotics
"ta gueule!"—"shut up!"

A Gathering of Gunmen

CHAPTER 1

The Panier district of Marseille was coming to life slowly. It was Saturday morning and the narrow warren of intersecting, steep streets was almost empty. Wet laundry hung from the grilled balconies and shuttered windows. A small pack of mongrels ranged the neighborhood, sniffing and pawing at the black plastic garbage sacks on the street corners. The sun was rising higher, beaming down on the ochre-tiled roofs and patches of damp pavement. Some of the small Arab cafés had been open since eight to serve a clientele of early risers. A truck had parked near the Vietnamese food shops to unload sacks of rice, fish sauce and packets of dried squid. A Senegalese street sweeper with a ragged hat pulled down over his ears was wielding his faggot broom in the gutter, driving a mound of wet refuse downhill toward the Place des Treize Coins.

Professor André Roux, a short, thin man with a sharp nose and a well-trimmed black mustache, was walking carefully over the cobblestones on his way to an archeological dig in the heart of the Panier. He kept his eyes on the ground to avoid dog droppings and slick stretches of sidewalk. Roux was a meticulous man who thoroughly enjoyed his work. He was employed by the city of Marseille and he'd been in charge of restoring the old Roman port discovered a few years earlier, thanks to a civic renovation project. His name was known to the public for his vehement defense of Marseille's archeological treasures in the face of rapacious construction companies and developers.

A heavily laden garbage truck inched along the street toward him. Roux flattened himself against a wall, automatically holding his breath to avoid the sharp odor of decayed food and sour wine. The truck passed with inches to spare. He followed behind it noting with distaste the trail of old wrappers and fluid waste it was leaving in its wake. Though his eyes were focused on the truck, his mind was elsewhere.

He had just returned from an archeological congress in London and he was anxious to see how his assistants and students were progressing on their latest dig. He'd risen early to inspect the site alone. He was always haunted by the thought that someone might interfere or make the wrong decision during his absence. A gust of wind swept up the street. He settled his wool cap more securely on his head and buttoned his leather jacket around his throat. Spring was the time for colds and he couldn't afford to be incapacitated.

He turned down the rue des Phocéens and hurried toward the plank and chicken-wire fence surrounding the dig. The buried Roman baths had been discovered after excavation had begun for a parking lot. A hard-fought political battle had ended in a partial victory for Professor Roux and his supporters. The City Council had given them six months to complete their work. They now had four months left.

The Professor paused at the gate, removed his gloves, and inserted a key in the padlock. The site was on an incline. The completed digging and probing had revealed a series of square baths lined with brick and ceramic tile divided by crumbling walls. The soft sandstone soil had made the work easier and much had been accomplished in a short time. He swung the gate open and closed it after him as the first fingers of sunlight played on the mounds of dirt and the ancient stones.

Roux wanted to insure that his students had exercised the proper caution in uncovering an indentation in the earth he'd discovered before his trip to London. He was certain it was another bath. He hoped it might contain some artifacts or a design that could help him situate the baths in a more precise historical framework.

He turned toward the site and gasped, his mouth open, his arms hanging slack at his side. "*Bonne mère,*" he murmured, blinking.

Three of the excavated baths were occupied. There was a man in each of them. They were flat on their backs. Roux moved closer, half-frozen by fear, driven by curiosity. He stared at each man in turn. They were all well-dressed. Two wore expensive overcoats; one had a felt hat on his head.

"Are you all right?" he said, hopefully, his voice cracking. It was a stupid question. He knew they were far from all right. "They're dead," Roux whispered to himself, "all dead!"

He moved closer and crouched over one of the holes. His analytical mind took over as the initial shock faded. He was looking for the cause of death. There was no apparent wound. The man's eyes were closed; his chubby face had the waxy, drained texture of death and his hands were folded, fingers interlaced on his chest. The professor stood up, noticing that all three had been laid out in the same manner. Each of them was grasping an identical yellow-blossomed mimosa in their lifeless hands.

Commissaire Aynard got through to Inspector Roger Bastide on his third attempt. Aynard, who had planned to spend a quiet weekend with his wife and family, was furious. The Préfet of Police had personally called him at home with news of the Panier killings. The game of bureaucratic one-upmanship Aynard had again lost. The routine—the proper chain of command—would have been for Bastide of homicide to call Aynard and for Aynard to inform the Préfet. Now the whole process had been reversed.

Bastide sat on the edge of his bed completely nude, listening to Aynard's rantings.

"Bastide, you must take things in hand," Aynard was shouting. "Do you want me to handle homicide myself? Killings don't end with the weekend. Have you ever heard of a murderer's truce? No? Neither have I. The Préfet himself informed me. What an embarrassment . . ."

Bastide smoothed his black mustache and contemplated his toes. His dark features were in complete repose, his hazel eyes half-closed. He ran a hand through his salt-and-pepper hair and turned, smiling, to his bed partner. Janine Bourdet was still fast asleep. He looked at the smooth odalisque of her hips under the sheet, the thick black hair on the pillow and the tanned arm hanging off the side of the mattress.

Bastide could tell that Aynard was running down. He had talked himself out of breath. Past experience told him that the Commissaire would soon have to reach for a tablet to calm his raging ulcer. Bastide timed his intervention perfectly.

"Monsieur le Commissaire," he said in a businesslike voice, "it happens that I am not on direct call this weekend. Nevertheless, you were unable to reach me because Mattei had just telephoned about the incident in the Panier. At this moment I'm preparing to meet him at the site."

There were a few seconds of silence as Commissaire Aynard digested this bit of information. Bastide decided to push his counterattack a bit further.

"If you recall," he continued, "my off-duty status this weekend is in direct compliance with your recent memorandum . . . the one that mentioned the importance of rest for your overworked staff . . ."

"Yes, yes," Aynard retorted impatiently, "I'm perfectly aware of my own orders. But the Préfet . . ."

"The Préfet, Monsieur le Commissaire, has an office full of eager acolytes who work the entire weekend and delight in sticking their noses into our business."

"*Doucement,* Bastide," Aynard replied, "we're all on the same team."

Bastide smiled to himself, knowing he'd planted a further worry in Aynard's suspicious mind. "Sir," he continued, "if you agree, I would now like to proceed."

"Very well," Aynard said grudgingly. "You've heard what this is about?"

"It sounds like a gang killing."

"What it *sounds* like doesn't interest me," Aynard snapped. "I want the facts, and quickly. Understood?"

"Yes, Monsieur le Commissaire." Why, Bastide thought as he replaced the receiver, couldn't they have kept Aynard in Lyon where he belongs?

Bastide rose and began to dress. He pulled on his gray slacks and yesterday's blue shirt, pushed his feet into an old pair of espadrilles and went to the kitchen to make some coffee. He put the espresso pot on the burner and peeled a tangerine, watching the first tourist launch of the morning cut through the calm water of the Vieux Port on its way to the Château d'If.

He frowned, reflecting on Aynard's call. Mattei had telephoned before he'd been to the scene. He'd only known what had been reported: three corpses laid out in the archeological digs in the Panier. Bastide had a premonition that this was the beginning of something big. Informers, unofficial tips and reports picked up in Paris, Lyon and Nice all indicated the strong possibility that Grondona, undisputed chief of the Nice underworld, was about to move on Marseille. The shooting of "Mr. Jack" Boldani in full daylight on the Canebière and the arrest of the financiers of the French-Sicilian narcotics connection in January had created a power vacuum in the city. Antoine Mondolino was struggling to keep his hold on the Marseille rackets but he was old and Boldani's death had made him cautious.

Bastide waited for the espresso pot to stop bubbling and poured himself a small cup of the strong coffee. He leaned back against the butcher chopping block, noting that the tress of garlic hanging over his cooking range was almost finished. He sipped the coffee and stifled a yawn. He and Janine had attended a dinner the night before at La Mère Pascal. Dominique, the proprietor, had been celebrating the first communion of her nephew from Allauch. They had eaten well and drunk too much wine. Bastide put his cup on the sink, took one last look at the Vieux Port, and returned to the bedroom in search of a necktie.

Janine was still on her side, breathing evenly. He decided not to shave, knowing she'd be awakened by his moving around the bathroom. He tiptoed to the washbasin and threw some cold water over his face and neck. He opened a drawer in a bleached pine commode in the bedroom and found a revolver. He picked up his shoes from the closet and selected a well-worn tweed jacket and shut the bedroom door gently. He'd asked Mattei to send a car from the Hôtel de Police. With luck, it should be waiting for him downstairs.

Barnabé, "Babar," Mattei crouched beside Dr. Colona, the police pathologist, watching him complete his cursory examination of the last corpse. Mattei was a broad-shouldered, handsome Corsican. When there were no women around he tended to relax his stomach muscles and let his belly protrude over his belt. The heavy, hand-tooled Manurhin .357 Magnum holstered on his right hip created another bulge under Mattei's wrinkled blue blazer.

"Perfect," Dr. Colona remarked, straightening up and wiping his hands on a small towel. The doctor had obviously dressed hurriedly. A pyjama collar protruded from his coat. "I'll go further once we get them into the morgue. But there's no doubt. It's a professional job. I would say a pistol, .22 long rifle. Each shot identical . . . below the right ear."

The doctor lowered his head and looked at Mattei over the top of his bifocals. "I'm afraid you've got your gang war," he said ruefully.

"What do you make of the mimosa?" Mattei asked, glancing over his shoulder at the curious crowd gathering on the rue des Phocéens.

The doctor shrugged. "I'm not a witch doctor," he replied. "I'm sure you can read the ju-ju signs of the milieu better than I can. Do you know who they are?"

Mattei stared for a moment at the body before answering. "The one with the hat is Bernardo Mille, one of Mondolino's 'pistoleros.' The type over there is Paul Frigano, the restaurant owner. This one, I don't know. Can I start disturbing them? I'd like to go through their pockets."

"Certainly, I'm finished for the moment. Call me later."

Mattei watched the doctor leave the site before turning back to the corpse. He lifted the overcoat and searched the man's inner pockets for a wallet. A uniformed policeman appeared, out of breath.

"Ah, Brigadier," Mattei greeted him, "move those people away from the fence. This isn't a freak show." The Brigadier hurried back to the gate, shouting to his men.

Mattei went through the wallet carefully, noting its contents: 900 francs in notes of 100; a Visa card; assorted family photos taken with an instant camera; and a dog-eared identity card. He pulled the card from its plastic framed pocket and read it. Auguste Imbert had died in his fifty-sixth year. He'd lived at the Avenue des Goums in Aubagne. He'd been a wine merchant. Mattei turned Imbert's head to the left and examined the wound. It was a perfect hole, small, blue and puckered, surrounded by a crust of dried blood. He could imagine the small slug driving upward into the brain, deformed and flattened by bone contact, ripping through the cortex to turn out Imbert's lights. Colona was right. Only gunmen who knew their business would rely on such a light-caliber piece. Mattei deduced the three men had been executed while in captivity. Even a pro couldn't place such perfect shots on the fly.

The Brigadier returned as Mattei searched Imbert's other pockets. He found an opened packet of Gitane cigarettes, an expensive gold lighter and a set of car keys. He took a small plastic bag from his pocket and filled it with what he'd found.

"You can move this one now," Mattei told the Brigadier before walking over the uneven ground toward the excavated bath occupied by Bernardo Mille's body. Mille looked strangely peaceful in his temporary tomb.

"Pauvre mec," Mattei muttered, beginning his search. "Not much fun on the receiving end, eh?" He'd known Mille would eventually end like this. There were too many killings on the gunman's record to allow him the privilege of a natural death. Mattei's practiced hand moved over the fatty rolls of Mille's body till it contacted a leather strap on Imbert's chest. He followed it to the empty shoulder holster. Mille had obviously gone to his last rendezvous armed.

"How's the undertaking business?" Inspector Bastide asked. He was standing behind Mattei, lighting a Havana cigar.

"Bonjour, Roger," Mattei greeted him. "Welcome to the Panier."

"Putain!" Bastide cursed. "It's a damn cemetery."

"You recognize our late playmates?" Mattei asked gesturing toward the occupied baths. "Mille, Frigano, and this lump is Imbert, Auguste . . . from Aubagne."

Bastide crouched beside Mattei for a better look at Imbert's corpse.

"What's he doing with the bad boys?" Bastide asked.

"I hope to find out soon," Mattei replied.

Bastide noticed the sprigs of mimosa. He whistled quietly and Mattei understood the significance of his reaction. It had been almost five years since the last major gang murders in Nice. The dead of the losing side had all borne the same trademark: a sprig of fuzzy, yellow-blossomed mimosa. The murders had established the Grondona family as the regulators of the Nice underworld and they hadn't been challenged since.

Bastide picked up a chunk of earth and squeezed it into dust. "They're making their move," he said flatly. "Don't expect any leave for the next few months."

"Do you suppose Mondolino knows yet?" Mattei asked.

"He'll hear soon enough. The reporters from the *Méridional* and the *Provençal* are on the other side of the fence but before they get back to their papers someone will have passed the word to Mondolino. Le Panier is one big underground telegraph. Who found them?"

"A city archeologist," Mattei explained. "He's over there by the gate. Want to talk to him?"

"Not now. Bring him into the office. I've got to get on the radio to the anti-gang people. They can share this windfall. Don't leave any of the mimosa behind."

Bastide walked to the gate and a policeman opened it for him. The street was crowded with gapers blocked on the far sidewalk by the portable barriers a police van had just delivered.

"Inspector," someone called. Bastide raised his head trying to identify who had called to him. Then he spotted the bearlike form of Michel Lanzi, a crime reporter from a leading Marseille daily. "When are you going to let us in?" Lanzi shouted, indicating a group of his colleagues waiting impatiently behind the police line.

Bastide walked toward them, head down, puffing on his cigar.

"Do you have a statement?" Lanzi asked, the morning sun glinting from his thick glasses.

"No statement," Bastide replied. "You can get something later at the Hôtel de Police. But you can go in now." He glanced at the photographers. "Do the families and your readers a favor . . . no closeups. Brigadier!" he called over his shoulder. "Let this pack in for ten minutes . . . then they're out."

Lanzi hung back as the others rushed for the gate. *"Alors?"* he asked, "who are they?"

"You'll recognize two of them," Bastide replied.

"Règlement de comptes?" Lanzi asked.

"Go see for yourself," Bastide replied, turning toward his car.

"It's les Niçois, isn't it?" Lanzi ventured, keeping pace with Bastide.

"You tell your own fairy tales," Bastide replied. *"I've* got work to do."

He increased his pace, leaving Lanzi behind, and slid into the police car beside Jean Lenoir, a young detective from the homicide division.

"What's up?" Lenoir asked eagerly.

"Three cold ones from the Mondolino gang," Bastide told him.

"Oh là, là!" Lenoir exclaimed. "That's not good."

"As you say," Bastide agreed, lifting the mike of the car radio to call headquarters. He got through to the central quickly but had no luck with the anti-gang squad. He was told they'd been called out on a special alert. He replaced the mike, wondering what could have pulled all of them away from the office. He didn't have to wait long for a response. As Lenoir drove down the rue des Phocéens and turned into the rue de la République they received an emergency call for Bastide. Automatic-weapons fire had been reported on the rue Henri Tomasi in Mazargues. There had been a death.

"Let's go!" Bastide said tersely. Lenoir didn't need any urging; he'd already flicked on the police klaxon and increased their speed. They streaked down the broad street, fishtailed through the slowing traffic and rocketed through a red light.

"Take the Corniche," Bastide ordered, opening the glove compartment and unfolding a street map to find the rue Henri Tomasi. They drove around the Vieux Port and up the hill past the Fort Saint-Nicolas. A second call told them there were now two dead. Bastide suddenly realized his cigar was out. He rolled down the window and tossed it onto the street. They skidded around a curve. Lenoir steadied the vehicle, passed two city buses and applied more speed as they sped down the hill toward the Prado beach. They slowed as they turned toward Mazargues hampered by the narrow streets and more traffic. Bastide cursed under his breath as he watched the slow, grudging reaction of drivers. They were either deaf or oblivious to the police klaxon. Lenoir was bumper to bumper with one sedan before the driver pulled over to let them pass.

When they reached the rue Henri Tomasi, Bastide recognized two cars of the anti-gang squad pulled up on the sidewalk. A blue van and several uniformed policemen were blocking the street. Lenoir pulled to a stop. Bastide jumped out of the car, listening for the sound of firing. There was none. Only the buzzing and static of police radios. He rushed forward and Lenoir followed. Two members of the anti-gang squad were coming toward them. One was wounded and being supported by a colleague. The wounded man's right leg was covered with blood.

"Give them a hand," Bastide told Lenoir, breaking into a run. A group of plainclothes policemen were gathered in the middle of the street. He recognized Joe Bellot, chief of the anti-gang squad. Bellot had just emptied his Magnum of empty shell cases. He looked up at Bastide's approach. In his pullover jacket and light slacks Bellot looked like an athlete who'd just finished a trying performance. His eyes were bright with excitement and tension.

"You missed it," he told Bastide, taking a deep breath.

"What the hell happened?" Bastide asked.

"Come on," Bellot said, gesturing, "I'll show you. What's left is yours."

Bellot led him past a Catholic school to a walled villa and pushed open a squeaking iron gate. There was a man face down on the concrete walkway, a halo of scarlet blood around his head. Two members of the anti-gang squad were standing over him.

"Look," Bellot said, holstering his Magnum, "over there."

Bastide walked to a small cactus garden and saw the dull mat finish of a Heckler & Koch submachine gun lying among the stones.

"The bastard's last shot caught Santelli in the leg," Bellot explained. "Luckily his magazine was finished or we'd be picking pieces of Santelli off the wall. The real damage is inside."

Bellot led Bastide into the villa. It was cold and dark. The polished wood floors were covered with Oriental rugs. The walls were hung with small etchings of old Marseille. There was a musky odor in the hall but when they stepped into the salon Bastide inhaled the cloying odor of fresh blood and the acid tang of urine.

"Oh, *merde!*" Bastide murmured. The far wall of the room looked as if someone had worked it over with a buzz saw. Individual bullet holes were difficult to identify. Slugs had chopped into the hardwood in compact patterns, ripping out furrows, splintering trim and exposing electric wires. The wall was spattered and smeared with blood. One body had slid to the floor in a sitting position but half the head was missing. A messy gob of gray-and-pink brain tissue was resting on the corpse's left shoulder. Exposed intestines were showing through the shredded material of the man's suit.

Bellot put his hand on Bastide's shoulder and guided him to the stairway. The second body was on the first landing, flat on its back. A Colt .45 lay nearby. A storm of automatic fire had caught the victim just above the waist. Bastide looked away and cleared his throat. They both walked down the stairs and out into the fresh air.

"Well," Bastide said, "what's the story?"

"We got a report of firing. At first I thought it wasn't our business. Then we checked the address. The villa belongs to René Bonta. That made it our business."

"Bonta? Mondolino's accountant?"

"Correct. René, *'le cerveau,'* as he was known in the milieu."

"Who's on the stairs?" Bastide asked.

"You didn't look closely enough," Bellot replied. "It's George Serp. You remember Serp. He was Mondolino's bodyguard until he took on some age and the old man assigned him to watch over Bonta."

Bastide nodded. "Serp was a great one for the horses," he said, remembering.

"Horses and whores," Bellot agreed. "He loved them both."

Bastide walked back to the body in the garden. "Any identification?" he asked one of the detectives.

"He's clean," the detective responded. "Not even a *franc* in his pocket."

"Did you hear about le Panier?" Bastide asked.

"I heard them calling Mattei earlier on the radio. What's up?"

"We found three of Mondolino's people laid out in an archeological dig. Bernardo Mille, Paul Frigano and a certain Auguste Imbert."

Bellot's eyes widened. *"Ça alors!"* he exclaimed.

"They had sprigs of mimosa in their hands."

"Bingo," Bellot murmured. "Grondona and Company."

"I'm afraid so," Bastide said. "Aynard better start requesting reinforcements and Colona will have to empty the morgue for new arrivals."

"If we could stop the bastards before they really get rolling . . ." Bellot said wistfully.

"You're a dreamer," Bastide replied as they walked back to their cars. "Mondolino isn't going to take this sitting down. He may be old but he's got his 'honor' to consider."

Jean Lenoir was on the sidewalk dabbing at his bloodstained jacket with a wet handkerchief. Bellot looked at Bastide and raised his eyebrows in an unspoken question.

"He helped Santelli get to the ambulance," Bastide explained.

"Ah, good," Bellot said. "Thanks."

"It was nothing," Lenoir replied, "but my wife will be furious. She bought me this jacket for my birthday."

"Allez," Bellot said, shaking hands with Bastide and Lenoir. "I'm off. We'll try to identify the H and K enthusiast. I've already ordered a twenty-four hour stakeout on Mondolino's villa. Are you informing Aynard?"

"Oh no, you don't," Bastide replied, shaking his head. "You were here first. The dead may be ours but you people have the smoking guns. You can contact the Commissaire."

Antoine Mondolino's old Provençal villa stood in solitary splendor among a scattering of boxlike high-rise apartment houses in Redon, an eastern suburb of Marseille. Over the years . . . despite pressures from the city government . . . he'd managed to retain his six *hectares* of land and preserve the tall pines and cypresses that screened the villa from the new developments and the ugly, flat-topped supermarket that had come with them. Mondolino had held onto the villa, deaf to his grandchildren's pleas to sell it and move out of Marseille. He had grown up in the villa. He intended to die in it. Even when he'd spent five years in jail in the 1960s he'd seen to it that no one laid a hand on the property.

The three-story villa had a peaked roof of russet tiles, thick walls of stone covered with ochre facing and an extensive, well-kept rose garden divided by gravel walks. It was cool in the summer and warm during the winter months. The dining room with its ancient, hand-carved oaken table was hung with dark oil paintings on religious themes by long-forgotten Italian painters. There was a large ebony crucifix over the entry door, brought back from the Ivory coast by Mondolino's brother, a Jesuit missionary. Antoine Mondolino used the dining room for his business dinners. One was now underway. There were four men at the table with Mondolino. They were eating their first course of *céleri-rave* in silence except for the clink of cutlery and the sound of wine being poured by a male servant.

Mondolino sat at the head of the table, a sagging figure in a heavy black suit. His head seemed too large for his body. His thick white hair was tinged with yellow as if it had been exposed to too much tobacco smoke. He ate methodically, forking the shredded celeriac into his mouth at regular intervals and pausing to wipe the mustardy mayonnaise from his plate with pieces of fugasse, the salty local bread, broken from the loaf in the silver bread basket. He rarely looked up. When he did his small dark eyes darted around the table, observing each of his guests as if he were trying to guess their thoughts. Mondolino was the only one at the table not drinking wine. A carafe of mineral water stood at his elbow. His servant took special care to see that Mondolino's glass was refilled periodically.

Paul Campagna sat to the right of the old man. He'd reached his place of authority in the Mondolino "family" due to an uncanny ability to remain one step ahead of the police and three steps ahead of his gangland rivals. Campagna had managed to emerge spotless in times of crisis be it a narcotics bust, the breakup of a prostitution ring or the collapse of a protection racket. He was always careful to insure that no direct or legal links could be traced to Antoine Mondolino. Campagna had begun his career as a small-time enforcer on the Marseille docks but promotion had come quickly. Few would have been able to link him now with the young, tattooed punk who'd learned to use a cargo hook as a deadly weapon. Campagna had become a model of the respectable citizen. He bought his expensive clothes from Sulka, his thick, graying hair was always blow-dried to perfection and his nails were manicured and buffed.

Marcel Perret sat on Mondolino's left. He was the investor, the launderer, the man who saw to it that illegal funds were cleansed and transferred into legitimate operations with high returns. Perret affected the relaxed intellectual look: heavy-framed glasses, wool turtleneck and a sport jacket.

The two other guests were opposites. Arnaud, "le Rouquin," Haro commanded Mondolino's "troops." He was tall, rawboned and redhaired. The two hitches he'd served in the Marine infantry as a sergeant had provided him with his expertise in weaponry and a gift for selecting the right man for the right job. Bachir Moukli, a middle-age Algerian with a taste for light cotton suits and ice cream shoes, owed his presence at the table to Mondolino's understanding of the ebb and flow of power in Marseille. Fifteen years earlier Moukli would have been lucky to get as far as the servant's entrance to the villa. But things had changed. Moukli represented the North African underworld of the city; a group that Antoine Mondolino found more useful as allies than as enemies.

The impersonal silence continued as dishes were cleared away and the fish course appeared: a large baked *dorade,* scored, napped with tomato sauce and covered with onion rings. Antoine Mondolino waited several minutes after the last man was served before posing his question.

"Is it good?" he asked, his throaty voice erupting from deep in his chest.

"*Magnifique!*" Campagna enthused, nodding his head.

"*Délicieux!*" Perret commented.

"*Parfait!*" Haro chimed in.

"*Quel parfum!*" Moukli added, "You'd find no better in Algiers."

Mondolino smiled at the unanimous hommage. The meal continued through a course of rare roast beef with firm new potatoes, a cheese board and a salad. There was no dessert but each guest was served a small cup of strong black coffee and a bottle of marc was left on the table. They filled their *digestif* glasses, passing the marc around the table, and turned toward Mondolino, waiting.

The old man took his time. He rolled his napkin with care, his bony hand shaking slightly and pushed it into an ivory napkin ring before reaching for his glass.

"To Bernardo, Paul and Auguste," Mondolino finally said, offering a toast.

They all drank and put their empty glasses down on the embroidered tablecloth.

Mondolino turned to Campagna and nodded, signaling for him to speak. "Grondona has made a monumental error," Campagna said. "We were willing to listen to reason but his ears were closed. He has gone too far. But his treachery doesn't excuse our laxity. The three friends we've just toasted were like our flesh and blood. We failed them. It must not happen again. Everyone must be mobilized. Our defenses must be tightened at the same time we hit back. Understood?"

There was a murmur of assent around the table and the bottle of marc was passed again.

"Haro," Campagna said, "tell us of tomorrow."

Arnaud Haro wiped his mouth with a napkin and cleared his throat. "Maurice Alberti, Grondona's son-in-law, is living his last hours," Haro told them. "Russo is handling the details."

"He has children?" Mondolino asked quietly, turning his glass of mineral water slowly on the tablecloth.

"Two," Haro replied. "And his wife is four months pregnant with a third."

"Perfect," Mondolino said quietly. "Now let us talk of the situation in Marseille."

Maurice Alberti stopped to admire some yellow jonquils and chat with a young man who was unloading them from a delivery van. The Nice flower market was a bright eruption of color, a vibrant watercolor brushed by an exuberant artist. Some of the vendors were still setting up their wooden stands, others had already begun to trade in a profusion of white, purple and pink stock plants, scarlet tulips and blue, yellow and red primavera. A patch of green plants divided the trays of pansies from the anemonies and cineraria. One stand featured cut branches full of apple and cherry blossoms and bright sprays of forsythia. There were thick pots of blue-and-rust-colored heathers. Bunches of yellow and pink long-stemmed roses were wrapped in wax paper and the fresh cut mimosa was piled like a golden snowfall for the customer's selection.

Alberti was walking to his law office from his apartment on the Boulevard Jean Jaurès. He took the same route each day when the weather was good. He found it a perfect prelude to his working day and a method of keeping in touch with the city he loved. Alberti was a short, stout man of forty who affected sober suits and an old-fashioned gold watch chain to impress his clients. He had the unlined face of a family man at peace with himself. Many of the flower vendors greeted him by his first name as he passed. He returned their salutations with a wave and a smile. He flattered himself that his popularity was not due solely to being Bartolomei Grondona's son-in-law. He had made his own name in Nice. He believed in keeping a respectable distance from Grondona's business. Grondona would have it no other way. When Alberti had married his daughter Teresa ten years earlier, Grondona had advised him to steer a different course.

"It will be best for Teresa," Grondona had said. "My world is not yours."

Alberti had been grateful and he'd increased the distance by dropping criminal law and concentrating on property transactions and disputes. His children saw their grandfather only on special occasions and feast days.

As Alberti reached the far end of the market he decided to buy some flowers to brighten up his office.

"*Salut*, Monsieur Alberti," an elderly, shawl-draped woman greeted him. "What will it be today? Roses? Or some of these tulips? They'll last a long time if you treat them right."

"*Bonjour,* Marie," he said, running his fingers over his chin. "The roses are beautiful. Let me have those red ones."

The black Citröen sedan moved slowly down the street, avoiding the parked vans and the stacked crates. It pulled to a stop, its engine running. A man got out, readjusted his three-quarter camel hair coat and turned up the soft collar. He was wearing dark glasses and his hat was pulled low on his forehead. He began to walk toward the last stall.

The vendor completed her wrapping and handed the roses to Alberti. He paid her and turned away, certain that the flowers would please his secretary.

"Maître Alberti!" someone called. Alberti swung around, expecting to see a client or someone from the court.

The man in the camel hair coat was seven feet from Alberti. He raised his right arm, leveled a target pistol with a silencer and pulled the trigger twice. The spaced thuds were lost in the tumult of the market. Even the old woman who'd sold the mimosa was oblivious to what was happening. Maurice Alberti sunk to his knees, dropped the bouquet and fell backward onto a pile of discarded carnations. The gunman walked quickly to the waiting Citröen.

"*Ça va?*" the driver asked as they pulled away from the curb.

"No problem," Tonin Russo replied. "Right eye and left forehead. His clients will have to find a new lawyer."

Bartolomei Grondona was in a state of high agitation. He paced the broad marble terrace of his apartment with an unlit, twisted Italian stogie clamped between his teeth. He was a corpulent man with a deep tan and smooth shaven head. His nose was a protruding monument of bumpy flesh, a deformed *brioche* some careless baker had hurried from the oven. René Polito, his old friend and assistant, stood with both hands on the balcony railing, staring down at the Promenade des Anglais, the beach of Nice and the broad blue green sweep of the Baie des Anges.

"Who could it be?" Grondona asked, pausing to tighten the belt of his blue-and-white-striped bathrobe. "There is no one else strong enough to challenge Mondolino. No one so stupid."

"At this moment," Polito replied, "I don't have the least idea. I hope to know soon." He was younger and darker than Grondona. His black hair was long but well-trimmed, his dark eyes set close together.

Polito's wool suit had been cut in London and there were stylish leather patches on the elbows.

Grondona stopped by a Roman amphora planted with red geraniums and ran his stubby fingers over the leaves. "I don't understand," he murmured. "I was going to take the peaceful path. I had decided to talk to Mondolino myself. You yourself said a war for Marseille would bleed us white. I was willing to be reasonable. Is that not right?"

"It is true," Polito agreed. "Someone obviously wants a war between us."

Grondona joined Polito at the railing. "We've got to make contact with Mondolino immediately," he said. "He must know it wasn't us."

"Do you think he'll believe us?"

"The old bastard must! If not, we'll have a war we don't want. The police will stand back and applaud while we kill each other."

Grondona struck a match and lit his cigar, staring out at the shimmering expanse of sea. "Could it be the Sicilians?" he pondered, "or the North Africans?"

Polito shook his head. "The Sicilians are thin on the ground in Marseille now. They took a beating two years ago. They have too many problems at home. Mondolino has the North Africans under control. He's got Moukli on his council. If they stepped out of line the old man would stamp on them."

"Any other ideas?" Grondona asked.

"No."

"Well," Grondona sighed, blinking through the acrid smoke of his stogie, "get to Campagna. Tell him it wasn't us. Tell him I want to meet with Mondolino urgently . . . someplace discreet. There is much at stake here for both of us. For once, we have the same enemy."

Polito was leaving when the doorbell rang. Grondona's white-jacketed valet and bodyguard ushered a visitor onto the terrace.

"*Salut,* Henri," Grondona greeted the newcomer without warmth. "What brings you here?" The visitor removed his hat as a sign of respect. His face was a mass of wrinkles and his thin gray mustache looked as if it had been stuck in place with glue. He was obviously nervous. "Well?!" Grondona demanded impatiently, "what is it?"

"It's your son-in-law," he replied gravely. "He was hit this morning on his way to work."

Grondona's fleshy face went white. Even his purple-veined nose lost its color. He took the unfinished cigar from his lips and dropped it onto the terrace tiles.

"Dead?" Polito asked.

The visitor nodded, his thin fingers kneading the brim of his hat.

"Bon Dieu," Grondona murmured, *"bon Dieu!* My poor Teresa!"

"Who did it," Polito demanded.

The visitor shrugged.

Grondona grasped himself with both arms and groaned. "My little girl a widow!" he muttered, "her children without a father. There is no God in heaven!" He took a handkerchief from his pocket and wiped his eyes. "Does she know yet?" he asked.

"I thought you should know first."

Grondona nodded. "You can go now, Henri," he said. "Wait outside." Grondona spoke only when the visitor had left. His voice was hard but controlled. "Who did it? There is no mystery. It was the whore's son, Mondolino, that stinking bag of old bones!"

"We are not sure . . ." Polito began.

"I am sure," Grondona shouted. "Bartolomei Grondona knows who murdered his son-in-law and made his daughter a widow. Who else could it be? Who would gun down an innocent lawyer?" He paused to blow his nose and viciously kicked the butt of his stogie into a drain.

"Very well," Grondona continued, nodding his head slowly, "the bastard has asked for it. There will be no peace. I don't know who stacked his people in the Panier but it will be nothing compared with what will happen now."

"Bartolomei," Polito pleaded, hands extended, "maybe it wasn't Mondolino. I know this has been a shock. I feel for you. But we must be certain. Let me meet with them."

"No!" Grondona bellowed, the veins of his neck swelling. "I forbid it. I want them all planted . . . for good. I want the old man to suffer as I have. Tighten security. We'll need more people in Marseille. Send only the best. Now get out of here."

Grondona looked out at the bay a long time after Polito had left. His jaw was working and his eyes were full of tears. He would have to hurry if he was to tell his daughter the news before she heard it from someone else.

CHAPTER 2

"Babar" Mattei sighed, waiting for the *patron* of the Café des Colonies to answer his question. The *patron* rubbed his hairy forearms and looked up at the cracked plaster of the ceiling, making a great show of heavy concentration. Mattei finished his coffee and glanced at his watch. It was almost noon but they were alone at the bar. Mattei guessed the regular customers had seen his car outside and decided to wait for his departure before drifting in for their usual *apéro.*

"I don't remember," the *patron* finally said.

"Unbelievable," Mattei commented, exasperated. "You were right where you are now. It was about six months ago when I was working on the murder of that American student. Two of them: one was older, all wrinkled, the other had a scar from his mouth to his ear and a lot of hair. They said they were from Lyon but they were lying. They were from Nice. No doubt about it. Bouche d'Or and Georges Astier were here too."

The *patron* began to wipe the formica bar top with application. "People come and go," he said, wondering how long Mattei was going to torment him. Running an underworld rendezvous like the Café des Colonies was no picnic. He was still trying to make up the losses he'd suffered during his own prison stay at les Baumettes and Mattei's visits were bad for business.

Mattei tried a different approach. He indicated a copy of *le Méridional* on one of the café's tables.

"You read this morning's paper?" he asked.

"Yes . . . the sports page."

"Oh," Mattei asked, "then you missed it?"

"Missed what?"

"Come now," Mattei said, "you skipped the front page. You didn't notice that the bodies of Mille, Frigano and Imbert had been found in the Panier?"

"All I know is that the Olympic of Marseille is going to have a new coach and that 'Golden Legs' won the race yesterday at Bonneveine."

The door swung open and Bouche d'Or hesitated on the threshold. The aging pimp's face turned blank. He stood off-balance for several seconds vainly trying to think of a graceful escape.

"Come in, come in," Mattei greeted him. He walked over and put his arm around Bouche d'Or's shoulder, propelling him toward the bar. "Give my friend a Ricard," Mattei beamed. "I'm glad you're here," he continued. "I'd like you to hear what I'm telling *le patron.*"

Bouche d'Or shifted uneasily, watching his drink being poured. He resembled a furless ferret. When Mattei relaxed his grip, Bouche d'Or moved a few steps away, a grotesque, unnatural grin on his face.

Mattei picked up the newspaper and held it up so Bouche d'Or could see the first page.

"What do you say to that?" Mattei asked.

"Sad," Bouche d'Or mumbled, reaching for his *pastis.*

"Exactly," Mattei agreed. "But things will become worse. We'll have a war on our hands. Nice versus Marseille. It won't be a game of football. It's Mondolino versus Grondona and I wouldn't want to be in the middle, would you?"

Bouche d'Or shrugged. The *patron* ignored the question.

"You see," Mattei continued, "I'm afraid you're already in the middle. When Mondolino finds out two of Grondona's people were in here six months ago he's going to get curious. He'll want to know why they picked the Café des Colonies. Was it because you serve such delicious coffee? Or was it because they had business here? If you were Mondolino, what would you think? First of all, you'd know that the coffee is concentrated camel piss. Then you'd get suspicious. When old man Mondolino gets suspicious it can be very dangerous."

"Listen, Mattei," the *patron* replied. "We're big boys. We can take care of ourselves. I might pay my taxes on time if you had other things to do but harass ordinary citizens."

Mattei laughed. He reached into his pocket, fished out some coins and paid for the drinks. "Pay your taxes?" He laughed again. "When you pay your taxes, virgins will reappear on the Côte d'Azur. Very well, the 'harassment' will now stop. I'd hoped you'd be more cooperative. But *tant pis.* For your own good I suggest you explain to

Mondolino's boys what those two hoods from Nice were doing here. *Au revoir.*"

The patron and Bouche d'Or watched Mattei drive off in silence. "Well," Bouche d'Or finally asked, "what do you think? Are you going to contact Mondolino's crowd?"

"I already have," the *patron* responded, shaking out a stained bar towel and hanging it on the spigot of the espresso machine. "Someone's coming by this afternoon. We've got nothing to fear. I can't control who comes into my café!"

Bouche d'Or was not reassured. He didn't like the patron's use of "we." "They'll want to know why you hadn't mentioned the visitors from Nice before," he suggested.

"Mattei's just trying to stir up trouble," the patron said. "I've done favors for Mondolino before. Nothing to worry about."

Bouche d'Or downed his Ricard hurriedly. "One of my girls is in the hospital," he said. "I promised to visit her today."

"Have another drink," the *patron* urged. "Wait for the others to arrive. Astier should be here soon."

"No thanks, I've got to hurry."

For several minutes after Bouche d'Or's departure, the *patron* stood with both hands on the bar, with his mouth pursed and a furrowed brow. He finally walked into the back room of the café and opened a tall cabinet built into the far wall. He rummaged through some old paint-smeared clothes and stiff brushes until he found what he was looking for. He lifted a packet, unwound its covering of oily rags and pulled out a well-cared-for sawed-off shotgun. The double barreled widowmaker's stock had been cut at the hand grip. The *patron* broke the weapon and reached up to a higher shelf for a box of shells. He loaded the shotgun, put two extra shells in his pocket and returned to the bar. He paused for a moment before concealing the weapon within easy reach under the counter. He wiped some oil from his hands with the bar towel and surveyed the empty street. It was late. He was surprised that none of his regulars had yet appeared.

Joe Bellot of the anti-gang squad and Roger Bastide had agreed to meet for lunch at Le Haiphong. The Vietnamese owner, a friend of Bastide's and a veteran of French special operations units in Indochina and Algeria, had reserved a table for them at the rear of the restaurant. He'd made a point of isolating them from the other customers. Dinh Le Thong was still a contract employee of the Direction de la Sécurité du Territoire and he knew when professionals needed to be alone.

Bellot arrived first. Thong greeted him at the door and offered to take his leather jacket but Bellot declined. As a compromise he handed Thong his wool scarf and followed him to the table. Bellot hadn't visited Le Haiphong before. He asked for a beer and surveyed the premises. He observed the lacquered red walls, the dragon paneling, the wood-paneled bar with its bouquet of plastic flowers and looked over his shoulder toward the kitchen door.

"*Voilà,*" Thong announced, pouring some Kronenbourg into a glass and putting the glass and bottle on the table. "The rear door is always double locked from the inside," Thong said softly. "Something I learned a long time ago in my own country."

Bellot watched Thong hurry to greet some customers and tried to remember what he'd heard about him in the past. Bastide had once said that Thong was worth a squad of paras when it came to a showdown. He also knew that the husky, gray-haired Vietnamese maintained a disciplined intelligence network within the Indochinese community in the Bouches du Rhône. He was pondering this when Bastide arrived.

"*Salut!*" Bastide said, sliding into their booth. "Sorry to be late. Aynard had me in the pan again."

Bellot chuckled. "What's his problem now?"

"The usual. He's wetting his pants about how Paris will react to our gang war. He hasn't panicked yet, but he's close to it. He's having visions of himself as a peacemaker between Grondona and Mondolino!"

Bellot sipped his beer and shook his head. He had the dark good looks of a tired Alain Delon. The bags under his brown eyes were the legacy of innumerable sleepless nights and interminable, fruitless stakeouts.

"Where did they ever find Aynard?" he asked, a note of despair in his voice.

"He's a clone of our system," Bastide replied, signaling to Thong for a bottle of wine. "A measure of politician, a pinch of Préfet, a dash of Machiavelli and two drops of policeman topped with frightened rabbit sauce."

Thong reappeared with a chilled bottle of rosé, uncorked it and poured a small measure in Bastide's glass.

"What's this?" Bastide demanded. "You're asking me to taste a rosé before pouring? *Mon ami*, you've been serving too many tourists!"

"You'll change your mind when you put this on your tongue," Thong reassured him. "It's a 1981 Sancerre rosé from Chavignol. Go ahead, taste it."

Bastide, still doubtful, raised his glass, sniffed the wine and filled his mouth. He raised his eyebrows in surprise and swallowed. He nodded his approval. "As the experts would say—aggressive but fruity," he told Thong. "I would say it's a rare but real rosé."

"I knew you'd like it," Thong smiled. "I've taken the liberty of ordering your lunch. I have a new chef from Bangkok. He's Vietnamese but he learned to cook Thai while waiting to come to France. You will be surprised. My niece will serve you. You will not be disturbed."

"A sympathetic type," Bellot commented when Thong had left them.

"Rock solid," Bastide said. "He saved my ass more than once in Algiers. But that's the past. Let's talk about our current problem. Joe, you and I will have to work together on this one, whether our boys like it or not."

"Easier said than done," Bellot said ruefully. "I don't have to tell you that some of my gang are 'cowboys.' They're always itching for action and I have to sit on them hard to keep them in line."

"I know," Bastide replied, "but this city already looks like the OK Corral. The least we can do is see that the body count doesn't include our own."

"Any ideas?" Bellot asked.

"Number one, we shouldn't try to act as buffers. If we're in the middle it will just mean double the fire power aimed in our direction. It won't do much good for us to pick up the small fry. We should go for them only when we have to—when the public is threatened. Our real target should be the head of the serpent—Grondona—the man who started it."

"You are a dreamer," Bellot said. "Grondona's like a goat in a clover field. We've been working on his case for six years. Result, one big zero. He's well protected. Friends in Nice, friends in Paris, clever advisers, everything. You won't find any compromising clues anywhere near Grondona."

Dinh Le Thong's niece brought them their first course. She wore a blue silk *ao dai* with the traditional high collar and split skirt. The black hair that fell to her waist was gathered behind her shoulders with a silver clip. She smiled as she served them a steaming, spicy soup with butterflied shrimp floating on its amber surface.

"That is *nice,*" Bellot remarked, watching the girl walk back to the kitchen.

"Easy," Bastide warned him, "Thong will have you on tomorrow's menu as grilled pork if you so much as touch her hand."

Bellot smiled and swallowed a large spoonful of soup. His placid face turned pink, his eyes widened and he reached for his beer, coughing and spluttering. *"Bon sang!"* he rasped, "it's pure fire!"

"Welcome to Thailand," Bastide said, sipping a small portion from his spoon. "At the least, it will open your sinuses."

By the time they'd finished, their eyes were watering and they were blowing their noses. Bellot ordered another bottle of beer and Bastide was halfway through his rosé. Their second course of green vegetables and chicken in peanut sauce was redolent of ginger and curry paste. It was not quite as peppery as the soup.

"I know Grondona is untouchable," Bastide said, clearing his throat. "For the moment. But suppose we try for one of his lieutenants? There's always a weak link."

"Just a minute," Bellot cautioned. "You're stepping into my territory. You're in charge of the cold meat; I go after the gangs."

"There you go," Bastide exploded. "That's our problem. You in your cage, me in mine. The barriers of administrative hierarchy. "Look," Bastide said, drawing two converging lines on the paper tablecloth. He put a jar of *nuoc mam* sauce where the lines converged. "That," he explained, "is Grondona. This line is you. This one is me. I start with a *macchabée* and work back to who did it. You're out to crack the gangs and put them out of business but your route is basically the same. So our paths meet. Why can't we work together?"

Bellot started to light a cigarette. Then, considering the furnace in his mouth, he decided against it. "We can try," Bellot finally said.

"But we've got to keep things quiet. It would be all over the Hôtel de Police in minutes if we were too obvious. Aynard would have our balls on the grill."

"I agree," Bastide said, "but we've got to work together. Is Mourand still your man in Nice?"

"Yes. He's a fount of knowledge on the Grondona 'family' but . . ."

"But what?"

"He tends to protect his turf."

"Don't we all?" Bastide sighed. "I've got to work with Gairaut. He's a good man but an invitation to a royal reception in Monaco is his idea of putting in a full day."

"It's going to be difficult smoking out Grondona's people on their own home ground," Bellot said. "He's got the city wrapped up."

Bastide agreed. He turned to order some coffee and Thong motioned for him to come to the telephone. Bastide walked to the bar to take the call. Bellot pushed his plate away, lit a cigarette and waited for Bastide's return. He didn't have to wait long.

"Mondolino's hit back," Bastide explained as he sat down. "Grondona's son-in-law is no longer with us."

"*Merde!*" Bellot cursed. "Mondolino doesn't waste any time."

"He knows where to put the knife where it hurts most. Grondona adores his daughter; anything that hurts her . . . hurts him."

Bellot paused while Thong's niece served them their coffee. He smiled at the girl. She blushed and hurried toward the kitchen.

"Remember those Heckler and Koch submachine guns your people picked up a few months ago?" Bastide asked.

"What about them?"

"You're still holding the courier?"

"Yes," Bellot told him, "one of them. He's in les Baumettes. A bottom-rung heavy. Grondona didn't even provide a lawyer. You want to see him?"

"I do," Bastide replied. "We've got to begin somewhere. Grondona's boys seem to feel at home in Marseille. I have a feeling that the *flingueurs* who filled the baths in the Panier are still with us, and preparing more hits. If I could only get my hands on one of them . . ."

Bellot stubbed out his cigarette and shook his head. "It's a nice thought," he said, "but even if we grab one he'll keep his mouth shut and go to jail like a good soldier."

"It's worth a try," Bastide said. "What's the courier's name?"

"Pignol, Bernard. A record of theft in Toulon and Nice. He's been around a long time. I'm going over to check with my stake-out on Mondolino's villa," Bellot said. "Thanks for the lunch."

Bastide walked with Bellot as far as the bar where they shook hands. Dinh Le Thong appeared with the bill when Bellot had gone. Bastide paid for their meal and left a generous tip for Thong's niece.

"Well," Thong asked, "what do you think of Thai cuisine?"

"I'll give you a report tomorrow," Bastide said, smiling. "But I know now why the North Vietnamese haven't invaded Thailand."

"Roger," Thong said quietly, putting his hand on Bastide's arm. "I have heard that Mondolino is calling in his debts. Bachir Moukli has put out the word in the Arab quarter that he needs some experienced strong arms. It appears Mondolino has let his organization slip lately. He doesn't have the muscle he can count on for a long haul contest."

"That jibes with what I've got," Bastide replied. "Grondona almost decapitated the Mondolino organization with the Panier killings. Have you heard anything about le Rouquin's activities?"

"No. Haro has been quiet lately."

"He's the one I'm worried about," Bastide said. "Anything you can pick up on him will be useful."

Thong nodded, a slight smile crossing his face. "You won't have to worry about us getting involved," he told Bastide. "We Indochinese will watch quietly while the dogs tear each other apart. Only when it is over will our bad boy pick up the scraps."

Janine Bourdet watched Théobald Gautier spooning down his vegetable soup and felt a strange, passive sadness. She had first been his mistress, then his companion. Recently she had begun to feel like his nurse. He had aged quickly over the past year, a *coup de vieux* signaled by a series of physical changes. He now had dentures; his step had become unsteady; he tended to forget things and he had no interest in leaving his apartment, even for the official receptions he used to enjoy so much. He had been kind to her and she felt a certain responsibility toward the elderly businessman. Her affair with Bastide had endured for three years. Gautier had known about it from the start. Janine had told him after her third meeting with Bastide. After a day of reflection Gautier had outlined a sensible *modus vivendi*, confirming their platonic relationship and allowing Janine to continue with Bastide if she promised a required minimum of discretion.

Théo Gautier was above all a realist. The same quality that had made him successful in the export-import trade allowed him to weigh his relationship with Janine and come down on the side of common sense. He needed her. He knew that the young, vibrant woman who had once been a perfect mistress could not be pulled down with him into the whirlpool of old age. She was too physically alive to lead the life of a nun and he preferred her liaison with Bastide to furtive affairs in isolated hotels with his younger business colleagues.

Gautier looked up from his soup and smiled. Janine was beautiful in the semi-darkness of the dining room. The ray of sunshine from the large window threw a soft light over her face, accentuating her high cheekbones and almond eyes. There was a fine sheen to her short black hair and the white Daniel Hechter blouse she was wearing revealed the line of her breasts. Janine returned Gautier's smile.

"What are you thinking about?" she asked.

"I am only admiring you," he replied, putting his spoon down carefully. "You provide me with much visual pleasure."

"Thank you, Théo," she replied. "Are you ready for your sole?"

"Fish again?"

"The doctor said . . ."

"The devil with the doctor!" he snapped, frowning. "He's a charlatan."

"Théo!" Janine reproached him. "He'll send you off on another cure if you continue like this."

She pressed the small kitchen buzzer under the table. "Grilled sole," she said, "just the way you like it."

He sipped his watered wine and frowned at the tablecloth.

His stout Portuguese cook pushed open the swinging door to the kitchen. She exhibited the filets of grilled sole on a silver platter trimmed with parsley and lemon slices before serving them. When the cook had gone back to the kitchen, Gautier raised his head and sighed.

"I am concerned about you," he said, something of the old authority returning to his voice.

"Concerned?" Janine asked, her fork halfway to her mouth.

"My dear," Gautier explained, "I am not completely ga-ga. I still control my business. I still have many important contacts in this city. Your 'friend' is entering a dangerous period."

Gautier had never referred to Bastide by name but Janine knew who he meant. Gautier tasted his fish, found it palatable and took a larger bite. His chewing had a certain dogged quality.

"We are about to experience one of the worst gang wars since the 1960s," he said. "I do not want you endangered."

"It doesn't affect me," Janine replied with a shrug. "He doesn't bring his work home with him."

"Now you're being unreasonable," Gautier replied with exasperation. "I am worried. Perhaps we can take a cruise, or a trip to the West Indies. Just leave Marseille for a time until the unpleasantness is over."

"Théo," she said, "my friend can take care of himself and no one is interested in me. Now, eat your sole and stop sounding like an old woman!"

Gautier grimaced and pushed his plate aside. "Now I am an old woman? That is a cruel description. It makes me angry."

She could see the hurt in his eyes. "I'm sorry, Théo," she said. "I didn't mean to offend you."

"It's of no great importance," he murmured, "but you mean a lot to me. You have been my mistress and my companion. Now you're almost a daughter. In a few days this city will become a shooting gallery. Your friend will be in the midst of it. Anyone close to him will be a target. I am not being selfish or jealous. You know that. I have great respect for him. But I do not want you to be hurt."

"I know," she said, touched by what he'd said. "I promise you to be extremely careful."

He wiped his mouth carefully and put his napkin on the table. "You have the character of a mule," he told her affectionately. "Will you remain with me for awhile after lunch?"

"Of course," she replied, smiling over the rim of her wine glass. "We can have coffee together and I'll tell you about the latest opera."

"That will be nice," he said without enthusiasm, secretly wishing he still had the desire and the ability to take Janine to bed.

Arnaud Haro was reconstructing the bloody disaster that had hit the Mondolino family. "Le Rouquin" had gathered the information carefully from his own subordinates and a network of dependable informers. Mille, Frigano and Imbert had been guilty of carelessness. They'd met for dinner at Le Cigale, one of their favorite restaurants overlooking an isolated *calanque* near Cassis. It had been a real *gueuleton,* an orgy of eating and drinking. The restaurant's owner, recognizing their semi-comatose condition, had offered to call for a cab but he'd been rebuffed. The three celebrants had staggered off to the unlit parking area to reclaim Frigano's BMW. The restauranteur had been surprised to find the BMW locked and still in place the next morning. There was no doubt in Haro's mind that les Niçois had been waiting for them in the darkness and had taken them with a minimum of effort.

The attack on Bonta's villa and the killing of Bonta and Serp was more straightforward. No great mystery there. But Haro was not sure if Grondona had used the same men for both actions. He doubted it. Thanks to the anti-gang squad one of the attackers would never see Nice again. Haro was anxious to find out who it was. It might clarify things. He had his contacts in the Hôtel de Police and it shouldn't be too long before he had the man's name.

Haro ran a hand through his red hair and glanced at the old Provençal clock ticking above the marble mantelpiece in Antoine Mondolino's study. He was due to meet some of Bachir Moukli's men at four in a bar on the rue de Blois and he would have to leave soon. It was at times like this that Haro's talent as a tactician was evident. He'd spread a detailed street map of Marseille on the floor before him. His blue eyes scanned the streets, the docks, the squares and the boulevards. He was trying to foresee Grondona's next move. He tried to put himself in Grondona's place. He knew his own forces were limited. At the most he could muster ten sure guns with a backup of about twenty unproven "soldiers": young punks, protection muscle and husky pimps who talked a good game. That was why he needed Moukli's help.

Grondona had cut them up like chopped beef within a twenty-four-hour period. The death of his son-in-law would surely infuriate him. Haro knew that his defensive and offensive actions had to be well balanced. They couldn't afford more losses. He also knew the main battlefield would be Marseille. All his efforts must be concentrated on finding and identifying Grondona's people in the city. He particularly wanted to know who Grondona had put in command. Once he knew that, it would be easier to anticipate their moves. Finding their base of operations would be difficult. Years before, when Grondona had allied himself with the Sicilians in an unsuccessful attempt to corner the Marseille hashish market, les Niçois had used a café on the rue Francis Davso. But Haro knew they'd never return to the same spot. He'd had a strange report from the patron of the Café des Colonies that two "visitors" from Nice had been in his establishment a few months ago but he discounted the report. He was awaiting a full description before passing it on to his lieutenants.

There were three prime target zones for les Niçois. Both sides of the Vieux Port and the Canebière, le Panier and the downtown area between the Place Castellane and the Porte d'Aix, and the dock area including la Jolliette and l'Estaque. The Vieux Port and the Canebière were nightclub, bar and hotel country. It was the operational zone of prostitutes, narcotics dealers and protection racketeers. Le Panier was important as a *planque,* a comparatively safe haven and fallback position for anyone under police pressure or rival gang threats. La Jolliette to l'Estaque took in the busy smuggler's paradise of Marseille, a cornucopia of expensive supplies and cargo protected by a porous security system; a paradise of payoffs and profits for the gang calling the shots.

If Grondona wanted Marseille he'd have to snatch these areas away from Mondolino. Haro glanced at the Sainte Marguerite sector on his map. He made a mental note to increase security around the Mondolino residence. He knew that the anti-gang squad had put a stakeout on the road leading to the villa. He folded the map, put it on the desk and walked to the door of the study. He took his tan jacket from the coatrack. Le Rouquin was unarmed. He rarely carried a weapon. He saw himself in the role of a general. He left his protection to his bodyguards.

Jacques Mourand of the Nice anti-gang squad walked past the silent flower market and turned into the dark, narrow streets of the old city. The sky was clear but it was a chilly night. He climbed a series of stone stairs and entered a small square. He paused in the shadows for a moment, examining the lighted windows of a café with a vine-hung trellis over its entrance. He saw the barman talking to two customers but he couldn't see if anyone was seated at the tables along the wall. He stepped out into the glow of a street light, walked directly to the café's door and pushed it open. Mourand returned the barman's greeting, strode to the only occupied table and sat down heavily.

"*Bonsoir,* Henri," Mourand said, smiling at the man opposite him. "I came as soon as I could."

Henri Barberi's wrinkled face showed no expression. He'd been very busy since he'd informed Grondona of his son-in-law's death and he was tired. His role as Grondona's unofficial contact with the police had often been useful to both parties but tonight he was uneasy. René Polito had asked him to deliver an important message to Inspector Mourand but, for the first time, Barberi was not sure Grondona knew what Polito had asked him to do. Now, as he looked across the table at the detective's self-confident, handsome face, he wondered what his boss would say if he knew of his mission.

"Have another Cap Course," Mourand said, "while I order a coffee."

"No, thank you," Barberi replied. "I don't have time."

"Listen, *mon vieux,*" Mourand told him, leaning across the table, "you asked me to come here. Now, what is it?"

Barberi smoothed his thin mustache and finished the last of his drink. "I have a message of importance for you," he said. "Polito wants you to know that we had nothing to do with the attacks on the Mondolino people."

Mourand sat back against the padded booth, his mouth half open. He waved a heavy hand in front of his face.

"Wait a minute," he said, "let me understand what you're saying. You're telling me Grondona didn't order those hits?"

"He did not."

"You're completely serious?" Mourand asked, incredulous.

"I am."

"Henri," Mourand said, "look at me. You're talking to Mourand . . . not some newly weaned detective just off the traffic beat. I don't believe in Père Noël or Père Grondona. I've been cleaning up the mess from your bloody games for a long time. One of these days I'm going to put you all on a diet of prison food. Now you're trying to tell me someone else has gone into the mimosa dispensing business?"

"It's the truth," Barberi said, looking down at his empty glass.

"Do I sense a bit of panic setting in?" Mourand asked. "Don't tell me the death of Maître Alberti has thrown the fear of God into your boss. Is he going to be asking us for protection from Mondolino?"

Barberi remained silent. He picked up his hat, creased its soft crown and squared it on his head. "I have told you all I can," he said. "What you do with the information is your affair. Good night."

The bright spring morning seemed to herald the approach of a warm summer. The sea was a deep blue and a strong offshore wind was churning up a cream of white foam along the Digue Sainte-Marie. Bastide had sent Lenoir down to the canteen for some coffee. The sun shining on the office windows revealed how long it had been since their last cleaning. Mattei had gone off to the morgue to wait for a positive identification on the gunmen killed by the anti-gang squad. Bastide was examining the list of weapons found four months earlier in the van driven by Bernard Pignol. In addition to the two cases of Heckler & Koch submachine guns and their ammunition there had been thirty assorted handguns and a case of grenades. The grenades bothered him more than the weapons. Rival gangs tended to use grenades when they were on the offensive and taking over new territory. They were useful in persuading nightclub and restaurant owners to change their allegiances. At first they exploded as a warning in the early morning hours when the establishments were closed. Then, if the warning was ignored, they smashed through the windows at peak time, killing and wounding customers and staff. The warnings were usually heeded.

Lenoir pushed open the office door, a steaming styrofoam cup in each hand. "Bellot asked if you could come down to his office," Lenoir said, handing Bastide his coffee. Bastide raised an eyebrow.

"What's his problem?" he asked. "Can't he make it up here?"

"He's alone in the office," Lenoir explained. "He said to tell you it's important."

Bastide cursed and gulped some coffee. He lifted his gray suit coat off the back of his chair and pulled it on. Commissaire Aynard had issued an order that all armed detectives were to wear jackets while in the corridors. A group of schoolchildren on a visit to the Hôtel de Police had become fascinated by all the visible firepower. Their teacher had complained to the Préfet of Police.

"Call Gairant in Nice," Bastide told Lenoir. "I want him to report twice a day on Grondona's activities. Make sure he slips a police photographer into the son-in-law's funeral. I'd like to know who shows up." He almost said something about Lenoir's mustache. After more than a year of growth it still looked like a fifteen-year-old's first attempt. But Bastide kept his mouth shut. It was the kind of niggling comment Commissaire Aynard would have made.

The anti-gang squad's office faced the rue de l'Évéché to the rear of the Hôtel de Police. Bastide went down the grimy concrete stairway to their door. He was irritated that Bellot had not come up to see him but the irritation turned to a subdued rage when he pushed open the door and saw that the office had recently been painted.

"*Salut*, Bastide," Bellot called as he entered. He was leaning back in his chair, feet on the desk, his heavy Magnum secure in a drop-away shoulder holster.

"When was this done?" Bastide asked, surveying the pristine walls.

"Last weekend," Bellot told him. "Not bad, eh? A bit of class. Mind you, we do receive a lot of visitors."

"I've had an order in for six months and nothing's happened," Bastide snapped. "Is the administrative officer your uncle?"

"No, but I often invite him to the firing range with us. He's frustrated in his work. He'd like to be one of us."

Bastide dropped into a chair and folded his arms. He ran his eyes over the torso silhouette targets pinned to a large board. Each target had a tight shot group in a different vital spot. A large colored poster of Clint Eastwood in his "Dirty Harry" role was displayed near the window. He shook his head.

"You people are your own best publicity," Bastide complained.

"We only post the best results," Bellot grinned, indicating the targets.

"What's so important?" Bastide asked.

"Prepare yourself for a shock," Bellot warned, suddenly serious. "René Polito sent word to us that Grondona and Company had nothing to do with the hits on Mondolino."

"But that's impossible," Bastide replied, sitting upright. "Who delivered the message?"

"Henri, 'the Prune,' Barberi passed the word to Mourand. Mourand takes it seriously."

"But Mondolino's already hit back!"

"That makes for complications." Bellot tapped a Gauloise cigarette out of its pack and lit it. "We might have a war without reason on our hands."

Bastide thought for a moment. "If Grondona wants peace there's still a chance," he said. "We've got to move fast."

"Agreed, *mon vieux,*" Bellot said. "But when I reported on the shootout at Bonta's villa, the Commissaire insisted I inform him immediately of any new development. I go nowhere without his blessing."

Bastide frowned. He knew Bellot was right but he would have preferred a few hours to work without the strictures of Aynard's supervision. "Very well," Bastide agreed. "Let's go see him now."

Commissaire Aynard had put aside his normally drab winter suit for a spring model. It hung on his thin frame like a tent. The light beige material was already spiderwebbed with creases. He greeted them with an abrupt nod and indicated they should sit down. He disliked impromptu meetings and their sudden call had disrupted his morning schedule.

He adjusted his rimless spectacles and glared at them like a school principal at a disciplinary session. "I'm listening," he said, his hands clasped on the desk.

Bastide let Bellot explain the details of the Nice contact with the Grondona gang, the ramifications of Maître Alberti's death and the slim chance that a truce was still possible. Bastide put forward his view that an attempt should be made to bring Mondolino and Grondona together before it was too late. He told Aynard that this gang war threatened to be the worst yet and predicted the violence would spill over in both cities with a heavy toll of innocent victims.

"So?" Aynard queried, reserving any comment.

"Monsieur le Commissaire," Bastide continued, "Bellot and I should work together on this one. He can go to Grondona. I'll contact Mondolino. It's worth a try."

Aynard looked at each of them in turn. "I wonder if you're both sane," he said. "You've either seen too many detective films or you've been struck with a heavenly light as peacemakers. Your combined experience should tell you that you're dealing with animals. In Lyon we see the rare gang war as a form of civic cleansing. We wait for the slaughter to slacken . . . then we pick up the survivors."

"Things are different here," Bastide volunteered.

"Really, Inspector?" Aynard replied, his voice full of sarcasm. "How is that?"

Aynard's manner irritated Bastide. He fought to control himself. Bellot shot a warning glance in Bastide's direction.

"The gangs are too strong in Marseille," Bastide replied. "They're part of the tradition; an unfortunate reality of local society with contacts, influences and mixed loyalties throughout the city. When the gangs bleed here, the city bleeds with them."

"No lectures, please," Aynard said with a dismissive wave of his thin hand.

Bastide ignored Aynard's comment. He decided to play on the Commissaire's particular sensitivities. "This gang war will spread far beyond Marseille and Nice," he continued. "Paris will be involved immediately." He noticed Aynard stiffen in his chair.

"You were not here during the last gang war," Bastide continued. "The Ministry was on the telephone constantly, day and night. There was much political pressure. Now, with the new government's tough line on crime, the pressure is sure to double."

The Commissaire was impressed. His ambition and desire to use Marseille as a stepping stone to a higher position made him particularly sensitive to the reactions and desires of his superiors in the capital. He removed his spectacles and rubbed his eyes.

"I understand what you want to do," he said, "but it's probably too late. Nevertheless, I will give you a maximum of three days. If, at the end of that time, nothing has been accomplished, I expect both of you and all your men to see that the . . . ah . . . breakage is kept to the minimum. You've understood?"

They both nodded in agreement.

"Now," the Commissaire continued, "if Grondona was not responsible for the killings in the Panier and at Mazargues . . . who was?"

"We don't know," Bastide replied.

"Of course you don't," Aynard commented. "And I don't imagine you will till your 'peacemaking' exercise is over."

"We're working on it," Bellot said. "All my people are on the street."

"So are mine," Bastide interjected. "This will be a parallel effort."

"Eh bien," Aynard said, standing up to end their discussion. "You don't have time to spare. I expect both of you to keep me informed."

CHAPTER 3

Bastide knew he'd been neglecting Janine and decided to do something about it. At first he'd planned to cook a special dinner but he'd abandoned that option and chosen a restaurant other than their usual rendezvous, La Mère Pascal. He decided both of them needed a change. Now as they settled into the Louis XVI ambiance of the Jambon de Parme on the rue de la Palud he knew he'd made the right decision. He'd pledged himself to make a special effort to please Janine; to shut out the frustrations and pressures of his day. He'd even agreed to order *kir royale* as an *apéritif,* a drink he normally considered too sweet.

Janine was resplendent in a new white silk dress. She was wearing the small jade earrings he'd given her. The tan she'd retained during the winter thanks to her skiing had been deepened by the spring sun. Her dark eyes sparkled in the candlelight. They were sitting at one of several tables on a raised dais at the far end of the room. It was a choice spot, allowing them a general view of the other diners. He knew she enjoyed watching people, inspecting the women's clothing and making sotto-voiced, humorous comments on the probable relationships and conversations of the other diners. The *maître d'hôtel* had made a special effort to make Bastide welcome. Bastide had no illusions. He knew it was his official position that kindled the smiles, the special attentions and the inevitable offer of a *digestif* following the meal.

He'd spent the last half of his working day with a visit to Pignol at les Baumettes prison. He'd come away almost convinced that Pignol had been telling the truth when he'd said he knew nothing of those behind the arms shipment or the planned use of the weapons. But the man must be hiding something. Someone had given him the assignment; someone had paid him. Bastide would have to think it out.

"Look," Janine said quietly, with a slight turn of her head, "the couple on the right, by the painting. Do you suppose he's a gigolo?"

Bastide followed her gaze. A squat, older woman in a bright, multicolored dress had raised her chubby face to speak with the *maître d'hôtel.* An angular youth shared her table, his bow tie skewed at an angle, his nervous hands demolishing a bread roll.

"That," Bastide replied, turning to Janine, "is a mother and son. She is a widow. He is doing badly in his last year in the *lycée.* If he was a gigolo he would be ordering. His wallet would be filled with her money."

"You sound like Inspector Maigret on a bad day," Janine countered. "It shows how little you know about women."

When the *maître d'hôtel* came to their table they ordered the traditional *jambon de Parme.* Janine settled on *rognons de veaux au marsala* and Bastide, after a long hesitation, picked a *tournedos périgourdin.* He'd been snatching food on the run for the last few days and he felt like something rich and solid. After perusing the wine list he offered Janine her choice of Burgundy or Bandol from the sun-warmed hills near le Castellet. She chose the latter. When they'd finished their *apéritifs,* the Bandol was uncorked, poured and approved. They toasted each other.

"Théo Gautier suggested I leave town for awhile," Janine told him. "He said you'll be in danger. He thinks I should keep my distance."

Bastide put his wine glass down slowly, staring at it. "He may be right," he said. "Things are already warm. They promise to become hot in a short time."

Their waiter appeared with plates of sliver-thin, pink *jambon de Parme* and crescent slices of juicy melon from Cavaillon. Bastide buttered a piece of roll, waiting for Janine's reaction.

"I think the proposal is ridiculous," she finally said, lifting a forkful of ham and melon to her mouth. "I've never run away from anything."

"There is the danger," Bastide replied. "There is also the fact that I'll be very busy. We won't have time to see each other. When we do the damn telephone is sure to interrupt our most delicate moments."

Janine smiled as she chewed and shook her head slowly. "Truly, Roger," she chided him, "you are impossible. We are talking about danger and you're worrying about 'delicate moments.' There are times when I think you're governed by your stomach and the region immediately below!"

He laughed, pretending to be shocked. "Mademoiselle," he said mockingly, "it is obvious you know little of my true personality."

"*Tu parles!*" Janine replied, narrowing her eyes. "I know you only too well. If you had your way you'd move your kitchen to the bedroom to save transit time."

The dinner progressed at an enjoyably casual pace. She enthused over the unctuous veal kidneys and Bastide's rare *tournedo* was perfect, napped in a dark sauce speckled with truffle slices. A second bottle of Bandol kept their conversation lively and led them into their cheese course.

An hour later, after lingering over their Armagnac and a slow walk back to Bastide's apartment, they made love with an unusual precise tenderness. The faint glow of a dim lamp cast a sheen over their intertwined bodies as they moved and turned, sharing each other as the tempo built slowly. A rush of desire finally plunged them into a series of pleasurable sensations that ended in a frenzied physical effort and mutual release. When Bastide regained his breath he turned his head toward Janine. She was lying on her back, both hands over her head, a slight smile on her full lips. He ran his right hand down her shoulder and over her taut breasts, followed the incline to her waist and modelled the curve of her hips like a sculptor seeking flaws in his own work.

"Go to sleep," Janine murmured, her eyes closed.

He moved closer till his lips touched her shoulder, shut his eyes and dozed off immediately.

Antoine Mondolino was acting as if he couldn't hear what Paul Campagna was telling him. His white hair framed his head in unruly tufts and his shirt collar was too wide for his thin neck. Shafts of light cut across the study. The few seconds since Campagna stopped talking had been marked only by the ticking of the clock and Mondolino's stentorious breathing.

"You say," Mondolino finally asked, "that Grondona claims he did not strike at our people?"

"Polito has passed the word to us . . . and the police . . ."

"Hah!" the old man shouted, wagging an unsteady finger in the air, "he is clever, that Grondona. Three steps forward, one step back. He has gone to the police too?"

"Polito says that is what happened."

"And Grondona . . . what does he say?"

"I presume Polito speaks for him."

Mondolino grimaced and pushed his plate of dry toast aside. He stood up, leaving the small tea table and moved toward his desk, his shoulders hunched and his head thrust forward. He turned suddenly toward Campagna, his eyes glittering with malice.

"What are we to make of this?" he demanded. "Am I to believe that despite what happened to his son-in-law he wants a truce?"

Campagna stifled a sigh and picked some lint off the sleeve of his expensive houndstooth jacket. There were times when the old man irritated him. "I can only tell you what Polito passed on to us."

"I know that. But I would like your view, *mon cher* Paulo. It is your job to advise me, is it not?"

"I believe it is important to verify this message," Campagna replied, "to make sure it actually came from Grondona himself. If you agree, I'll ask for a meeting with Grondona. It is worth pursuing."

Mondolino sat down and began to trace the gold leaf design of the Moroccan leather on his desk with one finger. "Very well," he told Campagna, "but be careful. It may be a trap. I don't want you going into Nice. If they do want to talk, they can come to you on neutral ground. Pick a public place and take some good men with you. But it must be Grondona himself. Anyone else would be a waste of time."

A soft knock on the door interrupted them. Marcel Perret stepped into the study. He was wearing a sweat suit and jogging shoes. "Sorry to bother you," he said, "but we just had a call from the Hôtel de Police."

Mondolino laughed at Campagna's sudden worried expression. It was more of a wheeze than a laugh and it ended in a fit of coughing. When he'd recovered he asked Perret what the police wanted.

"A detective, Inspector Bastide, has asked to see you," he explained. "He said it was highly important. It's about the Panier killings."

"Are they downgrading me?" Mondolino asked, frowning. "Antoine Mondolino talks with Préfets or Commissaires . . . not with common *poulets!* Bastide? That sounds familiar."

"He's the *flic* in homicide," Campagna explained. "He's done well on a few cases lately. *Un dur,* a tough one. But his request is unusual. I didn't think they were losing much sleep at the Hôtel de Police over our dead."

"Maybe they want to make a contribution to the widows," Perret suggested.

"That isn't amusing," Mondolino snapped. "What do you think, Paulo? Should I see this Bastide?"

"It might be interesting," Campagna said. "If what Polito said is true, the police have been told the Grondona family had nothing to do with the Panier or Mazargues killings. Bastide's request may be linked in some way."

"But where is Bellot?" Mondolino asked. "He's the boss of the anti-gang squad. He's the *flic* who's always bothering us."

"I don't know," Campagna admitted, "but the more I think about it, the more I feel you should see Bastide. We might learn something."

"Eh bien," Mondolino agreed. "Marcel, make the appointment for tomorrow morning. Paulo, I would like details on this Inspector before I meet with him. You will be with me. I never talk with a *flic* alone."

"Babar" Mattei parked his Mercedes sedan in the airport lot and crossed the street to the Marignane terminal building. Before activating the automatic doors to the terminal he paused to inspect himself in the plate glass. His recently cleaned blazer seemed a bit tight. The buttons were obviously straining at his waist. He ignored them and concentrated on his general appearance. Satisfied with what he saw he stepped inside. It was the usual madhouse. A feminine voice was announcing a flight departure over the public address system. Like most airport announcements it was scratchy and indecipherable. People were dawdling by the airport shops, rushing to their flights or pushing loaded luggage carts toward the exits. Blue-uniformed Compagnie Républicaine de Sécurité guards with walkie-talkies and heavy, holstered automatics were pacing the reception area in pairs. A chunky North African woman in a gray smock was pushing her broom over the wide expanse of floor, trying to keep up with the cigarette butts and wrappers deposited by travellers.

Mattei stopped at the magazine stand and bought a copy of *Le Soir,* Marseille's afternoon daily. He paused to leaf through it quickly. Since the Panier killings and the action at Mazargues, the press had tried to maintain a sensational momentum on the coming *"Guerre des Gangs,"* but the subsequent lull had pushed the story off the front pages. Mattei could see that *Le Soir*'s crime reporter had settled for a fourth page speculative item on the current situation. He folded the paper, slid it into his pocket and walked slowly to a small standup bar serving travellers who couldn't afford the lounge prices on the upper floor. This bar specialized in draft beer, *croques-monsieur,* hot dogs and ready-made ham and paté sandwiches. The majority of the customers were North African male workers returning home for a brief visit to their families, their rope-bound suitcases filled with food products and gifts unavailable at home.

Mattei found a place at the formica counter, ordered a beer and waited for Halimi to appear. He didn't have to wait long. He saw him coming through the crowd with his distinctive gait, a cross between a stumble and a rush. He was a short, stout man with curly black hair and the face of a cheerful clown. Halimi squeezed up to the bar next to Mattei, ordered a lemonade and produced a wrapped Arab pastry from his coat pocket. He took a huge bite of the honey and almond confection, filling his mouth like a squirrel, and gave a positive grunt of appreciation.

Halimi's father had been the mayor of a small town near Tlemcen during the closing years of French rule in Algeria. He'd remained loyal to the French and when the French had left the country he and his family had been forced to leave with them. Halimi's father and mother were now long dead but their only son was still in French service as a police informer. He'd telephoned Mattei that morning and a meeting had been arranged. It was difficult for Mattei to go into the Arab quarter without being spotted and Halimi had no desire to be seen with Mattei in the predominantly European sector of the city. Marignane Air Terminal, thanks to its mix of races and the many North Africans in transit, was an acceptable solution.

"So?" Mattei said, without turning toward Halimi.

Halimi almost emptied his glass of lemonade before responding. When he did he kept his eyes on the remainder of his pastry. "Moukli is feeding some of his gunmen into the Mondolino organization," Halimi muttered. "The word is out that there are jobs to be had."

Mattei knew that Moukli and Mondolino were now allies in the underworld but this was the first word he'd had on direct cooperation.

"Unusual," he said, lifting his beer glass.

"One of Moukli's people is making the selection," Halimi continued. "He's working with Haro, le Rouquin."

"What else?" Mattei demanded.

"Moukli doesn't want his men grouped together. He . . ." Halimi stopped talking as a nearby countryman reached over his shoulder for a straw. Halimi waited several seconds before he spoke again. "He wants his people seeded throughout the Mondolino 'organization.' "

"Why?"

"I supply," Halimi responded softly. "You evaluate."

"No ideas?"

"It's safer for them," Halimi suggested.

"Perhaps." Mattei sipped his beer and pondered the new information. It indicated a possible lack of trust on Moukli's part. It was hard for Mattei to believe Mondolino was recruiting Arab gunmen. He'd been ruthless in the past when the North Africans or Senegalese had attempted to widen their take in the city. A year ago the mutilated bodies of two North African pimps had been dumped in the early hours on the very street corner they'd hoped to take over for their girls. Unfortunately for them they'd encroached by forty feet into Mondolino territory.

Halimi finished his pastry, rolled the sticky paper into a ball and dropped it on the floor. "I must go," he said, before hurrying toward the doors.

Mattei paid for his beer and walked to a nearby booth to pay his parking charges. When he reached his car he sat behind the wheel for a moment, thinking. Mondolino obviously needed extra muscle to face the threat from Grondona and his Niçois, but to recruit Moukli's people? It indicated that the old man might be desperate. The identification of Antoine Imbert, the third corpse found in le Panier, as a wine merchant who liked to play at being a hood was a sign that the Mondolino people were scraping the bottom of the barrel.

Mattei sighed, turned on the ignition and drove up to the parking gate. As he slid his validated ticket into the automatic slot he remembered his wife had asked him to pick up some *figatelli* on the way home. She grilled these spicy Corsican sausages with thyme and served them on a bed of steaming *pommes mousseline.* If Mattei hurried he could make his purchase on the way back to the office.

Antoine Mondolino received Bastide in his rose garden. It was a calculated choice. The old man wanted Bastide to know he was not welcome in the villa and that any business they had together would not require either of them to sit down. Haro, le Rouquin, had opened the heavy, electrically operated gate for Bastide and escorted him to Mondolino and Campagna.

Bastide didn't like Haro. He was sure le Rouquin felt the same way about him. There had been an awkward moment at the gate. Haro was carrying a small metal detector that he obviously used on most visitors. He'd hesitated facing Bastide. Bastide solved the problem by flicking open his coat to reveal the holstered Magnum on his hip, then rebuttoned his jacket to indicate his intention to retain the revolver during his visit. Haro hadn't pushed him further.

Mondolino was showing Campagna a profusion of tight yellow buds studding a large rose bush at the end of a graveled path. They turned at Bastide's approach. Mondolino examined his visitor coldly.

"You can go," Mondolino told Haro, his eyes still on Bastide. "So, you're Bastide?"

"Inspector Bastide of homicide," Bastide replied. "Thank you for receiving me."

"You know Paul Campagna?" Mondolino asked, gesturing to his adviser. "We have no secrets. Now, what is it? I'm a busy man."

"So am I," Bastide responded. "I'll make it short. Bartolomei Grondona has passed the word to us that his people were not responsible for what happened in the Panier and at Mazargues."

"It is the time of miracles," Mondolino said, looking up at the blue sky. "Do you believe Grondona?" he asked.

"I'm not sure," Bastide replied. "But if you're both willing to talk we might avoid some premature deaths in this city."

"Not just this city," Mondolino cautioned, "but in Nice too! They'll call it Nice of the bloody gutters once we're through with them."

"Are you saying Grondona wants to talk?" Campagna asked calmly, hoping to quiet Mondolino.

"I would say he does," Bastide said, "but that is up to you . . . not us. The murder of his son-in-law . . ."

"Be careful, *flic,*" Mondolino cautioned, glaring at Bastide.

". . . affected him very much," Bastide continued. "But he obviously wants peace or he wouldn't be sending out these signals. Our question is . . . will you meet with him?"

"That is our business," Mondolino said shortly.

"It's also ours," Bastide replied. "If you don't reach an agreement, my men will be scraping your people off the sidewalk and fishing them out of the port. I know your situation, Monsieur Mondolino. Your 'family' is in trouble. You've lost some of your best men and you're having a hard time holding on to your territory. A gang war now could finish you."

"That is no way to speak to a respected citizen," Campagna countered. "The Mayor will hear of your attitude."

Mondolino's face was mottled with rage. His lips were quivering and he leveled his bony finger at Bastide. "Get off my property, you young bastard," he growled. "I'll have your head blown off if you snoop around here again!"

"I think you'd better leave," Campagna suggested. "He's not himself lately. He doesn't really mean . . ."

"Yes, I do, damn it!" Mondolino shouted. "Don't try to interpret my thoughts!"

Bastide took a notebook from his inner pocket and calmly recorded Mondolino's threats. When he put the notebook away he saw that Haro was returning.

"What's wrong?" Haro asked.

"Inspector Bastide is leaving," Campagna replied. "Show him out."

Before following Haro, Bastide turned again to Mondolino. "I hope you will make contact with Grondona," he said. "I also hope you'll give some thought to who was responsible for the Panier and Mazargues if it wasn't Grondona. You should also remember that we'll be looking for the killers of Maître Alberti . . ."

"That's enough, Bastide," Campagna warned. Haro began to move toward him, but Bastide held up his hand and shook his head.

"I wouldn't advise that," Bastide said. "I've only one more point to make. We don't like threats at the Hôtel de Police and I don't like them in particular. If you dare to talk to me again like that, *mon vieux*, I'll drag you in to marinate in a holding cell while Perret mobilizes your lawyers and influential friends. You've lost the common touch, Mondolino. It would do you good to renew acquaintance with the whores, pimps and pushers that helped put you where you are today."

Bastide turned abruptly and walked to the gate. Haro remained a few steps behind. "You think you're a tough one," Haro remarked, "but that was a mistake."

Bastide didn't reply. He waited, his arms folded as Haro pressed the button to activate the gate release.

"You just don't talk to Antoine Mondolino like that," Haro insisted.

Bastide stepped through the open grill and looked back at Haro. "Mondolino should not talk to an Inspector of the Police Judiciare like that," Bastide said. "As for you, Haro, I'd watch myself. If Grondona and Mondolino don't make peace you're going to be in the front line. I hope you have a good life insurance policy."

Maurice Alberti had been buried high above Nice in a cemetery surrounded by tall cypress trees and umbrella pines. It had been a painful moment for Bartolomei Grondona. Alberti's mother had refused to attend, blaming her son's death on the underworld connections of the Grondona family and Grondona's widowed daughter had sleepwalked through the whole ceremony in blank-eyed shock.

Grondona summoned René Polito to his apartment immediately after the funeral. "What is it you are doing?" Grondona demanded, his bald head thrust forward aggressively. "How dare you take such an initiative! I don't understand you, René. You deal with the enemy . . . and with the police. Are you mad?"

Polito swallowed to moisten his throat and tried to explain. "I wanted to prepare the ground for a truce," he said, talking quickly. "You, yourself, said you favored the peaceful path. I wanted to make sure there were no further mistakes while you decided our next move. If you wished to meet with Mondolino, the way would be open."

Grondona stared at Polito. "I don't know you anymore. You're speaking stupid. This is a bad day. My little girl's heart is broken; her husband is buried and I can no longer trust my old friend."

"That isn't true," Polito protested. "You gave direct orders for me to contact Mondolino."

"But that was before all this," Grondona said, indicating their mourning attire.

"Someone wants it this way," Polito pleaded. "They're planning to profit from it."

Grondona exhaled a thick cloud of cigar smoke and put his hand on the marble mantelpiece. An original oil by Chagall hung above them, its bright colors matched by a nearby vase of fresh-cut red tulips. Grondona stood in silence glaring at the Chagall, his jaw working.

"You see that painting?" he finally said. "It was a gift from Alberti and my daughter. He hung it himself, on my birthday. Now, I want it taken down. I don't want to remember the happy days."

"Will you meet with Mondolino?" Polito asked.

"No," Grondona replied.

"Will you let me meet with him?"

"No."

Polito let himself fall into an upholstered chair. It was a gesture of resignation tinged with despair.

"Very well, Bartolomei," he murmured. "It would be wise to send our women and children away. I suggest a planning meeting."

Grondona walked over to Polito and mussed his well-brushed hair. "*Enfin,*" he said, smiling. "That is the René I know. Yes, a meeting by all means. This afternoon at the Vesuvio. Keep it to a minimum."

Polito nodded in agreement but remained seated as if he'd lost all energy. Grondona put his hand on Polito's shoulder.

"I understand, René," Grondona reasoned, "you are worried. But remember this. We were not responsible for the Panier or Mazargues but *they* were responsible for Alberti. A café owner recognized Tonin Russo as he was driven off after the hit. It was Mondolino's responsibility to identify those who hit him in Marseille. He took the easy, stupid way and struck at us: not one of our people but an innocent, uninvolved member of my own family. That was too much. So, you ask, who did it in Marseille? Je m'en fous! Mondolino's built up a good reserve of enemies over the years. It could have been anyone. But he's gone too far this time. I don't want war but I want Russo."

Polito pulled himself erect and went to the door. "I'll arrange the meeting," he said.

"Good," Grondona said. "Make sure Barberi comes. I intend to send him to Marseille. 'The Prune' knows the city well."

The Gendarmerie firing range was in the Western outskirts of Marseille at the end of a high-walled, narrow road. It was a windowless one-story building, soundproofed and raised off the dusty ground on thick wooden blocks. It had an air of impermanence. From outside, the firing sounded like hammer blows from a metalwork shop. Inside, the din was deafening. Most of the marksmen wore special ear pads.

Bastide had come to the range to re-qualify with the Manurhin .357 Magnum. He'd already put his visit off for three months and Commissaire Aynard had complained that he wasn't setting a good example. The range monitor had promised Bastide to rush him through the firing routine once the elite Intervention Group of the National Police had finished.

Bastide sat impatiently on a bench, the stub of a Havana between his teeth and watched the three men teams of the GIPN hole their targets with well-placed bursts from their mini-Uzi's. Bright cartridges clattered onto the floor. Acrid smoke filled the dimly lit range. The firing died at the sound of the monitor's whistle. The marksmen cleared their weapons and drifted off the floor. One of the range staff wielded a push broom to clean the floor of cartridge cases.

"Holà, Bastide," the Monitor shouted. "It's all yours."

Bastide stood up, drew his revolver and loaded it with cartridges he'd taken from a trouser pocket. He pushed it back into its holster and adjusted his ear pads. He shook his arms like a swimmer preparing for a race and narrowed his eyes at the two fresh silhouette targets at the far end of the range. Each target depicted a gunman with a leveled weapon, ready to fire. The range monitor saw that Bastide was ready. He lifted his whistle and blew a short blast. Bastide's knees flexed, his arms came up, left hand supporting the right, the weapon an extension of his body as he pulled the trigger. He felt the Manurhin kick against the heel of his hand as he sent the heavy slugs ripping into the targets. He'd placed his shots where he'd wanted them before the whistle indicated his time was up.

"Let's do a walkaway," the Monitor shouted.

Bastide reloaded his weapon, holstered it and walked downrange away from the targets. When he'd gone twenty-five feet the whistle shrilled again. Bastide spun around in a combat crouch, the Magnum flashed from its holster and punched tight shot patterns in one of the silhouettes, just under the sternum.

"Not bad," the Monitor commented, with a smile. "Now, let's do some quick re-loads on three targets."

The strange, deadly ballet continued as Bastide completed his required performance. He did some firing with a Smith & Wesson and a Browning automatic. He burned two clips in a Mini-Uzi and a Heckler & Koch 94. The Monitor convinced him to try a few shots with a .38 caliber Derringer used for undercover work. It was a good thing it didn't count as part of his qualification. One of the two slugs he fired was well outside the target's kill area. When he'd finished he accepted a cup of coffee from the Monitor. They sat in the Monitor's cluttered office with three *gendarmes* among the disassembled weapons, gun oil and assorted shooting trophies, exchanging gossip and relaxing. Range firing had always taken a lot out of him. It exercised the body *and* the imagination. Once a policeman had experienced a life-and-death situation involving weapons, he could never approach the range with pure detachment. To many detectives, including Bastide, the crudely printed targets they faced took on an aspect of reality that insured their concentration and guaranteed a healthy sweat at the end of the session. For Bastide, who had served as a parachute commando in Algeria, range firing brought it all back. That was perhaps why he often missed his qualification deadline. Witnessing sudden death at firsthand had been repugnant to him. The spectacle of life being torn from a human being by the impact of steel-jacketed slugs had always filled him with an undefinable sadness. The way a shocked body shuddered prior to death was sickening, no matter what the provocation and guilt. His experiences in homicide had only strengthened these feelings. The blast of firing, the smell of gunpowder and the simple handling of a warm weapon brought back unpleasant memories.

"We hear there may be a gang war soon," the Monitor said. "Is it true?"

It took Bastide several seconds before he realized they were waiting for his reply. "It's possible," he said, putting his coffee cup down, and folding the completed qualification form the Monitor had filled out for him. "Anything is possible in Marseille."

"If that's the case," a husky *gendarme* commented, "you can have our share."

"There'll be enough for everyone," Bastide replied, pulling on his jacket and preparing to leave. "We wouldn't want the Gendarmerie to feel left out."

When Bastide had gone the Monitor shrugged. "No sense of humor," he commented laconically.

Bachir Moukli sipped his mint tea in a small Arab café near the Port d'Aix and kept his eyes on the beaded doorway at the far end of the narrow room. The café radio was switched to Radio Algiers and the announcer was describing a football game between Algiers and Oran. Four North African men were playing cards at the table nearest the door. The proprietor, swathed in scarves and a heavy wool sweater, was blowing his nose behind the bar. Three rolls of sticky flypaper were strategically hung from the linoleum-covered ceiling, each roll raisin-specked with long dead flies.

Moukli's cotton suit was well pressed. He was wearing a light blue shirt and a red necktie. With his high cheekbones, long nose and alert eyes he resembled a hunting falcon. The graying hair of his shaped sideburns had been dyed black.

The man he'd been waiting for appeared at the door and walked to Moukli's table. They greeted each other with a handshake. The proprietor brought a steaming glass of sugared tea to the new customer.

Ahmed Taroud would have been a handsome man if it were not for his blind left eye. Severe trachoma had given it a disconcerting opaque milkiness that Taroud had never attempted to hide with an eyepatch. The young Moroccan unbuttoned his spotted trench coat and sucked at his tea.

"I have seen Haro," he told Moukli. "He needs ten of our people. He has asked for the best."

Moukli smiled. "It is a strange sensation having Mondolino asking us for assistance," he said. "What did you tell him?"

"As you instructed. I told him we could spare five men now. More later."

"Yes, we must not make it too easy . . . nor should we anger the old man. Did le Rouquin speak of Nice . . . of Grondona?"

"He expects the worst. They know how much the son-in-law's death hurt Grondona. They are scouring Marseille to find Grondona's men."

"Have you heard if the police or the Mondolino people have made any progress in identifying our dead man?"

"No. And they won't. We hired the German in Tangier. He was an apprentice mercenary with no experience."

"I do not want that to happen again," Moukli said gravely. "We have been lucky. If someone had to die at Mazargues it is better it was the European and not one of us. I continue to worry about Pignol. All this has taught me a lesson. We use no more Europeans unless we absolutely have to."

Taroud smiled. "But we were again fortunate that it was Pignol they seized with the arms and not one of us. The police are sure the arms belonged to Grondona. It was a considerable loss for us but it could have been worse."

"Ahmed," Moukli smiled, "you are an eternal optimist. Do you realize how much it cost to replace those arms? How long it took? It set us back many months." Moukli paused to crunch a sugar cube between his teeth. "I am still concerned about Pignol."

"There is no danger there. He has been in prison for over three months. He has said nothing. The police think he's protecting Grondona. In fact, the only contact he met was the German who died at Mazargues. He gave Pignol his instructions and paid him his fee."

"You reassure me," Moukli said. "This is a difficult deception but things are going well. I expect Grondona to retaliate for his son-in-law's death soon. Then the real fireworks will begin. We must see that there is no slackening. I may decide to hurry things along. If I do, we shall go for Haro. I would feel much safer with him out of the way. Our people must be in a position to hit Mondolino hard when the time comes and strike Grondona in Nice when he is adequately weakened."

"You know," he said pensively, "the Algerian Tirailleurs liberated

Marseille in 1944. Now, with God's help, we North Africans will liberate it for the second time . . . for our own purposes."

"If Allah wills it," Taroud said softly.

The Pizzeria Vesuvio was just off the rue Bonaparte not far from the old port of Nice. Its facade was decorated by a primitive landscape of the Bay of Naples with an active Mount Vesuvio spewing red sparks and black smoke into a blue and tranquil sky. The green doors were locked. A hand-lettered sign in one window informed potential customers that the restaurant would be open at 7:30 p.m. One of Grondona's men was on guard outside, standing in a weak patch of sunlight. Two others were sitting nearby in an Opel sedan examining the racing form and chain-smoking cigarettes.

The meeting had begun in Vesuvio's back room, a dark parlor redolent of herb, garlic and overcooked tomato sauce. Bartolomei Grondona was outlining his plan for Marseille. René Polito and Henri Barberi had arrived with Grondona. Vincent, "le Baron," Ferro and Robert, "l'Anglais," Soames had been waiting for them. Ferro operated Grondona's casinos . . . those he owned on paper and those owned by straw men. He was a distinguished looking, gray-haired man, well-spoken and deferential. He handled all liaisons with local politicians, certain "contributions" to preserve the gang's influence and all official payoffs to those on Grondona's list. Ferro was also responsible for intelligence gathering on the Côte d'Azur. His network of bartenders, hotel clerks, prostitutes, policemen, maître d'hôtels and drug dealers kept him supplied with information essential to the well-being and efficient functioning of the Grondona organization.

Robert, l'Anglais Soames, who habitually wore dark glasses, even indoors, was a hirsute lump of muscle, the issue of a brief encounter between a British seaman and an Ajaccio hustler. He'd made himself indispensible to Grondona during the gang's successful struggle to take over the Roll-On-Roll-Off rackets of the coastal shipping trade. He now commanded Grondona's gunmen with a flair for detail and a taste for violence that had made him famous. He was proud of his nickname and seized any occasion to speak a unique form of fractured English that never failed to send his colleagues into storms of laughter.

"Henri," Grondona addressed Barberi who was sitting at the table like an expressionless mummy, "you will set up the Marseille operation. Find new headquarters. No cafés. Some place with space around it and good security, fast road access and not too far from the center of the city. The le Canet or Madrague areas might be the best. Arrange for a second *planque* near the Vieux Port. An apartment our people can use to store supplies and hole up in when necessary. How many guns do we have on the ground?"

"Three," Barberi said, his thin hands flat on the tablecloth. "Panizzo, duCroix and Soloman."

Grondona rubbed his bald head before fishing a twisted cigar from the breast pocket of his suit coat. He struck a match and took his time lighting the cigar. He turned to Soames.

"Robert," he said, "I don't want to march an army into Marseille. What would you estimate as an absolute minimum?"

"L'Anglais" took off his dark glasses and did some quick mental calculations. "Eight," he responded. "That would give us a total of eleven. If we count one man at each permanent location, it gives us nine guns for operations. That is the minimum."

"What do you think, René," Grondona asked Polito.

"I think Barberi would feel better with a few more," Polito said. "It would insure some flexibility and one man to guard a house or apartment is cutting it close. Remember, he's got to watch for Mondolino's boys."

"Very well," Grondona decided. "Make it fourteen. But remember, you can have reinforcements immediately if you need them. Understood?"

Barberi nodded in agreement.

"Any preference on weapons?" Soames asked.

"I'd like to keep this traditional," Barberi told them. ".45's and sawed-offs."

"You may need more firepower," Soames suggested.

"Whatever you need," Grondona replied, his head surrounded by a cloud of cigar smoke.

"We've received some MAC-10 .45 caliber submachine guns from Florida. They've been converted to full automatic . . . they can empty a thirty-shot clip in three seconds. I also suggest a Ruger

Mini-14 with a laser-lock sight for distance. You never know when it'll be needed."

"*Soit,*" Grondona said, "it's done. Now, Vincent, who can we depend on for information?"

Vincent Ferro produced a leather-bound notebook and ruffled the pages till he found what he wanted. "We have several dependable sources on our payroll," he explained. "They are working at the Préfet, the Mairie, Marignane Airport, the Chambre de Commerce and at two of the city's leading hotels. Of course, there are others in minor positions that can be used when needed. I believe you will agree, it would not be wise to alert them at this moment. The fact that they talk to us means they also talk to others."

Grondona chuckled. "Whores are the best informers," he announced with a broad grin. "Ask anyone who was in the Resistance . . . or worked for the Gestapo. But don't let me offend your sensibilities . . . go on."

"I will supply you with this list and recommendations on when and how to make the needed contacts," Ferro told Barberi.

"L'Anglais and I will work out a schedule," Grondona told them. "I can tell you now that one of our first objectives is the Vieux Port area. We will reach for Mondolino's heart and rip it out. The commercial port zone may be more profitable but a challenge to Mondolino at the Vieux Port will send a message to the bar and nightclub owners. I want those *boîtes* under new management."

The sound of a key rattling in the lock produced an instant silence. L'Anglais was on his feet in seconds, moving soundlessly toward the door with his silvered .45 drawn and ready. Barberi slid out of his chair, a stubby Beretta automatic in his hand. He motioned Grondona away from the table and toward the side wall.

"Who is it?" Soames demanded, flattened against the wall, gripping his weapon with both hands at shoulder height.

"*C'est moi,* Mario," a gravelly voice responded. The door opened slowly and the owner of the Vesuvio peered cautiously into the dark room. "*Bon Dieu!*" he complained, struggling with a large crate of lettuce and shutting the door with his foot, "can't I enter my own restaurant without a Colt up my nose? Who did you expect, the Minister of the Interior?"

The weapons disappeared as quickly as they'd been produced.

"*Mon cher* Mario," Grondona greeted the owner with a handshake, "we are almost finished here. Can you give us another ten minutes?"

Mario dropped the lettuce crate onto the table. "Of course, Bartolomei, of course," he said. "I'll go out front to prepare my oven. Will you stay for a pizza?"

"No, thank you," Grondona replied. "We have other business."

Mario shrugged and left them, still grumbling about his doubtful reception. They took their places again and waited for Grondona to speak.

"How much time do you need to set up in Marseille," Grondona asked Barberi.

"Three days."

"Make it two."

"As you wish."

"There is one special priority," Grondona announced.

Barberi raised his eyebrows, waiting to be told what it was.

"Tonin Russo is at the top of our list. I want his skin."

"Consider it done," Barberi replied with a grimace he meant to be a smile.

"Oh, and Henri," Grondona added, "take some fresh sprigs of mimosa with you. The quality of the Marseille variety is poor."

CHAPTER 4

Mattei answered the jangling telephone, put his heavy hand over the mouthpiece and motioned to Bastide. "It's the Commissaire!" he hissed.

"Merde!" Bastide put down his pen and reached for the phone on his desk. "Bastide," he responded.

"Inspector, your three days are up," Aynard informed him. "In fact, I've allowed you three days and a half. Any progress since your unproductive visit to Mondolino?"

"Bellot and Mourand are trying to contact Grondona in Nice . . ."

"But he refuses to see them," Aynard guessed. "Is that correct?"

"Up to now, yes, but . . ."

"No buts, no maybes, no extensions. We had an agreement. It's over." Aynard softened his voice. "I do appreciate your efforts but I could have told you neither of those scum would cooperate. I believe in letting my subordinates follow their hunches. Now we've lost three days. I want a written report from you and Bellot on your efforts, including the fact that I granted you the time you requested. I suggest you prepare for possible trouble. Of course, this 'gang war' of yours might never occur. Grondona and Mondolino have probably settled their own quarrel without our help. They're probably laughing at both of you."

"Monsieur le Commissaire," Bastide said, "I don't agree . . ."

"Somehow, I knew you wouldn't."

"Mondolino is spitting nails," Bastide continued, "and Bellot called last night to say Grondona has held a special meeting with his top people."

"That tells us nothing. If I know les Niçois, they're too lazy to budge from the Promenade des Anglais. They spend most of their time eating stockfish or fornicating with fat prostitutes."

"You don't know them at all," Bastide mumbled.

"What was that?" Aynard demanded, "what did you say?"

"I said, it is hard to know what is in their minds."

"Yes . . . well, we're not involved in mind reading. I want your report as soon as Bellot returns. In fact, call him and tell him to return to Marseille immediately."

"Yes, sir," Bastide replied. He put the phone down slowly.

"The Commissaire is unhappy?" Mattei asked.

"No more than usual," Bastide told him. "We're to give up on a truce."

"The man is a fool!"

"Babar, your insight is amazing." Bastide pushed his chair back and stood up. He pulled on his jacket. "Let's go to lunch. Talking to Aynard always makes me hungry. Where's Lenoir?"

"He's down in the canteen."

"I want him to call Bellot and tell him Aynard wants him in Marseille," Bastide said. While Mattei dialed the canteen he walked to a window facing the cathedral and the sea. An American naval ship was nudging its way into the harbor's mouth, signal flags snapping in the *mistral* winds and a thin smoke haze trailing from its funnel. Bastide wondered how much money the crew would feed into the Mondolino organization through its whores and bars.

"When will our windows be washed?" Bastide asked as they left the office.

"By the end of the week," Mattei told him.

"I don't believe it," Bastide said. "Those windows will still be dirty when we retire."

They walked down the hill past the ancient stone ramparts of the Fort Saint-Jean to the Quai du Port. The *mistral* ruffled the surface of the water and tapped the halyards against the tall masts of moored yachts. Reaching the Mairie they paused to watch one of the small white ferry boats leave its landing for the opposite side of the harbor, a five minute journey dear to the hearts of the Marseillais and a must for newly married couples leaving the civil ceremony at the Mairie.

Bastide raised his head to look up at the tall steeple of Notre-Dame de la Garde and its gilt statue of la Bonne Mère. Seagulls dipped and squawked over the Quai des Belges where the raucous fishwives had set up their temporary market. They'd been at work since their husbands had unloaded the catch earlier in the morning. Now they were folding their stands, clearing their wooden trays and sluicing down the sidewalk with buckets of salt water. A few diehards had chalked reduced prices on their blackboards and were shouting the news of great bargains in an attempt to sell their remaining squid, whiting and bass. The café terraces across the street were already filling with a lunch-time crowd. Bastide breathed deeply, inhaling the salt air, the pungent odors of fish, sun-warmed tar and bubbling caramel from a nearby candy vendor's wagon. This was his city. He glanced past the fishing boats to the Quai de Rive Neuve where a row of nightclubs fronted on the port. He examined the windowless facade of "Chez Eve" and frowned. Chez Eve and le Whiskey several doors away were part of Mondolino's holdings.

"You can feel summer in the air already," Mattei commented. Bastide was silent, still contemplating the tacky night clubs. "*Alors?*" Mattei asked. "What's up?"

"Nothing," Bastide replied. "Just thinking."

"Let's decide where to eat," Mattei suggested. "I don't want any exotic food today. Shall we go to Dominique's?"

"Yes," Bastide agreed, "we might as well."

"You don't sound enthusiastic. I thought you were hungry."

"I am. But I was considering the future."

Mattei glanced sideways at Bastide as they continued their walk. "You don't think it'll blow over?"

Bastide shook his head. "I don't."

"You tried," Mattei said. "If the Commissaire had a brain in his head he'd let you try again."

"He doesn't and he won't."

They reached la Mère Pascal and pushed open the old glass door. Dominique, the owner, was behind the narrow bar, black hair tumbling over her shoulders, both hands on her ample hips. The restaurant was redolent of fish soup, garlic and grilled meat.

"*Bienvenue,*" she said smiling. "It's been a long time. Come, have a *pastis* on the *patronne.*"

"*Bonjour,* Dominique," Bastide said, leaning across the bar to kiss her on both cheeks. "How goes it?"

"Not good," she told him, pouring a thin stream of Ricard into their glasses. "No one has any money. They all eat at home."

Mattei looked over his shoulder at the customers. "What do you call those," he asked, "ghosts?"

"Oh, at noon, things go well. But at night . . . no one. It's a disaster."

An elderly waiter came to the bar to order a bottle of rosé. "*Ça va,* Jean?" Bastide asked. "How's the foot?"

"Very painful," Jean replied, waiting for Dominique to hand him the bottle. "It was a bad winter." He took the bottle and limped away.

"Poor Jean," Mattei said. "He should retire."

"Retire?" Dominique replied. "How can he? He is alone. He has no family. This restaurant is his life. Without his job, he'd dry up and blow away."

Dominique gathered her thick hair with both hands, rolled it into a bun and secured it with two hairpins. Her neck was long and graceful, despite her plumpness. Mattei smiled. He'd always had a secret desire for Dominique. She was obviously aware of his feelings and not above a restrained flirtation when her husband was absent.

"What are we going to eat," Bastide asked, oblivious to Mattei's preoccupation.

"I have a *soupe aux moules* that will sharpen your appetite," Dominique announced, "and I'd recommend grilled fresh tuna with *sauce rémoulade.* Does that say something to you?"

"I should stick to grilled steak and salad," Mattei said, "to keep my weight down."

Dominique laughed, shaking her head. "Surely not," she said, reaching across the bar to tap Mattei's bicep. "You're all solid muscle. At least that's what the women say."

"*Eh bien,*" Mattei responded, "I'll go for the tuna."

They ate heartily at a corner table under a faded oil painting of a square-rigged ship. The thick slices of fresh tuna were grilled to perfection, crusted on the outside, pink and tender within. They napped the fish with a piquant *sauce rémoulade* dotted with capers and accompanied it with a bottle of white Palette from Aix. They talked about the latest terrorist attacks in Paris, the Italian wine scandal, the vagaries of "*co-habitation*" in the French government, and Mattei delivered a long harangue on the need for family discipline in the home. Neither of them mentioned business until their plates were cleared and Jean shuffled up with their coffee. Bastide pushed back his chair, lit an Upmann and blew a smoke ring toward the ceiling.

"Babar," he said, "do you ever think about history?"

"What do you mean?"

"The cliché about history repeating itself?"

"Who has time for philosophy?" Mattei said with a dismissive gesture.

"I was just thinking that little really changes," Bastide said. "Here we are with our satellites, our space probes, our great scientific advances but we might as well be existing in the Middle Ages. Look at us. We're sitting here, in what passes for a civilized country, waiting while two robber barons prepare to clash over control of this city. We know it will mean deaths and damage but we can do nothing about it."

"We can limit the damage."

Bastide smiled grimly. "That's probably what our ancestors said when the Saracens landed on the coast."

"Oh là là, Roger," Mattei reasoned, "you exaggerate. We can still arrest the bastards. We're not going to be passive!"

"I suppose you're right," Bastide replied, sipping his espresso. "We can arrest *some* of them."

"Bon sang," Mattei chided Bastide, "you are in a black mood!"

"Not really," Bastide answered, "but I think I've identified the problem, the negative ingredient."

"What's that?"

"People, Babar," Bastide said, reaching for his wallet. "They're the weak link . . . they don't change. Let's get back to the office. I want to make sure Bellot got my message."

Henri Barberi had found the location he was looking for in Haut Canet, within sight of the Autoroute Nord. It was an isolated, two-story house on one acre of walled property. The overgrown garden was studded with cypress trees. A cracked, empty fish pond decorated the front yard. The upper floor windows provided a clear view of the approach road and the doors and shutters could be secured with heavy bar locks. The owner, a friend of Christian Panizzo, was in a rest home and the house had been unoccupied for over a year. Barberi had put Panizzo and Soloman to work cleaning up the interior while duCroix had gone off in search of a *planque* near the Vieux Port. It had not been easy to find. The problem was to find a location near the heart of Mondolino's territory without risking immediate suspicion and discovery. DuCroix had finally settled on a furnished flat on a hill near the ancient Abbey of Saint-Victor. It looked down on the Vieux Port and off to the right duCroix could see the rooftops and narrow streets of their target area.

Barberi had waited till nightfall to inspect the location. He wanted to reduce any chance of his being recognized. The next morning, with Barberi's approval, duCroix had paid a security deposit and a month's rent in advance. He told the agent the apartment would be used by traveling businessmen. He'd moved in with his baggage that afternoon. By eleven o'clock the same Friday, Barberi and Soloman were sitting in a rented Volkswagen Golf, waiting for Tonin Russo to surface.

According to Vincent Ferro's informers, Russo always made his protection collections from the bars and clubs along the Boulevard des Dames after 8:30 p.m. When he'd completed his rounds he habitually sent his back-up off with the bag money and dropped into le Toucan for a drink. Barberi knew that Russo managed the prostitutes in le Toucan. One of them, a young blond from Normandy, was Russo's current mistress. They'd watched Russo enter the bar at ten-fifteen and he hadn't come out.

They sat in silence. Artur Soloman found it hard to make conversation with Henri Barberi. The older man had the personality of a depressed pallbearer. He felt uneasy in his presence. Their faces were occasionally illuminated by the headlights of passing cars that accentuated Barberi's wrinkles. Soloman's puffy, pale countenance resembled a clown's mask. A police van sped past, blue lights flashing, klaxon blaring. A couple emerged from le Toucan, paused to kiss under the flashing red neon over the entrance and hurried across the street to a small hotel.

"He's coming out," Barberi said without emotion.

Russo appeared on the sidewalk, buttoning his camel hair coat and squaring his felt hat. He paused to light a cigarette, tossed the match into the gutter and began to walk away from them. Barberi got out of the Volkswagen.

"*Allez!*" he told Soloman, before closing the door. "As planned."

Soloman started the engine, swung out onto the street and increased his speed. He passed Russo, being careful not to look in his direction, drove another half block and pulled into the curb. He turned off his lights and left the engine running, watching Russo's approach in the rearview mirror. He gauged Russo's pace, waited for several seconds, swung open his door and drew a Walther automatic. He held the pistol close to his side, circled the grill of the Volkswagen, and walked briskly toward the oncoming Russo. It was a full four seconds before Russo reacted. Soloman saw him hesitate and stop. He could also see Barberi moving up behind him. Russo looked over his shoulder, saw Barberi behind him and reached for his weapon. Barberi leveled his .45 and squeezed the trigger. The loud report echoed off the tall buildings. The impact of the heavy slug threw Russo flat onto the sidewalk, his right hand still inside the lapel of his overcoat, a dark stain spreading from the hole near his stomach.

Barberi stood over Russo, his Colt leveled at his head. The dying man had a disappointed look on his face. His eyes were blinking in disbelief.

"Cut your own piece of cake," Barberi ordered.

Solomon lifted his Walther and fired a shot into Russo's right eye. Barberi pulled a sprig of mimosa from his pocket and poked it into Russo's open mouth.

"Come on," Barberi said, smoothing his thin, gray mustache and turning up his collar. "Let's go."

As they got into the Volkswagen two approaching pedestrians crossed to the other side of the boulevard to avoid any trouble. Soloman accelerated and drove toward the Gare Saint-Charles. They would abandon the car in the station parking lot and take a cab to Haut Canet. Soloman gripped the wheel tightly to keep his hands from shaking. He was badly in need of a drink. Barberi laughed, making a sudden unexpected sound like the caw of a rook.

"Did you notice," he asked, "how they crossed the street? The Marseillais know when to mind their own business."

Babar Mattei parked his Mercedes behind the police ambulance. He and Bastide pushed their way through the curious crowd. Lenoir was already on the scene; the flashing blue-and-red lights painted strange patterns on his face as he turned toward them.

"We've got another flower child," Lenoir told Bastide. "Tonin Russo, one of Mondolino's heavies, complete with mimosa."

"Let's have a look," Bastide said, approaching the prone corpse and pulling back the plastic sheet. "*Eh bien!*" he exclaimed, examining the head wound and the blood-soaked overcoat. "He won't walk away from this one."

"Look!" Mattei pointed to Russo's hidden hand. "He was reaching for his *pétard.*"

"What's the story?" Bastide asked Lenoir.

"He'd been drinking in le Toucan . . . one of his favorite spots. The owner saw nothing suspicious."

"They never do," Bastide sighed, straightening up.

"A 9mm in the head," Lenoir said, "and probably a .45 in the gut."

"Very good," Mattei replied. "You're making progress."

"There's a blond in le Toucan who seems to be taking it very hard," Lenoir told them.

"Interesting," Bastide commented. "Babar, let's have a talk with her. You stay here," he told Lenoir. "Try to get the cold meat moving before the press arrives. If Bellot shows up tell him where we are."

The door of le Toucan was guarded by a uniformed policeman. The interior was dimly lit and red candles guttered on the tables in low smoked-glass containers. Four uneasy male customers stood at the bar. Six prostitutes had gathered in a protective circle around a far table. The palefaced owner was drinking a large whiskey. Bastide motioned for him to come to the end of the bar, away from his customers. Bastide and Mattei flashed their identification and introduced themselves. The owner was a young, balding man wearing circular granny glasses and a bulky blue linen suit with a necktie of the same material. He began talking before they could pose the first question.

"Nothing happened in here," he told them. "He came and left alone. I don't really know him. But I'll tell you what I can. When can my customers leave?"

Bastide held up his hand. "Not so fast," he said. "The night is young. Who is that blond," he asked, indicating a weeping prostitute at the far table.

"That's Flora," the owner told him. "She's a nice girl," he added without much enthusiasm. "Would you like a drink, Inspector?"

"*No,*" Bastide replied. "Babar, you have a talk with *le patron* here.

I'll go chat with Flora." He took off his trench coat, draped it over a bar stool and walked toward the women. Their heavy makeup was accentuated by the light of the candles. It added years to their age.

"Flora," Bastide said, "you stay where you are. You others . . . take the table near the door."

"Just a minute," a brunette with dyed hair and pink lip gloss said, facing Bastide defiantly. "Flora's for nothing in this business. I'll stay with her. She's had a shock."

"Walk, before you make me angry!" Bastide ordered, frowning. "You're not dealing with a social worker tonight!"

The brunette shrugged and pushed past him. Flora looked up at Bastide over a wrinkled handkerchief. He sat down next to her and gently moved the handkerchief away from her face.

"Mademoiselle," he said quietly, "I'm sorry about Tonin, but crying won't help him now. We'd like to find out who did it. We want you to help."

Her large brown eyes were slightly askew, her eyelids and cheeks smeared with mascara. She seemed to have a hard time focusing on Bastide, moving her head backward and forward. He noted the dilated pupils, the tongue continually moistening her lips. He guessed her constant sniffing was not due solely to sorrow. Like most of the local pimps, Tonin Russo kept his girls on the hook with carefully measured rations of heroin or cocaine.

"Was Tonin expecting trouble tonight?" Bastide asked. "Was he nervous?"

Flora shook her head and peered past him toward her colleagues.

"Don't worry about them," he said, "just answer my questions."

She folded her hands on her lap and began to rock back and forth in her chair. "We were going away next week," she sobbed. "He was taking me to Cannes. A fancy hotel. He gave me money to buy new clothes."

"Did he do that often?" Bastide asked.

"No. It was something special."

"A celebration. He'd been paid . . . a lot."

"For the Nice job?" Bastide asked, still speaking softly.

"You know about that?" she asked.

"Yes. The flower market. I suppose he told you about it?"

She stopped sobbing and drew herself erect, wiping her eyes with the back of her hand. "I don't know anything," she replied. "Who the hell are you?"

"Inspector Bastide of Homicide. What did he tell you? Did he tell you the man he hit had a wife, two children and a third on the way?"

"It's not true," Flora said, her voice cracking. "You're a lying shit!"

"As you wish," Bastide said. "What gives you pleasure? Are you snorting or on the needle? *Coco* or *héro?*"

"None of your business."

"Oh? Too bad. I'm only trying to help. But you're going in for a few days, *ma belle,* and our cells are free of powder. It will be a great test of your character."

She began to crack her knuckles. A sudden tick agitated the corner of one eye. Again, she looked over his shoulder at the other women.

"Forget them," he told her. "They don't have your problem. They'll all be free within the hour. You've got to think of yourself . . . now that you're alone. For God's sake, stop cracking your knuckles! Now, listen carefully. I'm going to make a statement. All you have to do is say yes or no."

"Tonin made a hit for Mondolino last week in the Nice flower market and he was paid well for his success."

She stared at him, her mouth half open, traces of spittle on her lips.

"Well," Bastide prompted her impatiently, "yes or no?"

"We were going to Cannes," she said in a little girl's voice. "I was going to buy new clothes."

"Flora!" he said roughly. "Fairy tale time is finished! Yes or no!"

"Yes," she whispered, "yes. Tonino was good at his job. But it had nothing to do with us, you understand. Now, can I go?"

"No," Bastide told her. "We're going to hold you overnight and tomorrow. What you've told me is interesting but it's got to be in writing."

"You promised . . ."

"I promised nothing. I'll do my best to see that you're on the street in twenty-four hours—*if* you cooperate. That's better than a week of *détox.*"

"*Salaud!*" she cursed, spitting at Bastide. She missed. Her saliva spotted the bodice of her skintight blue dress.

Bastide returned to the bar. "Have that one taken in," he told Mattei, indicating Flora. "We'll tackle her tomorrow morning when she's back on the ground." He glared across the bar counter at the owner of le Toucan. "How about our friend?" he asked Mattei.

"Pure as Alpine snow," Mattei replied. "If we stay here much longer he'll have a nervous breakdown. I have a feeling he and Russo were close but he denies it." Mattei walked away from the bar and Bastide followed him.

"I'm sure Russo was making a protection pickup," Mattei whispered. "I'm going to check the other bars on the boulevard."

Jean Lenoir appeared in the doorway. "Inspector," he called to Bastide, "they've taken him away. No press so far."

"Good," Bastide said. He looked down at the mimosa sprig in Lenoir's right hand. "What are you doing?" he asked. "Celebrating spring?"

"Well, I thought we'd need it."

"No word from Bellot?"

"No, sir."

"*Tant pis.* Pull the identity cards of *le patron* and all these expensive beauties," Bastide ordered. "Then they can pick them up tomorrow after we've talked to them. Take in that blond for a twenty-four-hour hold. Babar, let's get the hell out of here." He pushed open the door and took a deep breath of night air.

"Oh no!" Bastide groaned as they stepped onto the sidewalk. Two police reporters were sprinting toward them and a flashbulb froze their images against the backdrop of le Toucan.

Arnaud Haro paused in front of the Opéra to light a cigarette. His red hair was carefully combed and he was wearing an American-style seersucker suit. His bodyguard stopped ten feet behind him. The news of Tonin Russo's death had infuriated Mondolino. Le Rouquin had been forced to leave the villa to take an active part in the search for Grondona's men. He'd spent most of the morning seeding Moukli's recruits into the Mondolino organization. He'd urged them to use all their North African contacts in the search for Russo's killers.

Now, as he continued toward the rue Beauvau, he tried to put himself in Grondona's place. If he were Grondona, he'd have picked Soames, l'Anglais, to direct the Marseille effort. Haro had never met Soames but he knew a lot about him. He had a grudging respect for his professional ability. He'd passed the word for everyone to be on the lookout for the chunky gunman. He knew Soames would have to surface soon. Outsiders were noticed quickly in the Marseille underworld. They stood out like sharks in a piranha shoal. Soames would have to establish a base. Haro was sure the base wouldn't be far from Mondolino territory. It was only a matter of time till he found them but Haro didn't have that much time to work with. He turned into le Caveau and his bodyguard followed. Le Rouquin wanted to give the bar's owner a full description of Soames before he reported back to Mondolino.

Ahmed Taroud watched Haro enter le Caveau. He'd been following him at a respectful distance all morning. He hadn't been impressed with Haro's bodyguard. On only two occasions had the bodyguard turned to check for a tail and both inspections had been perfunctory. Taroud walked quickly to a public telephone booth near the Canebière, inserted coins and dialed a number. He spoke briefly, gave the name of le Caveau and hung up. He glanced at his watch, crossed the street to a kiosk and bought a copy of *Le Provençal.* He leaned against the wall of a bank building and opened the paper, keeping his good eye on the entrance to le Caveau. Twelve minutes later two men in black leather jackets stopped a motorbike at the far end of the street. They both wore visored crash helmets that covered their faces. A bulky saddlebag was slung behind the driver. The man riding pillion dismounted and began to examine the exhaust while the driver gunned the engine. The sidewalks were full of people. No one paid particular attention to the cyclists.

Haro was joking and laughing with the well-dressed *patron* of le Caveau. His bodyguard sat by the door. The bar was dark and expensively decorated in an attempt to reproduce the atmosphere of an English club. There were old hunting prints on the paneled walls, the bar stools were covered with real leather and a vase full of blue iris was centered on the bottle shelves. Le Caveau attracted a clientele of businessmen, bankers and shipping executives. It was one of the few Mondolino holdings that had a touch of class. The girls who worked the bar were specially selected and charged high prices. The garrulous customers unwittingly provided Mondolino with information on local business projects, investment trends and useful gossip on Marseille's leading citizens.

Haro finished his fruit juice, shook hands with the *patron* and signaled to his bodyguard. The bodyguard pushed open the front door and preceded Haro onto the sidewalk. He paused for a moment, surveying the street, gave an imperceptible nod and waited for Haro to exit. The two men turned to the left and began walking toward the Canebière. Ahmed Taroud stepped back into the shelter of a doorway, watching them, his heart pounding. He heard a muted rumble and watched the motorcycle pull out of the parking space. The man riding pillion held a towel-wrapped object on his knees. The bike swerved, steadied and gathered speed. The discarded towel fell to the street. The blue-black muzzle of a submachine gun was leveled at Haro.

Sensing danger, Haro's bodyguard swung around, a heavy revolver in his right hand. The pillion rider fired a burst. It sounded like metal being ripped. The window of a travel agency imploded, shards of glass shredding a poster of the Greek Islands. Haro threw himself onto the sidewalk and rolled under a parked car. The bodyguard remained erect and unflinching. His revolver cracked and kicked as he fired at the cyclists. The last rip of automatic fire tore the cardboard head off a life-sized, bikini-clad female in the display window. The motorcycle tilted in a sharp turn and disappeared around the corner.

Taroud saw Haro crawl from the gutter and brush off his pants legs. The bodyguard calmly reloaded his weapon. Someone screamed from inside the travel agency. People were coming out of the nearby shops and bars. Haro and the bodyguard exchanged a few words and walked swiftly toward the Opéra. Taroud heard an approaching police klaxon. He left the doorway and struck out for the Vieux Port, following the trail of the cyclists and examining the street for any sign of blood.

Bartolomei Grondona sipped his Campari and relaxed in the warm sun. He had taken his two young grandsons to Cannes to see a film. Now he was treating them to ice cream on the terrace of the Carlton Hotel. The film had been a Hollywood production full of gnomes, caves, talking rocks and sorcerers. He'd dozed through most of the screening but the boys had enjoyed it. That was what counted. Since the death of their father he'd made an effort to see them more often. The boys were discussing the film while Grondona's busy mind was considering the possibility of extending his organization into the world of cinema. He'd invested in a film in 1970 but it had turned out to be a *navet*, a turnip, as they said in film circles. He'd taken a loss. He'd found porno cassettes much more profitable. He controlled most of the outlets along the Riviera. The old Victorine studios in Nice had recently been reactivated and he was seriously considering a legitimate investment. It would provide him with another facade of respectability and he liked to mix with film people. He found them unconventional and exciting.

"Grandpère," one of the boys touched his arm, bringing him out of his reverie, "why did the dragon eat the dwarf?"

Grondona opened his eyes, massaged his bulbous nose and smiled. "I suppose it was because he was hungry," he replied.

The two boys giggled with delight. "But he didn't eat the princess," the other grandson said, filling his mouth with ice cream.

"Dragons never eat princesses," Grondona told them. "They taste awful."

The boys roared with laughter. From a nearby table, Grondona's two bodyguards observed the levity with straight faces, the steel frames of their dark glasses glinting in the sunlight. Grondona raised his head to watch some workmen raise a large poster above the terrace. It would soon be time for the Cannes International Film Festival. The length of the Croisette would be cluttered with advertisements announcing the various entries. Grondona made a mental note to make sure he was invited to the gala opening. A call to someone in the Mayor's office should suffice.

"Tonton René is coming," a grandson informed him, pointing his spoon at a BMW that had just pulled into the Carlton driveway. Polito handed his keys to the uniformed doorman and came in their direction.

"*Ciao*, René," Grondona greeted his colleague. "Have a drink with us."

"Yes," Polito replied, "I will." He sat down, his eyes sending a visual message to Grondona that his business was serious.

"Boys," Grondona said, "go look at the art exhibit inside. And don't forget to do pee-pee. We won't be stopping on the way home."

They obeyed their grandfather, pushing the ice-cream plates aside and hurrying for the swinging doors.

"Now what?" Grondona asked.

"Someone tried to bleed Haro," Polito told him. "Center of Marseille . . . in broad daylight."

"Barberi?"

"No. None of our people were involved. Barberi called me."

Grondona bit the tip off a cigar and spit it on the ground.

"Method?" he asked.

"Two *flingueurs* on a motorcycle. Used a chopper. They missed."

Grondona lit his cigar and shook his head. "I don't like this at all," he said pensively. "Some bastards are playing with fire."

"Mondolino will think it was us," Polito said.

"No doubt about it. Something smells bad." Grondona frowned. "Tell Barberi to sit tight. We'll have to tell Mondolino we weren't involved. I want to know what the hell is going on over there! Someone is trying to make fools of us all."

"I'll contact Campagna right away."

"No," Grondona told Polito, "nothing direct. Use the anti-gang squad. Get in touch with Jacques Mourand and have him pass the word to Bellot in Marseille. Let them be the go-betweens."

"You think Mondolino will believe Bellot?"

"Maybe not," Grondona replied, "but I want the *poulets* to know we made the effort."

The two boys returned, chasing each other over the terrace. They flopped down in their chairs, panting.

"Did you enjoy the exhibit?" Grondona asked.

"It was stupid," the eldest replied. "Fat ladies with no clothes."

Grondona smiled at Polito. "In a few more years you won't think such things stupid," he told his grandsons. "Now, we must go."

They stood up. One of the bodyguards hurried to a nearby Peugeot sedan and the other walked ahead of Grondona to the chauffeur-driven Citröen parked in front of the hotel.

"Call me after you talk to Mourand," Grondona told Polito. "I'll be at home."

Mireille Peraud's call caught Bastide in the shower. He rushed to the phone with a towel around his waist, leaving a trail of water on the waxed floor tiles. He hadn't heard from Mireille since their last chance meeting in Marseille when she'd offered herself to him. Everything had hinged on a follow-up telephone call. He'd never made it. Mireille's husband was at sea at the time. Bastide had let the opportunity go by. He'd wanted Mireille and his desire had only increased since her husband had been assigned to the naval base at Toulon. Listening to her voice he could imagine her at the other end of the line, the large blue eyes, the tawny hair and those enticing long legs. He'd known her since his university days. Her unexpected marriage to a young naval officer years before had hurried Bastide's decision to volunteer for duty in Algeria with a parachute regiment.

"A simple, informal dinner," she was saying. "Jacques has just returned from Djibouti and he would so like to see you." It was as if their last meeting on the rue Breteuil had never taken place. When they'd parted her last words had been, "if it's no, I don't think we should see each other again."

He'd reconciled himself to this and he almost resented the change of signals. "I . . . I don't know," Bastide told her. "We're particularly busy . . ."

He heard her clear her throat. "Roger," she said softly, "shall we forget our last meeting? It would probably be best. Pretend it didn't happen?"

"That will be hard to do," he replied, wondering what Janine's reaction would be if she knew he'd renewed contact with Mireille.

"You'll meet the Admiral," she said. "He's very nice. He served in Algeria too."

"Admirals don't interest me," Bastide told her. A pounding on the door made him jump and his towel slid to the floor. "Hold on," he told her, putting down the phone and retying the towel around his waist. "Who is it?" he shouted walking to the door.

"Bellot. Open up!"

Bastide let him in. "Just a minute," he said, picking up the telephone. "*Allo,* O.K. Tell Jacques I'll be glad to come."

"Perfect," Mireille said, obviously pleased. "Who's your caller?"

"Business," he said shortly. "Till Saturday." He hung up.

Joe Bellot was pacing the floor, perspiration beaded on his forehead.

"*Alors?*" Bastide asked, "what's the crisis?"

"That shooting on the rue Beauvau . . . the target was Haro."

"So? I'd go for him if I was Grondona."

"Mourand just called from Nice. Grondona swears they had nothing to do with it. He wants us to pass the word. He'd like to meet with Mondolino at a halfway point between Nice and Marseille. The exact location is up to the old man."

Bastide shook his head and sat down heavily in an armchair. "What the hell is this?" he asked. "Do they think we're a messenger service?"

"It might give us a little leverage," Bellot suggested, "buy us some time."

Bastide scratched the damp hair on his chest. Bellot was right. This new development just might allow them to bring Grondona and Mondolino together. Threatened jackals tend to run in packs. It was a slim chance but it was worth taking.

"We'll have to tell the Commissaire," Bellot said.

"Not right now," Bastide replied.

"But . . ."

"Listen," Bastide explained, "Mondolino will consider the attempt on Haro a personal insult. He's going to hit back. If we go to Aynard now we'll lose precious time. He'll want to argue. He'll want to sleep on it. We've got to get to Mondolino before his guns freeze one of Grondona's men."

"Mondolino won't believe us," Bellot said. "He'll think we're on Grondona's payroll. In fact, can we trust Grondona? He may be lying. If so, we'll look very stupid."

"He might think one of us is on the take," Bastide said, "not both of us. I don't think Grondona's lying. He smells an outsider, a threat, and if there's one thing these people can't stand it's uncertainty. They don't mind making mincemeat of each other but an unknown third party tends to shrivel their olives."

Bellot chuckled. "If we're going calling," he said, "you'd better get dressed."

Bastide jumped out of the chair and clapped Bellot on the back. "Help yourself to a drink," he said, walking to the bedroom. "Mondolino isn't much of a host."

Bastide's telephone conversation with Paul Campagna had been brief and glacial. When Bastide told him they had to see Mondolino, Campagna had laughed and suggested they would do better to seek an audience with the Pope. Bastide had insisted, stressing the urgency of his message and its importance. Something in Bastide's voice had eventually convinced Campagna and he'd grudgingly agreed to receive them, but he'd made it clear that Mondolino might refuse to let them past the gate.

"The last time I was here," Bastide told Bellot as they parked, "the old man threatened to blow my head off."

"*Formidable,*" Bellot said. "You wait to tell me this now?"

"Just crankiness," Bastide smiled. "It comes with old age. Look . . . we've got a reception committee."

Haro, le Rouquin, was waiting for them, his arms folded.

"*Bonjour,*" Bastide said as they waited for Haro to open the gate. "Congratulations on your miraculous escape."

Haro didn't reply. He shut the gate once they were inside and walked ahead of them to the villa. Campagna was on the terrace.

"Now listen to me, Bastide," he began, "Monsieur Mondolino has been napping. He isn't feeling too well. He's agreed to see you both, briefly. If you don't upset him . . . like last time."

"I'm sorry," Bastide replied.

"It might be better to pass your message through me."

"No," Bastide told him, "that would be impossible."

"I admire your courage," Campagna remarked sarcastically.

"It comes with the job," Bastide shot back.

"And lack of brains," Campagna countered.

"Shall we go in?" Bellot suggested.

There was a strange odor in Mondolino's study. It reminded Bastide of the dry stench of puffball mushrooms. A clock ticked on the marble mantelpiece and the curtains were drawn. The old man bared his dentures from the depths of his leather chair.

"So," he said, the attempted smile gone, "you've come again . . . and you've brought Bellot along. I must say you're persistent. After your last visit I almost called the Préfet of Police to complain of your attitude. Some of the things you said were libelous. You're a strange animal, Bastide. What's so important this time?"

Bastide sat down uninvited. Bellot did the same. Campagna remained standing, one manicured hand caressing his silk tie.

"I've come with the same message," Bastide told Mondolino, "but this time there is more urgency. Grondona says he had nothing to do with the attempt on Haro. Someone else was responsible."

Mondolino tilted his head slightly and pursed his lips. "This is curious," he said, "You've come twice now with messages from Grondona. I don't understand. Can't the man speak for himself? Does he have to use the police as a buffer? Is he that afraid of me?"

"He wants to talk," Bellot said, ignoring the questions. "Just the two of you. You obviously share a common enemy."

"I'm not sure Tonin Russo would agree . . . if he was still alive," Mondolino replied. "Grondona's enemies are my friends. I know this town. If there was someone playing the clown, I'd be told . . . quickly."

"Russo was a payback for Alberti," Bastide said. "You know that. But someone wants you and Grondona in a full-scale war."

Mondolino exhaled heavily. "Everything is possible in this life," he said.

"Will you meet with Grondona?" Bastide asked.

"Don't push me," Mondolino said. "I move at my own pace. Grondona can always come here to see me. He is the one who wants to talk. Marseille is an open city."

"He's willing to come halfway," Bellot told him. "The location is up to you."

"We'll see, eh Paulo?" Mondolino said to Campagna. "We'll consider it."

Campagna nodded in agreement.

"So now," Mondolino said, "I go look at my rose garden. Haro will see that you find the street."

"Will you let us know when you make your decision?" Bastide asked.

Mondolino pushed himself out of his chair with a sudden effort and straightened his back. The old man's shining eyes reminded Bastide of a defiant rat that had bitten him on the hand during a wartime search in the Casbah.

"You're out of it now," Mondolino told him. "If we decide to meet with Grondona, we'll contact him directly. Don't expect any progress reports."

"This way," Haro said, indicating the door.

As they passed Campagna, Bastide raised his eyebrows in a question, hoping for an indication of Mondolino's intentions. But Campagna's face only mirrored his normal distaste for the police and Bastide in particular.

CHAPTER 5

Bartolomei Grondona sat behind his highly polished walnut desk and wrestled with his professional conscience. Before the attempt on Haro he'd been preparing an all-out assault on Mondolino. Now he'd ordered Barberi to lie low and do nothing. Tonin Russo's death had eased some of his anger following the hit on his son-in-law. He was having second thoughts on the risks and attrition of a sustained battle for Marseille. The mystery of the unexplained killings was a real worry. Someone was in the middle, using them both as dupes. He didn't like it. Someone had managed to convince Mondolino that Grondona was responsible. There was no question of further action until the interloper was neutralized.

Grondona recognized the danger of hesitation. He'd known his men were unhappy when he'd put the brakes on. They were chafing at the bit. He was concerned about Barberi. Each day he remained in Marseille doing nothing increased the chances of his being localized and dealt with by Mondolino. Vincent Ferro and René Polito had approved of his decision but they weren't the problem. He'd learned long ago that it was dangerous to frustrate the violent ones. They were liable to take any change of plan as a sign of weakness. They were like spoiled children if told to keep their weapons holstered. He opened a leather-bound account book and began to check the receipts from one of his casinos. The gross was definitely down. He could blame the political terrorists for that. They were keeping his clients away from France. He cursed under his breath, remembering the time he'd consented to sell some arms to a representative of the Direct Action Group. He'd hardly made a profit and the fools had bungled a bank robbery two weeks later. Fortunately the purchaser had been killed by the CRS and the weapons hadn't been traced. But he'd sworn never to deal with terrorists again. They were untrustworthy. If he had his way, they'd all be shot on sight.

René Polito knocked on the door and entered. "We've heard from Mondolino," he told Grondona. "They're willing to talk. At Draguignan."

"Why Draguignan?"

Polito shrugged. "It's a halfway point. Campagna has set the time at 11:00 a.m. next Sunday at the American war cemetery."

"American cemetery!" Grondona exclaimed, throwing up his hands. "What is this comedy?"

"The cemetery's open to visitors at that time," Polito explained. "We'll meet Mondolino and Campagna at the memorial shrine. They don't want anyone else from either organization in the grounds."

Grondona stood up and shook his finger at Polito. "I don't like them telling us what to do," he growled.

"We asked for the meeting," Polito reminded him. "But there is one condition they insist on."

"Bordel!" Grondona cursed, "you're joking?"

"Mondolino insists we exchange guarantees. He'll send Haro to Nice for the period of the meeting if we send Soames to Marseille."

"The decrepit old bastard doesn't trust me," Grondona said with an air of disbelief. "It's a direct insult!"

"I don't think so," Polito said. "It's a mutual safeguard."

Grondona leaned on his desk, both fists clenched. "You are a witness," he intoned gravely. "I am accepting this insult with the calm of a leader . . . for the benefit of all." He shook his head before a slow smile spread over his tanned face. "The American cemetery! A strange choice. Is the old man gaga? Should we look for a hidden meaning in this?"

"I don't think so. But Mondolino did work with the Americans after the liberation."

"Work with them? He stole them blind! In July of 1945 he hijacked an entire convoy of quartermaster trucks loaded with cigarettes and chocolate near Miramas. He's probably heard that marble is bringing a good price and wants to harvest the cemetery tombstones!"

"Do you agree," Polito asked. "Can I call Campagna? We only have two days."

"Soames won't like it," Grondona replied.

"L'Anglais will follow your orders," Polito reminded him, "and we'll have Haro."

"Eh bien, I agree," Grondona replied. He left his desk to pour himself a Cognac from a crystal decanter on the nearby bar. "I am curious to see Mondolino again after all these years," he said pensively. "He must be ancient."

Babar Mattei stood in front of the map he'd tacked to the wall near his desk and admired his handiwork. A series of red pins represented Mondolino's holdings throughout Marseille. They were thickest near the Vieux Port and the lower Canebière and scattered in the areas of the commercial docks and the industrial zones. The blue pins intended to represent Grondona's encroachments in Marseille were still in their round box.

"Look," Mattei called over his shoulder to Bastide, "Mondolino's empire." Bastide put his hands behind his head and leaned back in his chair.

"What about the yellow pins?" he asked.

"Those mark the casualties," Mattei explained.

They were both in shirtsleeves, holstered weapons exposed. It was the first hot day of the season and they'd managed to force a window open and jam it with a wooden block to insure maximum airflow.

Mattei smoothed his sideburns and returned to his desk. He'd made an unpublicized effort to eat less and exercise for the past week. He could tell his waist had diminished slightly, but he'd made up his mind not to mention it till someone noticed the change. Bastide was working on a long overdue report. It covered the brutal murder of a hitchhiker near Cassis. The girl's half-clothed body had been found in the *garrigue* by the side of the highway. The murderer, a salesclerk at a supermarket, had been very careless. He'd thrown his bloody clothing out with the garbage and taken a shower at 3 a.m. His jealous wife, suspecting an affair, had snooped in the garbage bin later that morning. She'd turned him in. When Bastide and Mattei had confronted him at the supermarket he'd collapsed and been sick over a crate of newly arrived Belgian endive.

"Do you think Mondolino will agree to meet Grondona?" Mattei asked.

"I hope so," Bastide replied without looking up.

"Are Bellot's people watching his movements?"

"They are. But not too closely. We can't risk blowing the whole operation."

"What did Aynard say about it?"

Bastide smiled and said nothing.

"Oh no!" Mattei groaned, "you haven't told him yet? You're mad!"

"If they go ahead with the meeting, we tell him. If not . . . nothing's happened."

"He's sure to find out."

"We'll worry about that when it happens."

"Did Bellot agree?"

"Bellot's a good man. Of course he agreed."

Mattei glanced up at the wall clock. "I've got to move," he told Bastide. "Halimi has something for me. He sounded excited."

"Halimi's always excited," Bastide commented, without looking up from the report. "Have you noticed how his reports become more important and more numerous at the end of the month? He's trying to meet his racing debts."

"He was right about Moukli teaming up with Mondolino," Mattei said. "We've checked. Some of Moukli's people have been escorting Mondolino's protection collectors. One of them now supervises Mondolino's girls on a choice piece of sidewalk near the Prado."

"Anything new on Haro's narrow escape?"

"He lost no time in leaving the scene. One of the customers who'd seen the whole thing from inside le Caveau was talkative. Once he'd opened his mouth, *le patron* was forced to confirm it."

"How could they have missed?" Bastide asked. "Bellot told me they made *Gruyère* out of the wall and came close to wiping out the travel agency next door."

"I'll wager they were young," Mattei said, preparing to leave. "You put a UZI or an H and K in their hands and they expect the weapon to do their work for them. A witness said the bike was weaving and the shooter was using his H and K like a hose. I'll see you later."

Bastide finished editing the last lines of his report. He was tempted to send it down to the typist pool but he knew that would only mean delay and errors. He decided to type it himself. He moved to Mattei's cluttered desk, pushed aside a copy of a men's magazine open to a lascivious color display of a nude model, and centered the ancient IBM machine. He was about to strike the first key when something Mattei had said stopped him cold. It was the remark about Moukli's cooperation with Mondolino. Bastide leaned forward, both forearms on the typewriter. Moukli had been nibbling at the edges of Mondolino's territory for years. Six years before he'd been ambitious enough to crowd the Sicilians. That had been a mistake. Torn to pieces by their own gang war, the Sicilians had paused long enough to administer a punishment that had put three of Moukli's men under the ground and sent him into temporary hiding in Algiers. Last year Moukli had worked his way into Mondolino's inner circle. Could Moukli be involved in the Marseille killings? Bastide stood up and walked to the window. The sea sparkled under the bright sun. Three yachts were beating out toward the Château d'If, hobbyhorsing into the chop. No, he told himself, Moukli would be mad to take such a risk. One false step would wipe out all he'd accomplished and neither Mondolino or Grondona would rest until they'd put him on ice. There were a few other possibilities. Some of the Sicilians were still nosing around. They'd never forgiven Mondolino for pushing them out. They were past masters at revenge. The Senegalese were another group Mondolino had broken. They'd maintained a remunerative hold on prostitution west of the Canebière for almost ten years but Mondolino had closed them into a tiny enclave and stripped them of their authority after three days of concentrated bloodletting. Then there were the old, deposed "families" of the Marseille underworld: the Guerinis, the Renuccis and the clan of Corsicans, all resenting Mondolino and capable of putting guns on the street if they thought the time was right.

Bastide sighed. If Moukli was trying to put the two gangs at each other's throats, a Mondolino-Grondona meeting would be the last thing he'd want. He walked back to the typewriter, reflecting on Moukli's ambition and tenacity. He lifted the first page of the report, read a few lines and put it aside. It could wait. He'd decided to talk with Bellot about Moukli.

Bachir Moukli's fifth-floor apartment had a panoramic view of the city.

To the west it looked down on the Porte d'Aix, to the east Notre-

Dame de la Garde rose from the distant heat haze like a gold-topped finger. The street noise was muted by split bamboo shades and the potted palms on each windowsill. Several fat canaries flitted and trilled in a large cage in the corner of the cluttered sitting room. Moukli paused by the cage and shook some seed into the feeder.

"I want those two fools on the next ferry to Algiers," Moukli said angrily. "We cannot afford amateurs."

"I'll see to it," Ahmed Taroud replied, his good eye following Moukli's movements. "They were much too eager, too nervous."

"You told me they had experience," Moukli snapped. "They couldn't break a pipe in a shooting gallery!"

"They were recommended by Ali."

"Ali has become undependable. He sits in his villa at Sidi Ferrouch growing fat on whiskey and *foie gras.* He sends us children. It was extremely fortunate that Haro's bodyguard missed them. Now, to more important things. You say Haro is going to Nice?"

"That's what his bodyguard told me," Taroud replied. "Haro's ordered him to remain in Marseille."

"Strange."

"It is. Célestin, the bodyguard, is upset. He's not too bright. He thinks Haro is displeased with his work."

"He has every right to be," Moukli replied. "Does he know why Haro is going to Nice?"

"No. That bothers Célestin too. He says no one will tell him."

Moukli left the birds to sit on a soft red satin couch. "I don't like it either," Moukli said. "Mondolino has said nothing. I know there has been a meeting. I was not invited. This is serious. I want you to go directly to Haro. Try to find out more. Tell him we are providing our people and we expect to be informed of new developments."

"Would it not be better for you to see Mondolino?"

"Not for the moment," Moukli responded. "Now go. And keep me informed." Moukli saw Taroud out and returned to his canaries. He stared at them, provoking a nervous excitement within the cage. Distracted by their movements he went into his bedroom, took a wide-lapelled cotton jacket from the closet and put it on in front of the mirror. If Haro was going to Nice, he had to know why. Either Mondolino was planning a major assault on Grondona or he was making an approach to the Nice gang leader. Moukli opened an ornate, mother-of-pearl box and took out his Star 9mm automatic. He checked the clip and the safety before slipping it into the waistband of his trousers. He buttoned his jacket, straightened his flowered tie and noted that more gray had appeared in his hair.

His mind was still fixed on Haro's trip. Any negotiations between Mondolino and Grondona could mean the collapse of his plan and extreme danger for himself and his men. It could force him to accelerate his actions. He decided to give Taroud till nightfall to produce more information. If Taroud didn't succeed, he was determined to approach Mondolino in search of answers. Meanwhile, he had to alert his men.

Halimi greeted Mattei with a grin and remained in the shadow of a heavy stone pillar away from the flickering votive candles. They'd met near a side altar of Notre-Dame de la Garde. Halimi had suggested the location. He was certain he wouldn't find any fellow Muslims in the Basilica. The vaulted interior was cool. It smelled of incense and deteriorating flowers. Visitors' footsteps echoed off the stone walls. A clutter of ship models hung over the main altar: blue-and-white fishing boats, dark brigantines, multicolored coasters and gray destroyers; all had been offered to la Bonne Mère for her grace in saving the lives of threatened mariners or insuring that those who had perished found their way to heaven.

Mattei dropped some *francs* through a slit in the candle rack, selected a candle, lit it and pushed it down firmly into a holder. He made a quick, automatic sign of the cross.

"A very reliable source has identified some of Grondona's men in Marseille," Halimi whispered. "They've taken an apartment not far from here, near Saint-Victor."

"Reliable source?" Mattei asked. "*Bon sang!* You sound like a journalist. I'm not paying you for any 'reliable source' garbage! You're supposed to be a *direct* source."

"Patience," Halimi advised. "I am a direct source. You don't think I'd come here with unconfirmed information? I went to the apartment building myself. I watched. Do you know of Henri Barberi?"

"The Prune?" Mattei asked, suddenly more than interested.

"None other."

"He's here . . . in Marseille?"

Halimi nodded. "He is here along with two others. I followed them to a small restaurant in Endoume. I knew it would interest you."

"Can you identify the others?"

"One of them is the Jew, Soloman . . . from Morocco. He worked with the Sicilians in the past. I didn't recognize the other."

Mattei knew Henri Barberi. The cold-blooded, laconic killer had been with Grondona from the very beginning. His date of birth was unknown but he was well past retirement age for an active gunman. Mattei recalled his file photo. Barberi's thin, deeply lined faced gave him the appearance of an Egyptian mummy wearing a rat's fur mustache. If Barberi was in Marseille it meant Grondona was planning trouble. Mattei guessed that Barberi had already been in action. Tonin Russo's death definitely had the Barberi touch.

"Your Jesus always looks so sad," Halimi remarked, gazing up at a plaster statue near the altar. "He has a woman's hands, you know."

"What else did you see?" Mattei demanded.

"Not much. I don't think Barberi is staying in the apartment. He left them after they returned from the restaurant."

"You didn't follow him?" Mattei demanded.

"I am not paid enough to take unnecessary risks," Halimi replied. He took a plastic bag from his pocket and shook some candy-coated peanuts into his hand. He offered some to Mattei.

Mattei waved them aside. Halimi shrugged and filled his mouth.

"Which restaurant in Endoume?" Mattei asked.

"Chez Giselle on the rue d'Endoume. It's run by a Niçoise. A small place known for its *pistou.*"

A moon-faced nun paused nearby, smiled at the two men and knelt before the altar. Mattei motioned for Halami to follow him to a shelf filled with religious literature and brochures.

"What else did your *source* tell you?" he asked.

"Nothing. It was a simple stroke of good fortune that he managed to recognize Barberi. He'd known him in jail when Barberi was doing time for that garroting attempt at Cavalaire."

"What do you make of it?"

Halimi raised his eyebrows and made a dismissive gesture. "I am flattered you ask my opinion but I make nothing of it."

"Don't get wise with me!" Mattei snapped, exasperated.

"Shhh," Halimi cautioned, his fingers to his lips. "We are in a house of worship."

Mattei fought the urge to grab Halimi's lapels and shake him. Of all the informers he'd known in his long police career, none managed to irritate him more than Halimi.

"What do you have on Moukli?" Mattei asked, controlling his temper.

"There is nothing new. His men are now working with Mondolino. It appears to be a profitable alliance for both parties. I think I should leave now."

Mattei watched Halimi hurry off, his peculiar gait drawing the attention of a group of tourists near the exit. Mattei followed more slowly. He stepped out of the basilica into the bright sunlight, walked to the parapet and looked down on the city. The fishing boats and tour craft were moving like water bugs over the surface of the Vieux Port. A supertanker was passing off shore on its way to the oil complex of Lavera. The fenced hulk of a Sherman tank was still in place several hundred yards down the steep hill, left as a monument where it had been hit by German fire during the 1944 liberation of Marseille.

Mattei was thinking about Barberi. If they moved fast they might be able to pick up all the Niçois before there were more killings. They could get them on weapons charges if nothing else. But Bastide might have other ideas. Mattei left the parapet and hurried down the broad stone stairway toward the parking area, settling his cap more securely in deference to the freshening afternoon wind.

Jacques and Mireille Peraud lived in a small villa with a large garden high above Toulon. A succession of naval officers had owned or rented the house and each seemed to have left some exotic plant behind. Stepping out onto the terrace was like walking into the fragrance of the tropics. Bastide hadn't realized that the dinner was a celebration of Jacques Peraud's promotion to Capitaine de Frégate. It had been a particularly festive occasion with champagne, speeches and toasts. He'd arrived for the dinner in a dark mood. He'd made the mistake of telling Janine where he was going. Janine and Mireille had never met but they detested each other. He and Janine had argued. It had begun slowly and increased in tempo till they were both shouting. She'd slammed the door to his apartment so hard a ceramic jar filled with dried flowers had tumbled from a bookshelf and smashed on the tile floor.

Before their argument he'd even considered a last-minute excuse for not driving to Toulon. He'd been uneasy about leaving Marseille. There were indications that the Mondolino-Grondona meeting might be scheduled for the next day. But he'd been drawn by his desire to see Mireille and a need to prove his independence to Janine. He'd promised himself to leave the dinner early.

"Beautiful, isn't it," the Admiral remarked, appearing at Bastide's side.

"It is," Bastide agreed, enjoying his cigar and watching the blinking lights of the city and the port. They'd come out onto the terrace for their after-dinner coffee and Cognac. The Admiral was a stocky Breton with sandy hair and bushy Celtic eyebrows. His face was marked by years of sea, sun, wind and drinking. Bastide had taken a liking to him. He was the type of man who said little and listened well.

"Peraud tells me you were in Algeria," the Admiral said. "Those were strange days."

"They were," Bastide agreed. He seldom talked about his wartime experiences. They were a portion of his life that had been stored away, like old letters in an attic.

"You were with the 'Paras,' weren't you? During the battle of Algiers?"

"Yes," Bastide replied. "It was not fun."

"I know," the Admiral told him. "I spent a few days in the city. I heard the explosions at night. We were briefed at headquarters, but they didn't tell us much. You were fighting a special kind of war."

"I'd never want to see it again," Bastide said.

The two men stood in silence for a few moments thinking their own private thoughts.

"I'm very pleased with Peraud's promotion," the Admiral finally said. "He's an excellent officer."

"I imagine he is," Bastide said. "I like Jacques."

"And you . . . you're a police inspector?"

"Yes, homicide."

"It must be fascinating work. When I was young I almost opted for the police instead of the navy."

"You made the best choice," Bastide told him.

"Perhaps," the Admiral said, "but la Royale, for all its attractions, gives one a fairly limited perspective on life."

Bastide was about to reply when Mireille interrupted their conversation. A slight evening breeze molded the sari-like blue dress to her body. She wore two heavy gold bracelets. A double string of pearls accentuated the fine line of her throat."

"You two look so serious," she said, smiling. "I imagine you're talking business."

"You're right," the Admiral chuckled, "this isn't the place for such things. Where is Jacques? I must speak with him about his next assignment."

"He's at the bar," she replied.

"Excuse me." The Admiral left them alone.

"Next assignment?" Bastide asked.

"Yes. It isn't official yet but it seems we may be going to Washington where Jacques will be assigned as a Naval Attaché."

"Congratulations," Bastide murmured, feeling a twinge of regret.

"Thank you. But I'm not sure I want to go. I've heard about the diplomatic life: the receptions, dinners; the emphasis on rank and the infighting among the wives. I'd be much happier here in Toulon."

"I thought you were bored here."

She sighed, glanced around to insure they were alone and put her hand on his. "When I said we shouldn't see each other again I didn't know how much I really want you," she told him. "It's been pure torture the last few months."

He couldn't resist running his fingers gently along her upper arm. "Do you realize how long this sparring has gone on?" he asked. "It's like a play with no last act."

"The difficult thing is . . . I'm not sure I'm in love with you, Roger. It's stupid. Is it purely physical?"

"How can it be," he replied. "We've never made love. That's our problem. It might not work at all."

"But if it did, what then?"

He shrugged, irritated with himself for not having a ready reply and for playing such a juvenile, romantic game.

"Perhaps the time has now come," she said. "It's selfish but I know the pleasure we could share."

"I have commitments too," he said hesitatingly.

"You're speaking of Mademoiselle Bourdet?" Mireille said, a sudden edge in her voice. "Surely, you're not serious?"

"What do you mean by that?" he demanded.

"You consider her a commitment?" Mireille asked. "You surprise me, Roger."

He said nothing, hoping she'd say no more, but she did.

"She must make you very happy in bed," Mireille remarked. "I imagine experience counts."

Bastide's eyes narrowed with anger. *"Salope!"* he snapped at her before leaving the terrace.

"Roger," Jacques Peraud called to him from the bar, "a glass of champagne?"

"No, thank you," he replied, "I must leave now." He said goodby to the Admiral, his pudgy wife and the other guests.

Peraud walked with him to the door where they shook hands. "Come back any time," Peraud told him. "We're always pleased to see you."

Bastide knew Mireille had followed him but he left without turning to say goodby.

Bartolomei Grondona's Citröen was parked near the iron gate of the cemetery. Antoine Mondolino's aging black Cadillac was about sixty feet away. The two drivers had remained behind the wheels. They smoked, glanced at each other occasionally and waited. It was a clear day full of the odor of sun-warmed, fresh-cut grass. The well-kept cemetery grounds rose in a slight green incline bisected by row after row of white marble crosses and an occasional Star of David. A large American flag billowed from a tall pole at the far end of the cemetery. The unusual silence was broken by intermittent bird song and the hum of bees from the blossoming shrubbery.

Antoine Mondolino walked slowly along a graveled path toward the dome-shaped memorial shrine. The old man wore a baggy black suit, a blue shirt and a loosely knotted red necktie. His shock of white hair was unkempt and he handled his cane as if it was an unwanted accessory. Paul Campagna walked at his side, pacing his progress to

Mondolino's and glancing ahead at the two men waiting for them at the memorial.

Bartolomei Grondona watched Mondolino's approach and shook his head. "He hasn't many years left," he murmured. "I'm surprised he's still on his feet."

"Don't underestimate him," René Polito cautioned, "his mind is still good."

They both walked to meet Mondolino and Campagna. Campagna helped Mondolino up the few steps to the marble terrace. The four of them stood in silence for several awkward seconds.

"*Ciao,* Antoine," Grondona finally said.

Mondolino acknowledged the greeting with a jerky nod.

"Shall we sit down?" Grondona asked.

"As you wish," Mondolino replied, moving toward a nearby bench. He paused and lifted his cane. "You two," he said to Polito and Campagna, "wait over there."

The two gang leaders settled onto the bench. Mondolino put his cane between his knees. His small eyes darted over the cemetery, taking in the crosses, the paths and the rolling grounds. Grondona raised his purple-veined bun of a nose toward the sun and took a deep breath.

"What a beautiful day," he said. "I am glad you could come."

Mondolino grunted, gave Grondona a sidelong glance and made an impatient gesture with a gnarled hand.

"You want to talk," he said, "talk."

"We have problems," Grondona said. "We share a common enemy."

"I do not know this," Mondolino replied. "It is only what you tell me."

"We did not do the thing in the Panier or that of Mazargues," Grondona said. "We were not responsible for the attempt on Haro. On my honor, Antoine, I swear this is true."

Mondolino lifted his cane and poked at a passing ant until he'd crushed it. "And Tonin Russo? He died of heart failure?"

"We did Russo. I admit it. You know why. You sent him after my son-in-law."

Mondolino sighed, staring at the tip of his cane.

"Those dead are at peace," Grondona continued, "but not the

others. We must work together to find the true assassins. They want us to bleed each other. Then they will move in. Surely, you must agree. Have you no idea who we're facing?"

"If it is not you," Mondolino replied, "I know of no others. They are ghosts to me."

"It is your city," Grondona said, "but we are both involved. We can help. I will tell you something, Antoine, to prove my sincerity. I have men in Marseille. Barberi and some others. I will order them to work with Haro."

Mondolino glared at Grondona for a few seconds. "You sent them after me?" he asked.

"Not after you," Grondona told him. "Following my son-in-law's death I didn't want to lose anyone else. You would have done the same."

"You want an alliance?"

"It is not what *I* want, Antoine; it is what *we* must do to survive."

"When we find these people and end their games, will I have to face you in Marseille? You've wanted my city for many years."

"No longer, Antoine," Grondona replied. "I have my hands full in Nice."

"You swear that . . . on your mother's grave?"

"I swear it on my sainted mother's grave."

Mondolino looked toward Campagna and Polito standing on the far side of the memorial. They had paused to look up at the multicolored mosaic of the allied landings in southern France.

"We are both men of honor," Mondolino said. "We will do this job together."

"Good," Grondona replied.

"It might be the Sicilians," Mondolino mused. "We will have to rake the streets for them."

"You can have all the men I can spare," Grondona told him. "Polito will work with Campagna and I'll send Soames over to work with Haro."

"And Barberi," Mondolino asked, "who will keep him in check?"

"He will follow the orders of Soames."

"Isn't Barberi too old for his job?"

"He remains one of the best."

A large green bus pulled into the cemetery parking lot. Mondolino and Grondona watched the tourists debark, make their way through the gates and move up the path toward the memorial.

"Americans," Grondona murmured disapprovingly.

"I thought they weren't coming this summer because of the terrorists," Mondolino said.

"They come every year to visit their dead," Grondona explained. "Some of them have fathers or brothers buried here."

The first wave of tourists reached the memorial and flowed over the terrace. A stout woman in slacks paused to fan herself with a straw hat and squinted up at the list of units involved in the landings. She lost interest quickly and turned to watch Grondona and Mondolino.

"George!" she called to her husband, "take a picture of those two old Frenchmen. They're really picturesque."

George, bald, equally stout and colorfully arrayed in plaid seersucker trousers, moved to the bench with an ingratiating smile. He unlimbered his expensive Hasselblad camera and had begun to focus when René Polito stepped between him and the two men on the bench.

"No photo," Polito said firmly through a fixed smile. "I regret."

"But . . ." the American began.

"Very personal," Polito explained. "Very sad story. But no photo."

"O.K., pal, suit yourself." The American turned to his wife and shrugged. "They're camera shy," he told her.

"That's just dumb," she said, glaring at Polito. "They probably want you to pay."

"It is time to go," Mondolino said, mustering his energy to rise from the bench. "Shall we eat together?"

"I would hope so," Grondona replied. "I have reserved a table at la Calèche. Will you be my guests?"

"As you wish," Mondolino said, pushing himself erect.

"If your theory on Moukli is correct, he'll have to move soon," Joe Bellot said. He was sitting on the edge of Bastide's desk smoking a cigarette. Bastide brushed some bread crumbs off his lap and drank from an open beer bottle. It was a quiet Sunday in the Hôtel de Police. Most of the offices were empty. Mattei was out looking for Barberi and Bastide had assigned Lenoir to watch Moukli's movements. Now they were waiting for a report from Draguignon on the Mondolino-Grondona meeting.

"How can Moukli do it?" Bellot asked. "He doesn't have the muscle."

"He might," Bastide replied. "Don't discount Arab solidarity. They'd like to see one of theirs at the top of the heap. He'll have a good reservoir of manpower when it comes to a showdown. If the Tunisians, the Algerians and the Moroccans decide to back Moukli, Mondolino could be in trouble."

"If that ever happens," Bellot speculated, "Grondona would step in to help Mondolino."

"I'm not sure. It depends on today's meeting. Grondona might decide to play Moukli's game . . . stand back and wait to strip the bones when it's all over."

Bastide's telephone rang and he picked it up. "It's Mourand," he told Bellot, "for you."

Bellot took the phone. He began to scribble notes on a piece of typing paper. "Yes," he said, "I understand. Yes . . . go on."

Bastide finished his beer and dropped the bottle into a wastebasket. He rolled up the sandwich wrapper and tossed it after the bottle.

"Very well," Bellot was saying. "Stay with them and call me when they part." He hung up and shook his head. "You won't believe it. Mondolino and Grondona are having lunch together in Draguignan. Mourand says they met at the cemetery for a long talk and drove into town together in Grondona's car. Campagna and Polito followed in Mondolino's Cadillac. They're still at the restaurant."

"A meeting of old friends," Bastide said sarcastically.

"It sounds like it."

"I wonder if Moukli knows about this?"

"If he doesn't, he's the one in the shit."

"If the meeting has gone as well as Mourand reports," Bastide said, "and if I'm right about our sheik, it's a question of hours before Moukli lights a fire. He'll be looking for targets and Barberi's a natural. I better find him."

"Take a backup," Bellot suggested.

"No, I'll radio Babar and meet him wherever he is. We'll haul Barberi in for questioning on the Russo killing. Who knows, it might save his life."

Bachir Moukli decided to move when Taroud returned from the Mondolino villa. The bodyguard, Célestin, had been drinking alone in the kitchen and Taroud had pumped him for all the information he could get. Eighteen minutes later, Taroud knew that Haro had gone to Nice as a guarantee of Mondolino's good faith. More important, Célestin hinted that a truce between the two gangs could usher in a new era of underworld cooperation and peace. No one had told Célestin what was happening but he'd listened to the conversations and the old cook had a loose tongue. Taroud's judicious use of flattery and a continual flow of alcohol had insured Célestin's volubility. He'd even repeated what Mondolino's chauffeur had said about the planned meeting at Draguignan and he'd remembered the cook had been told her employer would not be home until after dark. Taroud's report confirmed Moukli's worst fears. He was now facing an alliance of the two most powerful gangs on the coast. If he didn't act quickly they could crush his organization like an empty eggshell. Moukli had decided to hit one of Mondolino's holdings. He saw it as an easy chance to demolish any truce between Mondolino and Grondona.

The Brasserie Alsacienne on the Boulevard Garibaldi was a busy remodeled restaurant and bar. Paul Campagna had acquired the property for Mondolino through an adroit squeeze play on the former owner. The aged, dark wood paneling and moleskin-covered booths had been torn out and replaced with an Art Nouveau decor. The overhead lighting reflected off bright strips of brass running along the pastel walls. A variety of beers on draft, good, solid Alsatian food and quick, efficient service had made the Brasserie a highly profitable venture. The manager, a thick-necked former Legionnaire from Strasbourg was "known to the police" for his activities but his booming laugh and an innate sense of public relations had already made him something of a local character. He'd developed a faithful young clientele among the *bon chic-bon gens bourgeois* of Marseille who favored the Brasserie as a late night eating spot.

By 5:10 p.m. on Sunday evening Taroud had gathered the men he'd need. At 6:30 p.m. they were in place. Taroud stood at a food stand across from the Brasserie eating a sandwich of *merguez-frites.* The street traffic was sparse but there were a number of pedestrians on the sidewalks. The heat of the day was fading and the city's lights were blinking on in zigzags of garish neon. Taroud could see the Brasserie's white-coated waiters serving brimming steins of beer. He watched the manager moving from table to table chatting with his customers.

The attack was set for 7 p.m. Taroud had chosen grenades and given strict orders that none of his men were to enter the Brasserie. A gunman with orders to kill the manager was window shopping at a record store about 100 feet away from the food stand. The three other men were nearby. They had grenades and black Balaclava hoods in their pockets. A get away car was parked around the corner on the rue de l'Académie with its engine running, a driver behind the wheel. It was to be used only if one Taroud's men was wounded.

Bastide joined Mattei not far from Saint-Victor. Mattei had been checking some of the Corsican bars off the rue de la Corderie when Bastide contacted him by car radio. Barberi was nowhere to be found. They'd decided to meet at the apartment building described by Halimi. The anti-gang stake-out told them he'd seen Soloman and Panizzo leave the building at noon. There had been no movement since then and no sight of Barberi. Mattei had suggested they pick up Soloman but Bastide refused. He wanted Barberi. Now, as they sat side by side in the front seat of the unmarked police sedan, Bastide was plagued by an unusual tension. Even the sputtering and static of the radio irritated him. Something was about to happen but he had no idea what it might be. He'd smoked his last cigar and the *Gruyère* sandwich he'd eaten in the office sat heavily on his stomach.

Janine had left town. She'd gone off on a cruise to the Greek Islands with Théo Gautier. He'd found a note in his apartment when he'd come back from the Peraud's dinner. "I need to think," was all it had said. At first, Bastide had felt deserted but considering his immediate preoccupations Janine couldn't have picked a better moment.

Mattei was leafing through one of his favorite erotic publications pausing occasionally to turn the magazine upside down for a unique view of interlaced bodies posed in unlikely positions.

"*Allez!*" Bastide said suddenly, "we're wasting our time. On the way back to your car tell that stake-out to notify us the minute Barberi shows. I'll see you at the office after I pick up more cigars."

Mattei climbed out of the car, put his magazine under his one arm and came around to the driver's window. "I'll stay awhile," he said. "Barberi may surface yet."

"Let me know if he does," Bastide replied. "And don't try anything on your own. He works with a filed trigger."

Bastide started the engine, swung the car around and drove down the hill toward the Vieux Port. He felt better on the move but he was still puzzled by his own restlessness. He decided to drink an espresso laced with brandy when he bought his cigars. It might help him to relax.

The deadly ballet began at 6:56 p.m. The three men who had been loitering on the Boulevard Garibaldi pulled on their hoods and converged from three directions on the Brasserie Alsacienne. They walked rapidly, keeping out of the bright light. Taroud watched as they slowed their pace, produced the grenades, armed them and lobbed them at the wide windows. The crash of glass almost covered the baritone rip of the H & K in the hands of the marksman. Taroud saw the manager go down behind the bar before he sheltered behind the food stand. Seconds later the grenades exploded. The blast blew out the front of the Brasserie, filling the air with splintered glass and wood fragments. Thick clouds of gray smoke obscured the street. Taroud turned and walked up the rue des Mages. He could hear screams and shouting. He stopped to light a cigarette, glancing over his shoulder at the confused scene. Pinpoints of flame were showing through the smoke and the streets were filling with people. Two men hurried past him toward the shattered Brasserie. "What happened?" he called after them. They didn't turn around.

Bastide had driven to a *Bar-Tabac* on the Canebière to buy some Upmanns. He'd just recovered his change when the explosions shook the bar's glasses. A display of pipes fell to the floor. "*Bon Dieu!*" the woman at the tobacco counter murmured in awe, "what was that?"

Bastide rushed out the door, paused to get his bearings and sprinted up the Canebière, past the Grand Hôtel Noaille toward the smoke haze hanging over the Boulevard Garibaldi. People dodged out of his way. A middle-aged man shouted after him, telling him to be more careful. He rounded the corner and saw the smoke and flames billowing from the Brasserie Alsacienne. Wounded customers were lying on the ground, others were staggering from the doors, smoke-smudged and bloody, coughing and crying, their clothes torn and scorched. He moved closer and felt the soles of his shoes sticking to the pavement. He was walking through a viscous sooty layer of scarlet blood. Two uniformed policemen were carrying a moaning, half-naked woman away from the smoke. Her hair had been scorched and her face was swollen with severe burns.

Bastide saw a hooded man leaning against a nearby plane tree. The man pushed himself from the trunk and made his way unsteadily to a tree further away. Dark, shining stains spotted the man's clothing.

Bastide hurried forward, drawing his revolver. "*Halte,* police!" he shouted, leveling his Magnum.

The man turned, slid down the tree into a sitting position. The dull muzzle of an automatic pointed in Bastide's direction. Bastide fired twice. The roar of the Magnum was deafening. The hooded man's body spun away from the tree. Bastide felt his stomach turn over. He moved forward cautiously, crouched over his target and felt for an artery pulse. A uniformed policeman with a Browning automatic in his hand hurried to Bastide's side.

"Don't waste time," Bastide snapped. "There may be more of them!"

A secondary gas explosion sent a second acrid cloud of smoke and debris onto the sidewalk. There were more screams as the rescuers dragged the wounded further away. Bastide holstered his revolver and reached over to tug at the dead man's hood. He peeled it off, lowering the man's head gently to the pavement. He was a North African.

"Roger!" Mattei shouted, jumping from his car. "You all right?"

"*Ça va,*" Bastide replied, without looking up, continuing to examine the corpse and the blood stains on the clothing. He opened a slash in the suit coat gingerly and probed for a wound. A jagged shard of glass was embedded deeply in the flesh of the upper arm. He checked another wound and found the same thing.

"*Putain!*" Mattei cursed. "He's a *bicot!*"

"He is North African," Bastide replied with irritation, "if that's what you mean."

"How many times did you hit him," Mattei asked. "He looks like a sieve."

"Flying glass did most of it," Bastide explained. "He was too close to his own grenade."

Mattei crouched beside Bastide and began a pocket search. He glanced at the dead man's face and reached up to close the staring eyes.

"Moukli's work?" Mattei asked.

"I'm afraid so," Bastide replied, standing up, trying to keep his hands from shaking. "He's decided to put all his chips on the double zero."

CHAPTER 6

The attack on the Brasserie produced a siege atmosphere. Marseille pulled in on itself defensively in expectation of the coming storm. The underworld, the city officials, the police, the workers, even the long established bourgeois had learned to live with gang skirmishes. The burned-out front of a bar or the officially chalked outlines of a corpse on the pavement didn't interrupt the daily routine. They were integral parts of the city's environment, fragments of local folklore. The "*coup de Brasserie*" was different. It was a direct notification that the killings in the Panier and Mazargues were not isolated, one-time attempts to challenge Mondolino's supremacy. The Brasserie had been the newest jewel in Mondolino's crown. Its destruction had been a double-handed slap to the old man. Marseille held its collective breath waiting for him to accept the challenge.

News of the attack reached Mondolino in Brignolle where he and Campagna had stopped to visit an old friend on their way back from Draguignan. A preliminary report from Marcel Perret over the Cadillac's car telephone provided the details. Campagna did the talking, relaying Mondolino's questions and orders. One priority was the identification of the assailant killed by the police. Campagna suggested that Perret make use of a contact in the Hôtel de Police with access to the morgue. Mondolino called for a meeting at his villa.

It began at midnight, despite Bachir Moukli's empty chair. The alliance with Grondona was fully discussed. Haro, freed from his hostage role in Nice, was ordered to integrate Barberi and his men into the Mondolino gang and share his operational control with Soames, l'Anglais. The professorial Perret reported on the damage and casualties at the Brasserie. Campagna made it clear that Grondona had agreed not to set foot in Marseille during the "*nettoyage*" but René Polito would be standing by to negotiate any problems.

When the administrative details were finished, Mondolino fixed his eyes on Moukli's place at the table.

"Where is he?" he demanded.

"He has the flu," Perret explained.

"Bring Moukli here," Mondolino said. "I want to talk with him."

Perret glanced uneasily at Campagna.

"I'll get him," Haro volunteered. "Is he at home?"

"That's what I was told," Perret replied.

"Very well," Mondolino said to Haro. "Go now."

There was a long silence after Haro had left the room. Campagna was the first to speak. "You have suspicions?" he asked.

Mondolino poured himself some mineral water and drank it. Campagna noticed that the old man's hands were steady. He seemed younger, as if he'd drawn on some secret reserve of inner strength.

"Paulo," Mondolino replied, "Bachir is an ambitious man. We crushed him once. I'm sure he's not forgotten it. Put yourself in his place. With Grondona and me knocking heads like two goats . . ." He left the sentence unfinished and raised his hands, palms out.

"He'd never dare," Perret said.

Mondolino laughed, coughed, brought up some phlegm and wiped it from his lips with a handkerchief. "You don't know the North Africans like I do," he explained. "They may appear docile but they have fire in their bellies. Have you never noticed Moukli when he sits with us? He says yes, he smiles, he even flatters me, but the dislike bubbles just below the surface. I may be wrong. I hope I am. But I should have thought of it sooner. We all should have thought of it sooner."

"We should have warned Haro," Perret said.

"No," Mondolino said, shaking his head. "I don't want to warn Moukli in advance. Haro is a good soldier but he wears his feelings on his sleeve."

The telephone rang in the hall. Mondolino turned to Perret, indicating he should reply.

"Paulo," Mondolino said, "if I am correct about Moukli it must all be done quickly. First Taroud and each of the men he has given us. I would want Moukli alive, for a limited time."

Perret came back into the dining room, heavy glasses pushed up on his forehead, his mouth working nervously. "The man killed at the Brasserie," he told them, "he was a North African."

"Strange coincidence," Mondolino remarked, smiling across the table at Campagna.

Mattei took off his dark glasses to watch Henri Barberi enter the apartment building near Saint-Victor. It was 8 a.m. Lenoir was sleeping beside him in the unmarked police sedan. They'd relieved another stake-out team at midnight and taken turns observing the building. Mattei poked Lenoir in the ribs. The young detective sat bolt upright, blinking his eyes and smoothing his sparse mustache.

"*Debout*, sleeping beauty!" Mattei told him. "Barberi's just gone in."

"Shall we pick him up?" Lenoir asked, his voice still heavy with sleep.

"Not without help." Mattei put his glasses back on, picked up the radio mike and called for a backup.

It was a bright, clear morning. The sun was rising over the tiled roofs, illuminating the pastel-colored walls of the old *quartier*. Gray pigeons were cooing and pecking at refuse in the gutters.

"Oh ho!" Mattei said, leaning forward, his head close to the windshield. "Look at that!"

Barberi was leaving the building accompanied by Soloman and Panizzo. Mattei called in again, outlined the situation and secured the radio mike.

"Come on," he told Lenoir, locking the car door, "let's go for a walk."

They took different sides of the street and hurried after the three Niçois. Mattei could see Barberi talking, emphasizing his words with his hands. They slowed when they reached the rue d'Endoume and turned left. The two detectives adjusted their pace accordingly. It suddenly came back to Mattei. Barberi was one of the men he'd seen six months earlier in the Café des Colonies when he was handing out *auto-portraits* of the killer in the Feldman case.

A passing delivery truck hid Mattei's quarry from view as they crossed to the rue Sainte. Then it pulled ahead and he saw them enter a corner café. Mattei stepped into a ship chandler's doorway and motioned for Lenoir to join him. Lenoir crossed the street, hands deep in his jacket pockets, trying to look inconspicuous. He stood a few feet from Mattei looking at the display of brass fittings and bright-yellow life jackets.

"Get the car," Mattei said. "Radio the name and location of the café. Hurry up, they won't be dawdling over their breakfast."

The sun on the café's windows made it difficult for Mattei to see what was going on. He could make out Barberi and his men standing at the bar but he didn't want to shade his eyes for a better view. It would be too obvious. He walked up the street to a *pâtisserie,* bought a *croissant* from the rosy-cheeked woman behind the counter, and took up a new position opposite the café. Halfway through the buttery *croissant* he realized he was breaking his diet but it didn't worry him. Tailing someone burned up calories and eating kept him from smoking cigarettes.

A dented white sedan with rust spots on the doors pulled to the curb about forty feet away. He glanced at the car casually, noting it had parked illegally and wondering if a traffic warden would arrive in time to give the driver a ticket. He was about to turn his attention back to the café when the occupants of the Peugeot stepped out onto the street.

"Putain de merde!" Mattei cursed under his breath, his hand unbuttoning his blazer.

Four of them. All North African. Two wearing long raincoats. On a sunny day? He knew why. They were hiding something heavy—something deadly. He only had seconds to make a decision. Without a backup his choice was extremely limited. He stepped off the curb and crossed the street to the café, pushed the door half open with his foot and drew his Magnum, raising it shoulder high to insure easy visibility.

"Police," he shouted, "hands on the bar!" He glanced out of the corner of his eye at the North Africans. They'd stopped by their car, hesitating. He felt like a sardine in a sandwich. If either Barberi or the North Africans began firing he'd be the first casualty.

"You're mad!" the barman shouted in protest.

"Ta gueule!" Mattei responded, noting that Barberi and his men were following his orders. He heard car doors slamming behind him and turned to see the white sedan careen away, leaving a residue of smoking rubber on the asphalt.

"Petit Jésus!" Mattei murmured, holstering his weapon and stepping into the café.

"What is all this?" the barman demanded. "You playing cowboy?"

"Get me a coffee," Mattei growled, "and relax."

He wiped the perspiration from his brow. "Barberi," he said, "bring your friends over here to the table. Let's have a quick talk."

The three gunmen took their hands off the bar and walked toward Mattei. He indicated the chairs and they sat down. Barberi was the only one wearing a hat. His face was expressionless but he kept his eyes fixed on Mattei. The barman brought Mattei's coffee. He was about to continue his protest but Mattei motioned him away.

"Keep your hands on the table," Mattei told them before turning to Barberi. "It's been a long time," he said, dropping a sugar cube into his espresso. "Our last meeting at the Café des Colonies wasn't very sociable. Remember? You told me you were from Lyon."

"What do you want?" Barberi asked. Soloman studied the ceiling and Panizzo glared at Mattei.

"I just want a bit of quiet," Mattei responded. "It's been a busy morning. In fact, I just saved your collective ass. If you'd been more alert you'd have noticed some very bad boys outside. I think they belong to your associate Monsieur Moukli."

Soloman stopped his contemplation of the ceiling. Panizzo's frown deepened. A slight twitch at the corner of Barberi's thin mouth was the only signal of his reaction.

"Two of them were wearing raincoats," Mattei continued. "I imagine their hidden ordnance would have spattered you all over that bar mirror by now if I hadn't been here."

Barberi pinched the bridge of his nose. "Are you holding us for some reason?" he asked. "If not, we have business."

"I'm sure you do." Mattei lifted his cup and drained the coffee in one long draft. As he put the cup down he glanced out the window. Where the hell was Lenoir? He didn't relish sitting along with three of Grondona's top guns.

"Listen, *flic,*" Barberi said without emotion, "we do not have the time to humor you. Tell us what you want . . . or we're leaving."

Mattei leaned forward and drew his revolver from its hip holster in one smooth movement. He kept it under the table, the thick barrel in direct line with Barberi's crotch.

"No one is leaving," Mattei said quietly. "We're going to sit here and wait for my backup. Then we're going to the Hôtel de Police where you can tell us all about Tonin Russo."

"*Salaud!*" Soloman cursed under his breath.

"That is one man's opinion," Mattei commented.

Commissaire Aynard was strangely passive. Joe Bellot had briefed him earlier on the Draguignan meeting, playing it as if his knowledge was the result of normal surveillance. Bastide had reported on the Brasserie attack. He'd made it clear that indications pointed to Moukli as the spark in the gangland tinder. Bastide almost had the impression that Aynard wasn't listening. Either the sudden rush of facts had been too much to assimilate or his doctor had prescribed a powerful tranquilizer to ease the pressure on his ulcer.

"Very well," Aynard said, when Bastide had finished. "What do you suggest?"

Bastide's mouth fell open. He closed it, peering closely at Aynard. "What?" Bastide asked. It was the first time Aynard had asked his opinion on anything.

"If you were sitting in my chair," Aynard said, "what would you do?"

"Well . . ." Bastide replied, hesitatingly, "I'd go after Moukli . . . with all I've got. Get him off the streets before all hell breaks loose."

"You wouldn't leave that to Grondona and Mondolino?"

"No. It would mean too much breakage."

"I see." Aynard put his fingers together and narrowed his eyes.

Bastide's mind was racing. He could hardly believe it. He finally had a chance to make some solid recommendations and he couldn't come up with the right words. Precious seconds passed before he remembered a thought he'd had that morning while he was shaving.

"I'd also tell Mondolino and Grondona what I planned to do," Bastide said. "I'd ask for their cooperation."

"Explain your logic," Aynard demanded, like a professor questioning a student on his thesis.

"They'd have to know or they'd get in the middle. If they do we'll have blood from the Arenc to Saint-Anne. If they cooperate, we profit from their resources . . . information and people."

"Would they cooperate?"

"It's worth trying."

In the heavy silence that followed, Bastide heard a dying fly buzzing on Aynard's windowsill, the clicking of the electric wall clock and the Commissaire's shallow breathing.

"If I were still in Lyon," Aynard finally said, "I wouldn't consider such a proposition." He paused to replace the top of his fountain pen. "You don't consider it strange to make an alliance with the gangs?" he asked Bastide.

"I wouldn't consider it an alliance," Bastide told him. "It would be a temporary arrangement. No handshakes, no flowers. We know who we're dealing with."

"Unorthodox, nevertheless."

"I agree." Bastide had the feeling Aynard might be setting him up for ridicule or a possible reprimand. He was waiting for the Commissaire to lash out at him, brand his suggestion an aberration and order him out of the office.

"Very well," Aynard said decisively, "I do not entirely agree but this is Marseille. Things are different. I will have to talk to the Préfet but you can prepare yourselves. This is primarily an anti-gang squad matter but with so many murders involved you are also concerned. You and Bellot will continue to work together and I will see to it that you have any support you need from other sections. Prepare everything and check with me in two hours."

"Are we authorized to contact Mondolino and Grondona?" Bastide asked.

"Once I give the green light," Aynard told him. "If, by any chance, either of these gentlemen have problems of protocol because of their 'high' positions and want to deal with me directly, tell them it's out of the question. *That* I will not do. If they refuse to cooperate or envisage eliminating Moukli's men on their own, we'll come down on them like an avalanche. Understood?"

"Understood," Bastide agreed, dumbfounded by the change in Aynard.

"That's all, Inspector," Aynard said, nodding toward the door.

Once alone the Commissaire opened his desk drawer and removed a long tube of tablets. He dropped the tube into his wastebasket. He hadn't told Bastide that he'd be entering the Hôtel Dieu that evening for an operation on his ulcer. Only his superiors and his secretary knew of his plans. He felt tired, vulnerable and surprisingly uninterested in what might happen to Marseille during the next twenty-four hours. He had no great expectations for the results of the operation. Clearing the top of his desk for the Commissaire who'd replace him temporarily, he reflected that his continued presence in Marseille would probably produce a new hole in his stomach.

Arnaud, le Rouquin, Haro and Robert, l'Anglais, Soames met in a tea salon on the rue Paradis. The tall, red-haired Haro and the husky, dark Soames had drawn curious, surprised glances from the chubby women who frequented the salon for their afternoon treat of rich cream *éclairs* and fruit tarts. The presence of the two men disturbed them. They seemed alien to the environment. But it was just such an environment that Haro had chosen for their first meeting. No snooping detective or police informer was likely to spot them in le Poussin Bleu.

"So," Soames said, "Moukli has disappeared?"

"Momentarily," Haro replied. "His apartment is empty. His servant has gone. Someone has left a huge portion of seed for the birds. It appears he won't be returning to the apartment for some time."

"It is Moukli then?"

"I would have some doubt but for one thing. His men have also evaporated. All those he sent to work with us failed to appear today. I've tried to locate them. No luck. No excuses."

A slow smile spread over Soames's face. "You were going to butt them anyway," he said. "They must have sensed it."

"I think Moukli knew what was coming. The guilty are always sensitive."

Soames tasted his tea and grimaced. "Why can't the Marseillais make a decent cup of tea," he demanded. "This is supposed to be Earl Grey and it tastes like pollution from the Étang de Berre. You're not drinking yours?"

"I never drink tea," Haro told him.

"You have a good reputation," Soames said, changing the subject. "We know of you in Nice."

Haro acknowledged the professional recognition with a brief smile.

"I can say the same of you . . . in Marseille."

"Shall I ask questions or do you want to talk?" Soames asked.

"You ask the questions."

"I have fourteen guns. Is that enough?"

"For the moment five or six will do. You can hold the others in reserve."

"How difficult will it be to find Moukli and his people? Will it take long?"

"I don't think so. We're already working on it. I don't think they've gone far. But he's no one's fool. He'll try to hit us first."

Soames nodded and bit into a chocolate cookie with his white, even teeth. "Most of my men don't know Marseille," he said. "Barberi does. You can depend on him. But we'll take our lead from you. You give us the targets and the location, we'll do the rest."

"Mondolino wants Moukli alive," Haro explained. "He has some *personal* business with him."

"I understand. Tell me about the police. How much interference can we expect?"

"Enough to make it difficult," Haro replied. "The anti-gang squad under Joe Bellot is active. Not too bright, but eager and trigger happy. Inspector Bastide runs homicide. He's tough and he moves fast. Look out for him. My boss makes it his policy to avoid trouble with the police. If it comes to a showdown he prefers us to go along quietly. He's got a battery of lawyers prepared to spring us. Tell your men to keep their hands off their weapons in any confrontation. The anti-gang cowboys would like nothing better than a live target."

"Are they going to interfere?"

"If they have to. It's our job to see they aren't around."

"Suppose one of my men is hit?"

"We've a good specialist with his own private clinic. No problem there."

Soames finished his tea and topped off the cup from the pot. He smiled at a woman who'd been staring in his direction. She flushed and turned away. "Did you see the pearls on that crow?" Soames murmured. "They'd buy a good week of play at one of Grondona's casinos." He craned his neck looking toward the plate-glass window fronting onto the sidewalk.

"Look," Soames said, indicating Haro's bodyguard. "I think your shadow wants to see you."

Célestin was standing with his nose a few inches from the window, making fluttery gestures with one thick hand. In a few more seconds he would have the attention of every dowager in the salon. Haro threw some money on the table and Soames followed him to the door.

"What the hell is it," Haro demanded. "You look like the village idiot!"

"Monsieur Mondolino sent a message," he explained. "Mattei of Homicide has picked up Barberi and two other Grondona people. He wants you to find out what the charges are."

"I don't like that," Soames said grimly, "I don't like that at all."

Bachir Moukli had turned an old wine cellar on the rue de Refuge into a redoubt. The street-level windows had been shuttered and reinforced with iron bars. The thick outer and inner doors at the top and bottom of the steep stone stairway were each guarded by one of his men. Moukli sat at a wooden table in the center of the cellar. It was bare exept for a telephone, a telephone book and a plastic Cinzano ashtray. The whitewashed stone walls reflected the light from the bare bulb over the table. The damp air was thick with cigarette smoke. The strong black tobacco blended with the odor of sour wine to produce an acrid, oppressive pall in the low-ceilinged cellar. Ahmed Taroud stood in front of the table and two other North Africans were leaning against the wall. Taroud had just reported on the abortive attempt to eliminate Barberi and he was waiting for Moukli's reaction.

Moukli's eyes narrowed as he contemplated what Taroud had told him. He was in need of a shave. His paisley necktie hung loose and unknotted from his collar.

"I didn't expect the police to interfere so soon," he finally said, almost as if he were speaking to himself. "First they drop Hassan at the Brasserie. Now they save Barberi. It is all wrong. I'm after Mondolino and Grondona. I don't want a battle with the police!"

Taroud said nothing. His blind eye glistened in the raw light, unblinking, as he waited for Moukli to continue.

"Who was it this time?" Moukli asked.

"The Corsican . . . Mattei."

"First Bastide and now Mattei." Moukli spoke the names as if they were tainted. "I expected trouble to come from the anti-gang squad, not homicide. What are they doing in all this?"

"Death is their business," Taroud replied.

"It's also ours," Moukli said. "This is going badly. We cannot afford further delays. If the police get in the way again treat them as enemies."

"Is that wise?"

Moukli shook his head. "We have no choice. The next forty-eight hours are crucial."

The telephone rang and Moukli snatched it from its cradle. "*Allo,*" Moukli responded. He listened, nodding his head. "Yes, very good. Yes, quickly." He put the phone down. "We've found Barberi's other *planque.* It's out in Haut Canet. There is only one man there. Go, immediately. Rendezvous with Mohammed at the Esso station off the Autoroute Nord. Eliminate this person and leave a present for Barberi's return. Call me when you're finished."

Taroud pointed to the two men near the wall, indicating they should follow him and vaulted up the stairs past the sentry.

Pierre Ducroix had just made himself a large sandwich. He'd sliced a crusty *baguette* down the middle, buttered it, layered it with slices of *Gruyère* and salami and applied a thick coat of Dijon mustard. He put the sandwich on a plate, carried it into the villa's front room and sat down in front of the small color television set. He poured himself a full glass of red wine from an open bottle and tried to catch up on the soccer game he'd been watching. A sawed-off 12 gauge shotgun was on the floor at his feet. The match between France and Wales was important to Ducroix. He had 600 *francs* riding on a French victory. He bit into the sandwich and leaned forward, intent on an upcoming penalty kick.

Taroud and his three men circled the villa and halted at a rear wall. The narrow street was quiet. Taroud muttered a few words in Arabic. One of his men joined his hands to provide a foot lift. He boosted Taroud up the wall. He hung there unsteadily, searching for a handhold between the jagged glass shards imbedded in the cement. Then he lifted himself with a great effort and brought one foot up till he found a purchase on the top of the wall. He dropped from sight into the garden. The others followed him.

The Welsh were playing rough. One of the French players had been carried off the field. Ducroix listened to the chant of protest from the French supporters and added his own comments. He wiped some mustard from his lips and tensed for the next play.

The thin wire flashed before his eyes. His brain sent a tardy alarm message but the garrote closed on his throat before his muscles could react. He thrashed in place, heels drumming on the faded carpets, eyes bulging as the wire bit into his flesh. His frantic fingers punctured the chair's upholstery. Taroud applied a final pressure, pulling the garrote's toggles tight until Ducroix was limp and still.

"Get him out of here," he said, unwinding the bloody wire. "He stinks."

His assistants dragged Ducroix's body out into the kitchen. Taroud moved quickly to the front door. He crouched down, examining the entrance, running his fingers over the doorjamb, noting that the door opened inward. He took a fragmentation grenade from the pocket of his baggy raincoat and put it on the floor. He reached into the same pocket for a coil of thin plastic fishing leader and a small box of carpet tacks. He picked up the grenade, moving it up the molding to the left of the door till it was about two feet off the floor. Satisfied, he put the grenade down and dug in his pocket for the adhesive tape.

He taped the grenade firmly in place and pushed a sharp tack into the soft wood at the inside base of the door. He unwound the coil of line, threading one end through the grenade's pin, and led it down to the tack. He took up the slack slowly, tightening the line and securing it. Taroud straightened, inspecting his handiwork.

"*Voilà,*" he murmured, "that should do it."

One of his men stood mesmerized in front of the television. "What are you doing?" Taroud demanded. "France two, Wales nothing," the man replied. "It's a good game."

When Antoine Mondolino laughed it sounded like his body was breaking up. Grating sounds came from deep in his chest and dissipated into staccato raspings by the time they reached his open mouth.

"I don't believe it," he said, dabbing at his eyes with a crisply ironed handkerchief. "*You* are going to protect us. *You* are going after Moukli?"

"That's it," Bastide said, straight-lipped. "This is going to be our responsibility. We don't want a gang war in Marseille."

Joe Bellot stood beside Bastide in Mondolino's study, his arms folded. Paul Campagna was on the other side of Mondolino's desk. He looked as if he'd been presented with a difficult riddle.

"You want our help?" Campagna asked.

"Correct," Bastide responded. "It's very simple. Moukli started this trouble. We're going after him. We want you and Grondona to step aside. But we need all the information and support you can give us. The sooner we cooperate, the sooner it'll be finished."

"You're too late, Inspector," Mondolino said, glancing at Campagna. "I'm afraid Moukli's days are numbered. Of course, I don't know who is tracking him, but I don't think you'll have to worry about him much longer. Why don't you go back to your Commissaire Aynard. Tell him we appreciate his concern but we can take care of our own problems."

Bastide glared at Mondolino, his jaw clenched, trying to dominate his anger.

"Listen well, old man," Bastide said speaking slowly, "I may be simply another Inspector of Police to you but this is my city. It was also my grandfather's and my father's city. If you and your scum don't do what we say there will be a war. But this time it won't be you, Grondona and Moukli. I'll be in, Bellot will be in it and every *flic* in Marseille will be involved. The Commissaire told me to warn you that we'll hit you like an avalanche and we will. In fact, I'm beginning to hope you'll remain as stubborn and stupid as you are now. It will be much simpler if we know who our enemies really are."

"Oh là là!" Mondolino said, feigning shock. "That is no way for a servant of the people to talk."

Bastide addressed himself to Campagna. "You refuse to cooperate?" he asked.

"You heard Monsieur Mondolino," Campagna replied with just enough hesitation to indicate a certain lack of enthusiasm.

"You're making a mistake," Joe Bellot told them. "My men are on the street now. If your boys get in the way . . ." He shrugged his shoulders.

"Come on," Bastide said, "we're wasting our time." He turned and left the room.

"Too bad," Bellot commented before following Bastide.

Campagna hurried after them to open the door.

"Inspector," he whispered as he let Bastide out, "I'll try to reason with him. He's old and he tends to live in the past. I don't think he realizes how things have changed."

Bastide paused, searching his pockets for a cigar. He found it and struck a match. "We can't wait," he warned. "But call us if he changes his mind."

When Campagna returned to the study Mondolino was smiling. "Imagine," he said, "the police offering us protection. It's hard to believe. They've lost their balls—turned into old women." The smile disappeared. "I don't like Bastide," Mondolino said, frowning. "He has no respect for age. He talks to me as if I were a street corner hoodlum. If his meddling continues he should be taught a lesson. One his colleagues will remember."

"You've always said the police shouldn't be touched."

"That's true, Paulo, under normal circumstances. But in an emergency one takes calculated risks. Do you remember that detective from Toulon in nineteen seventy? He pistol-whipped my nephew and the boy lost an eye. We handled that correctly. They found the detective floating off the Quai Stalingrad and a lot of tough cops began to act like kittens."

"This isn't the same," Campagna said. "Bastide is only doing his job."

The old man examined Campagna quizzically. "I don't like the way he does his job," he snapped. "What's gotten into you? Are you becoming softheaded?"

"No, but I believe we have enough problems with Moukli without battling the police."

"Paulo," Mondolino said wistfully, "you will never lead an organization. You're too cautious. You listen to lawyers when you should be listening to your heart. There is a time to be passive and a time to strike. I promise you, if that Bastide interferes again, I'll deal with him."

Dinh Le Thong listened carefully to what his diminutive visitor had to say. The man was a dark-skinned Cambodian with a wide, flat face and black, bowl-cut hair. They were sitting in the warm kitchen.

A large stockpot bubbled on the stove. Thong's niece was setting tables in the restaurant, singing a Vietnamese love song in a high, fluctuating voice.

"Mondolino's people have located three of the Arabs that had been working with them," the Cambodian told Thong. "They will go after them tomorrow."

"How do you know this?" Thong asked.

"My sister sleeps with one of Mondolino's men. He drinks. He talks too much."

"Where?"

"The Arabs take coffee every morning in the Café Agadir on the rue de l'Étoile. My sister's lover says it's a sewer full of rats that needs cleaning. He told her he didn't care how many Arabs he killed."

Thong rubbed his cropped head and offered the Cambodian a cigarette. He lit it for him and put the packet back in his shirt pocket. "You have no idea what hour this might be?" he asked.

"No. Early, I suppose."

"I thank you," Thong said. "What you have told me is useful. Anything your sister tells you will be of interest."

The Cambodian joined his palms together, bowing his head. Thong led him into the restaurant, opened the drawer of the cash register and handed him several 100 *franc* notes. When the man had left Thong picked up the phone and dialed Bastide's number at the Hôtel de Police.

The morning was fresh but warm. The Arab and Armenian traders on the rue d'Aix were setting their display trays out on the sidewalk, filling them with cut-rate clothes, kitchen utensils and cheap running shoes made in Taiwan and South Korea. Stout North African women with large rattan shopping bags were hurrying to the market and their men were leaving for a hard day of work on construction sites and civic projects. Laughing children were lined up for the buses that would take them to school.

Haro ordered his driver to double-park on the rue des Dominicaines and got out of the car. His bodyguard and another man joined him from the backseat. He had decided to direct this operation himself. Mondolino wanted no errors or slip-ups. If Haro's plan was working, and it should be, three more of his men were approaching the rue de l'Étoile from the other direction. As he turned into the short street he could see his scout walking toward them. The Café Agadir would be on the man's right. Haro paused, keeping his eyes on the scout's progress. He watched him stop in front of the café to light a cigarette. He tossed his match into the gutter and nodded an affirmation before he resumed walking.

"Go!" Haro said, waving the two men behind him forward. Two other gunmen hurried toward the café from the other end of the street. Haro moved forward till he could see the café's entrance. He folded his arms and leaned against the facade of an old hotel.

"You're up early, carrot-top." Bastide stood behind Haro with the muzzle of his Magnum caressing Haro's neck. Mattei stepped forward, running his hands over Haro's body, searching for a weapon.

"He's clean," Mattei said.

"Come on," Bastide ordered, pushing him along the sidewalk. "Call off your wolves!"

The gunmen had almost reached the café. Bastide saw Bellot and his men appear at the bar corner.

"Call them off, damn it!" Bastide demanded, jabbing Haro with the Magnum. Haro said nothing. Haro's bodyguard turned, saw Bastide and Mattei and froze.

"Stop," Bastide shouted. Mattei crossed to the other side of the street, edging forward. "Police! Flat on the ground, all of you!"

Shutters banged overhead as residents pulled them closed. A mother reached out of a passageway and jerked a young child to safety. The rue de l'Étoile was suddenly clear of pedestrians.

One of Haro's men disappeared into the café. Bastide swung Haro around by his collar and pushed him toward Lenoir. "Watch him," he said.

There was a burst of fire from the café. Haro's bodyguard drew his .45. "Drop it!" Mattei ordered, his Manurhin braced. Célestin's Colt blasted a chunk of plaster into the air above Mattei's head. Bastide fired from a crouch, his Magnum bucking in both hands. He missed Célestin but hit the man behind him. Bellot dropped Célestin with a shot between the shoulder blades. He fell on his face, his .45 discharging when it struck the pavement. The street was blue with smoke and the acrid odor of gunpowder. More plainclothesmen were pounding up the street toward the café.

"Watch it!" Bastide shouted at Mattei as they both moved forward, weapons extended.

An Arab appeared at the entrance to the café. He was holding on to the doorway with one hand. His bearded face was bloodied. The sun glinted off the nickled automatic in his right hand.

"C'est fini!" Mattei bellowed. "Give me your gun."

The man staggered, regained his footing and shook his head as if to clear it, spattering blood on the wall. Mattei moved forward, hand outstretched.

"Doucement," he said softly, "give it to me."

Bastide watched the bright automatic being raised. It seemed to be happening in slow motion . . . a sequence from a bad dream.

"No!" Bastide shouted, hoping to distract the gunman. The seconds were passing. The automatic was almost in line with Mattei's head. Mattei leapt for cover. Bastide squeezed the trigger twice, blinking at the shock of the reports. The Arab was thrown back into the doorway by the impact.

"Merde!" Bastide murmured, the Magnum hanging slack in his hand. He saw Bellot, his weapon held high in both hands, peer cautiously into the café. Mattei moved to join him. Bastide followed, stepping over Célestin's body, noting the rivulet of slow-moving, crimson blood in the gutter.

"An *abbatoir,"* Bellot said as he reached the doorway. The dead Arab was lying on his back, both eyes open, half of his lower jaw missing. Bastide took a deep breath and stepped inside. Haro's gunman had caught Moukli's men at the bar. They lay in a tangle of limbs and smashed coffee cups. The Arab Bastide had dropped at the door had obviously fought back. Haro's man was writhing on the floor, his knees drawn up to his chest, bloody hands clutching his stomach.

"Get him to an ambulance," Mattei told one of the detectives.

"C'est pas beau," Bellot remarked, shaking his head.

"Babar," Bastide said, reloading and holstering his Magnum, "bring Haro in here."

"With pleasure," Mattei said, hurrying out the door.

Bastide put one hand on the bar. He felt sick and angry. This wasn't police work. It was slaughter. Mattei returned, pushing Haro ahead of him. His hands were handcuffed.

"Are you content?" Bastide asked. "Are you happy now? Take a good look, you bastard! Here," he said, pushing Haro toward the bar. "Walk in the blood. That's it, get your shoes dirty. I ought to make you roll in it."

Chez Angele was crowded and noisy. The long, narrow dining room was hot from the pizza oven and the general gaiety was punctuated by popping wine corks. Bastide and Mattei weren't joining in the ambiance. They were devouring their pizzas in silence. Neither of them had found time for lunch and they were both hungry and exhausted.

"You know," Mattei ventured, "after a day like this the thought of retirement is welcome."

Bastide looked across the checked tablecloth but said nothing.

"I have an uncle in Corsica," Mattei continued. "He's a widower and had no children. I'm his heir. When he goes I get his property near Calvi. Fifteen *hectares* of almonds and olives, an old farmhouse with thick walls and a solid roof. You can see the sea from the second-floor windows. There are songbirds in the woods."

Bastide pushed his half-finished plate aside and poured some Chianti into their glasses.

"Five dead," Bastide said grimly, "and we've got nothing to show for it."

"At least Haro's off the street."

"Hardly worth it, was it?"

"You make it sound as if it's our fault."

"Wait for tomorrow's papers," Bastide said. "We'll be blamed."

Mattei shook some peppered oil from a cruet onto the last of his pizza and popped it into his mouth. "What you need is sleep," he said. "Let's get out of here."

It was after midnight when Bastide returned to his apartment. He poured himself an Armagnac, opened the doors to the balcony and took a deep breath of fresh air. A full moon hung over the city, tinting the roofs with a silver light and softening the shadows of the narrow streets. There was a party of some kind going on at the floating Yacht Club moored to the Quai de Rive Neuve. He could hear laughter and the clink of glasses. It was strange how far sound could travel once the rush of traffic had diminished. He yawned, remembering how tired he was. He finished his Armagnac in the kitchen, washed the glass and retired to the bedroom. Stripping to his shorts, he brushed his teeth and fell into bed.

The repetitive ringing of the telephone jolted him from a deep sleep. He flicked the bedside lamp on and checked his watch. It was 2 a.m.

"Bastide," he murmured groggily.

"Roger, are you all right?"

It was a bad connection. Janine sounded as if she were speaking under water.

"I'm fine," Bastide told her, "and you?"

"I heard about the shootings on shortwave," she told him. "Were you there?"

"Yes."

"I knew it! I'm coming back."

"No! Janine, listen to me. Stay where you are. It's better that way."

A buzzing on the line interrupted them momentarily.

"You don't want me to return," she said. He could hear the resentment in her voice.

"No, it isn't that. Be reasonable. It's going to get worse. Please, listen to me. Ah . . . give me your telephone number." He grabbed a pen and wrote the number on a pad. "The Hotel Thalassa? You'll be there tomorrow night. Good, I'll call you. If I can't get through call me here . . . late. How is Greece?"

"I think I should come back."

"Bon sang! Don't you understand? It's better for both of us if you're not here!"

There was a click followed by a steady hum. Janine had hung up. Bastide sighed, turned off the light and fell back onto his pillow. In the few minutes he remained awake he realized he'd handled the call badly.

It was 2 a.m. and Halimi was late for their meeting. Mattei was exhausted. He'd spent the afternoon and most of the night trying to squeeze information out of Henri Barberi. He'd used every trick of the trade but the elderly gunman had sat in a straight-backed chair, his wrinkled face emotionless, his mouth shut. Mattei was convinced that Barberi had perfected a method of sleeping with his eyes open.

The only time he'd spoken during the interrogation was to ask for his hat. When Mattei retrieved it Barberi had squared it carefully on his head and resumed his sphinx-like attitude.

Mattei was alone in his Mercedes. He'd parked at the top of the Cours Julien. He was fighting to keep himself awake. Earlier he'd been able to watch late diners leaving the small restaurants along the Cours. It had been a welcome diversion. Now the restaurants were closed and the street was dark. A few cats were rat hunting among the garbage cans. Mattei closed his eyes for several seconds, drifting off to sleep. He caught himself in time and sat up straight. He'd decided to stretch his legs when Halimi arrived. Mattei opened the door and Halimi slipped in beside him. Halimi smelled of lamb fat. Mattei rolled down the window.

"I am late," Halimi said. "The end of Ramadan. A big family feast. I could not leave earlier. What is so urgent?"

"I've been here for over an hour," Mattei complained. "You're supposed to be dependable!"

"I told you. It was . . ."

"Never mind." Mattei cut him off.

"Who do you know among Moukli's crowd?"

Halimi did a delayed double take before he responded. "None of them are my friends," he said.

"I don't care about friendship," Mattei told him. "Who do you know? Who can you get to? Be careful, I'm too tired for any bull-shit!"

Halimi's baby face wrinkled with earnest thought. "There is a fel-low called Asnir. I see him when I play the horses. But he is not an important man. He drives for Moukli . . . from time to time."

"He plays the horses?" Mattei said with obvious interest. "Good, that means he's hungry."

"I don't understand," Halimi said, pulling a small plastic bag from his pocket. "Would you like some preserved orange slices? Very tasty."

"Bugger the orange slices," Mattei said, grabbing the bag and throwing it into the backseat. "If Asnir plays the horses, he needs money. We need information. Can you make a deal with him?"

"It's possible. But risky."

"We'll make it worth your while."

"What do you want to know?"

"Moukli's whereabouts and his next move."

"Aieee!" Halimi murmured, exhaling. "That may be too much to ask. Asnir is not suicidal."

"Very well. We'll settle for the next move. That's more important."

"I know why you're anxious," Halimi said. "The owner of the Café Agadir gave me a full description of what happened. I presume you expect Moukli to hit back?"

"Correct."

"And you would like to stop him?"

"Brilliant, Halimi! Your mind strikes sparks."

"Oh, you know, it is not too difficult," Halimi said, "but this will be most dangerous . . . for me and Asnir."

Mattei drew a thick sealed envelope from the breast pocket of his blazer. *"Voilà,"* he said, handing the envelope to Halimi. "This is more than you've ever handled. Police funds and all well-counted. You're to account for every *franc.* I expect to hear from you at least once a day. If you 'mislay' any of it, you'll go into a meat grinder!"

Halimi poked the envelope into his shirtfront. "Let it be known that I cannot guarantee anything. Asnir may refuse; he may be taken sick, he may drop dead tomorrow . . ."

Mattei reached over and gripped Halimi's puffy cheeks, squeezing them till his lips puckered. "Get out," Mattei ordered, "and get to work!"

He pushed Halimi out of the Mercedes and started the engine.

"Wait!" Halimi shouted as Mattei pulled away from the curb. "My orange slices!"

CHAPTER 7

Paul Campagna frowned as Bartolomei Grondona loosed a string of profanities. He held the phone away from his ear so Antoine Mondolino could hear.

"What is happening over there?" Grondona demanded. "I gave you my full confidence. I've done my part. What is the result? Barberi, Soloman and Panizzo are in jail and Ducroix is dead. I don't like this. Let me talk to Mondolino!"

"He's not here," Campagna lied. "He is not well."

"Dommage," Grondona snapped. "My thoughts are with him. But I wonder . . . should I still trust you?"

"It has been difficult," Campagna explained. "We've suffered two dead and Haro is in the hands of the police."

"It sounds like bad planning," Grondona said. "All this to smash a tea drinking Arab? It's too much to believe!"

"The police interfered. They have warned us to remain passive."

"You're joking? Surely you're not obeying them? Listen Campagna, I'm sending René Polito to Marseille. He is to remain with you and be present for every decision. No move will be made without his agreement. I also want Soames to replace Haro. At least l'Anglais has a brain in his head. You can tell Mondolino those are my terms. If he does not agree I'm pulling everyone out. You'll be left to face Moukli and the police alone."

"I'll have to speak to the *patron,*" Campagna told him.

"Do it and call me back. Tell him to consider my demands carefully. If it continues like this you and Moukli's people will all be dead or in prison and the Senegalese will be running Marseille!"

Campagna put the telephone down slowly.

"He sounds agitated," Mondolino commented, folding his unsteady hands on the desk.

"What do you think?" Campagna asked.

"What do I think?" Mondolino sighed. "I think we must agree. We need him and now that Haro isn't available we need Soames. Polito is a reasonable man. He can be handled."

Campagna examined himself in the mirror over the mantelpiece and straightened his tie. "We'd be helping them build a power base here," he said. "Grondona could be more dangerous than Moukli."

"I know that. But we don't have much choice. When Polito arrives I want Perret to stay with him wherever he goes and whatever he does. Pick the best of Haro's men and tell him to stick with Soames, as 'guide.' We don't want l'Anglais getting lost in Marseille."

"You want me to tell Grondona we agree to his conditions?"

"Oh, not yet. Let him marinate a bit. Call him this evening. Now . . . explain what happened at Haut Canet."

Campagna sat down and lit a cigarette. "When we heard that Barberi had been picked up by homicide we sent someone out to the house he'd rented to warn whoever was left and clean up any evidence before the *flics* got there. We found one of Barberi's boys garroted in the kitchen, stiff as a stockfish. Luckily, our man had gone in the back door. The front door was booby-trapped with a grenade."

"He didn't leave it there?" Mondolino asked.

"No. He cleared it and brought it back with him."

"And the *macchabée?*"

"It's been removed. Should be in a lime bath by now."

Mondolino nodded his approval. "So," he said reflectively, "it was Bastide who ruined things at the Agadir?"

"Yes. Bastide and the Corsican, Mattei. They grabbed Haro and Bastide dropped Célestin. Bellot was also involved."

Mondolino's small eyes were shining. "I have a job for Soames. We'll see if he's as good as Grondona says he is. I want Bastide's skin!"

"I wouldn't advise it," Campagna said, pulling himself upright in his chair. "It's not the time . . ."

"You're wrong, Paulo," Mondolino told him. "It *is* the time. That *salopard* has been under our feet too long. I've had patience but this is too much. No *poulet* has ever spoken to me like he has. Now, he's gone too far. It's time the fools in the Hôtel de Police learned a lesson."

"But we can't afford a war with the police!"

"War? Who speaks of a war? We'll leave it to l'Anglais. Of course," Mondolino smiled, "if there is any trouble . . . he isn't one of us. They'll charge it to Grondona's account."

"Polito will never agree."

"Polito won't be involved," Mondolino said. "I am sure Soames will agree to a private arrangement."

Bachir Moukli was preparing his revenge. He'd done his planning in the smoke-filled wine cellar, sending messengers out into the city and receiving reports when they'd returned. His worktable was cluttered with empty soup bowls, half-finished bottles of wine and filled ashtrays. Four of his men were gathered in a corner of the cellar cleaning their weapons. Disassembled Heckler & Koch 94's lay on the canvas they'd spread on the stone floor. Ahmed Taroud sat at the far end of the table hunched over a hot bowl of *chorba.* He spooned the rich, coriander-flavored broth into his mouth, chewing on the bits of chicken and watching Moukli study a diagram drawn with a red marker pen. The cuffs of Moukli's white suit coat were edged with grime and there was a stain on his necktie. Taroud shifted his gaze to the men in the corner. One of them was pushing cartridges into the box magazine of a Heckler & Koch.

"Wipe those bullets carefully," Taroud warned. "We don't want any jamming." He finished the soup and cleaned his mouth with the back of his hand. "Well," he said to Moukli, "are you satisfied?"

Moukli looked down his hawk nose in Taroud's direction, blinking away the smoke from his cigarette.

"I think we are ready," Moukli replied.

"You're certain?"

"It is the only course to take. We could continue this eye-for-an-eye business for a month. It would only weaken us and in the end someone with more power could move in. We must kill the snake by cutting off its head."

"Mondolino's villa could be a fortress."

"I don't think so. He has always felt secure in his own city. No one would dare hit *le vieux.*"

"It might be better to wait till he travels again," Taroud suggested. "Easier to get him in the car."

"He seldom goes out. We can't wait."

"It will have to be fast. The police could be there quickly."

"If we do this right, there will be no warning," Moukli said, "no noise. Come over here. Let us go over everything together."

Something unusual had caught the attention of Bellot's stake-out. He'd been sharing the watch on Mondolino's villa in Redon for more than a week. It had been a boring assignment. Now he shifted his weight in the driver's seat of the unmarked police sedan to get a better view in the wing mirror. The street sweeper had spent more than fifteen minutes near the villa. Now, he'd put his broom aside to light a cigarette. The detective had done enough surveillance to recognize the technique. Normally, a street sweeper would have pushed his collection of refuse and leaves along the gutter and been well clear of the villa in a maximum of four minutes. This man was obviously observing Mondolino's property. More important, he was a North African.

The street sweeper went back to work, flicking his broom at some paper and moving beyond Mondolino's driveway. He took the small canvas bag from his shoulder and crouched down to remove a wrapped sandwich and a Thermos bottle. He sat against the trunk of a plane tree to eat. The detective was tempted to confront the man but decided it would be more profitable to watch.

Twenty minutes later the street sweeper finished his lunch, stuffed the Thermos and sandwich wrappings back into his bag and moved off down the street. The detective sighed, checking his watch. Perhaps he was too edgy. Stake-outs did that to him. The street sweeper was probably just another lazy city employee. He turned to look over his left shoulder, scanning the street. A mother pushing a baby carriage, some schoolchildren on their way home for lunch and . . . a North African leaning against the bus stop shelter across from the villa's entrance. The young man was wearing a red jogging suit and running shoes. He'd opened a newspaper and seemed absorbed in his reading. The detective smiled to himself. This was interesting. He would see just how much time passed before the jogger decided to take a bus.

"*Western à Marseille,*" the Socialist paper's headlines screamed. "*Tuerie* rue de l'Étoile!" the Communist sheet bannered. "*Succès de*

Police" the conservative daily proclaimed. Bastide chewed on his cigar as he stood by the window reading the reports. "One must ask if our police have turned into cowboys. Do we want John Wayne back from the dead and third-rate Rambos on our streets?" an editorialist asked.

Bastide threw the papers onto his desk.

Joe Bellot pushed the door open. He was out of breath from running up the stairs. "The North Africans are watching Mondolino's villa," he said. "They're working in relays. Very professional."

"That's not good," Bastide remarked, sitting down. "They must belong to Moukli."

"They're planning something," Bellot said. He detailed the stakeout's report. Bastide crushed his cigar butt in an ashtray.

"If they're working in relays we should be able to tail one of them back to the source," he said. "I'll put Lenoir on it. Are you thinking what I'm thinking?"

"They wouldn't go after Mondolino?"

"Why not? Put yourself in Moukli's place. He's been hit hard. He doesn't have much time left."

"I'd better get my people out there," Bellot said, starting for the door.

"Wait!" Bastide shouted. "We don't want to flush them now. Moukli is desperate but not crazy. I doubt if he'd try anything in broad daylight."

"You may be right but I can't take chances. My job is prevention. I can't wait to clean up the mess. I'll put in a minimum of men discreetly."

"If you must," Bastide replied. "This could be the grand finale if we play it right."

"Are you going to tell Aynard?" Bellot asked.

"Haven't you heard? The Commissaire's in the hospital for an operation. We won't see him for awhile. Commissaire Bigeard from Narcotics is sitting at his desk. He's tied up with his own problems. He doesn't seem too interested in ours."

"*Tant mieux,*" Bellot murmured. "You look tired, Roger."

"I am. Look, if you *must* send people out there tell them to be careful."

The telephone rang. Bastide picked it up, motioning for Bellot to stay. "It's Mattei," he explained, his hand over the mouthpiece. Bellot paced the floor impatiently while Bastide quizzed his assistant. He was smiling when he finally replaced the receiver.

"Money talks," Bastide said, rubbing his hands together.

"*Alors?*" Bellot asked, showing his irritation.

"Mattei made an investment in Halimi and we already have a return," Bastide explained. "Moukli's planning something for tonight."

"But where is Moukli? If we knew that we could grab him now."

"The driver is no fool. He obviously values his life. If he tipped us on Moukli's *cache* it wouldn't take long for them to trace it back to him. A *sortie* against Mondolino is another thing altogether. Even some stupid detectives could blunder onto that."

"I've got to go," Bellot said. "I'll call in once my boys are in place."

Bastide nodded and picked up the phone. He'd send Lenoir to Redon. If they were lucky, one of Moukli's men might lead him to something interesting.

Lenoir parked his car in an alley near Mondolino's villa and walked fifty feet to the main street. He knew an anti-gang stake-out was in place and he didn't want to clog the thoroughfare with police vehicles. He found what he was looking for. There was a North African waiting at the bus stop. A young man in a jogging suit who matched the stake-out's last report. Lenoir scanned the street until he found Bellot's man. The car was parked at some distance, its rear to the villa entrance and the bus stop. The stake-out was obviously using his wing mirror. A simple ploy but it usually worked. Lenoir wondered if he should advance his car to the corner but decided against it. If the jogger hopped on a bus he could get to his vehicle and follow the bus without too much trouble. If he walked off there was little chance of losing him. It would be a problem if someone picked him up in a car. Lenoir leaned against a wall to wait.

Three buses went by over a period of half an hour but the jogger was still there. Lenoir was daydreaming about his coming vacation in Spain when the fourth bus appeared and slowed for the stop. The jogger folded his paper and moved behind two other people waiting to board. Lenoir watched him climb into the bus and sprinted for his car. He started the engine, engaged the gears and cut the corner sharply, keeping the moving bus in sight. It was more difficult than he'd imagined. The further they got into the city the heavier the traffic and the more frequent the stops. He had to maneuver into the bus and taxi lane to examine the debarking passengers. Each time he did, protesting taxis blew their horns. By the time the bus reached the terminal behind the Bourse, Lenoir was perspiring profusely. His eyes were strained from trying to locate the jogger. He stopped abruptly and jumped out of the car as the bus doors were opened. He watched the passengers step down onto the pavement. No jogger. He vaulted into the bus examining the empty seats.

"Lose something?" the driver asked, eyeing him with suspicion. Lenoir ignored the question and left.

"Hey!" An officious controller hurried toward him. "You can't park there!"

Antoine Mondolino was having an early supper. He sat alone at the long dining room table eating a cheese omelet. His yellow-tinged, white hair needed cutting and his shoulders were hunched over the plate. His mind was full of problems but he was having difficulty isolating them. The past few weeks had impressed him with how old he really was. De Gaulle had once said that old age was a "shipwreck," and he'd been right. The thought that his hold on Marseille was threatened haunted him. It was a nightmare he'd never anticipated. If only his son were still alive. His sole male child had been killed in a stupid motorcycle accident ten years ago. If he were here, Mondolino mused, he'd be at my side to keep watch on the cretins that surround me.

He left his plate unfinished and rang for his servant. The plate was cleared and a bowl of stewed fruit was left for him. Mondolino drank some mineral water and thought about his wife. She'd died one year after his son and he missed her. He'd had his share of mistresses in the past but at least he'd been able to talk to his wife. Now there was no one. He left the table for his study and found Robert Soames waiting in the hall.

"Ah," Mondolino greeted him, "what is it you want?"

"Monsieur Campagna said you wished to see me."

"Yes. Come into the study."

Mondolino settled behind his desk and gestured toward another chair. "I want you to replace Haro," Mondolino said. "Grondona says you're very good."

Soames was tempted to smile but he didn't. He knew that Grondona's demand was responsible for Mondolino's summons. "Thank you," he replied.

"Bachir Moukli has made a big mistake," Mondolino said. "He is like a bull full of *banderillas* with only a short time to live. It's time for the *estocade.* You will be the *matador.*"

"I understand you want him alive?"

"No, I've changed my mind. The sooner that scum is no more, the better. You'll have all the help you need. Campagna will see to that."

"Haro told me the police are a problem."

"It's true." Mondolino sighed. "I wanted to talk with you about it." The old man hesitated, his eyes boring into Soames as he evaluated him. "I know you are loyal to Grondona," Mondolino began, "and I respect that. But I have a proposition for you."

Soames raised an eyebrow waiting for Mondolino to continue.

"I have a personal request, a special task for you," Mondolino said. "The one called Bastide. Roger Bastide . . . an Inspector."

"A policeman?" Soames asked, surprised.

"A policeman and a fool," Mondolino said.

"Monsieur Mondolino," Soames shook his head slowly, "such work is against my principles. I learned when I was young that action against the police brings trouble. It's unprofessional and extremely dangerous—like stamping on a hornet's nest with bare feet."

"I understand all that," Mondolino said, impatiently. "Normally, I would agree with you but this is a special case."

"Have you mentioned it to Monsieur Grondona?"

"No. This is between the two of us. No one else will be involved. You can name your price, the currency you desire, and whatever location you choose: Switzerland, Andorra, Monte Carlo. It could be gold if you wish."

Soames's suspicions were matched by a strong temptation. He would be betraying Grondona's trust. He knew that the Mondolino-Grondona alliance was temporary. He wondered if Mondolino's proposal was the first move in a campaign to fragment the Grondona organization. But if the old man was sincere he too would want their arrangement to remain secret. The thought of naming his own price was enticing. Grondona wouldn't last forever and Soames himself wasn't getting any younger. There was nothing more sad than an aging gunman. He'd seen them cadging drinks in the shabby bars near the port of Nice and taking any job offered for little pay. Their slow reflexes and cobwebbed brains usually put them in jail for the rest of their lives or they were found lying dead in an empty lot.

"Well?" Mondolino asked.

"Twenty-five-thousand American dollars in my account on the Isle of Jersey and the equivalent in Swiss *francs* in a numbered account in Zurich." Soames made his demand as if he'd been thinking it over for days. He was sometimes surprised by his own decisiveness. He saw Mondolino wince.

"Agreed," Mondolino said, clearing his throat to make his voice heard.

"I will be entirely alone," Soames stated as if he were reading clauses in a contract. "No one else is to know of this arrangement."

"Correct." Mondolino made a mental note to tell Campagna to keep his mouth shut. He would also have to bring Perret into it to handle the transfer of funds. Surely Soames didn't think he, Mondolino, would be rushing off to the bank to handle the transactions?

Soames watched Mondolino carefully. He knew Mondolino wouldn't and couldn't keep the project to himself but he'd learned that it was wise to let others think you were not too smart. It was a distinct advantage to be underestimated by a potential enemy.

"I would like one half of each sum immediately," Soames said. "The rest when the job is completed."

"That can be arranged," Mondolino replied. "So, we are agreed?"

Soames nodded and extended his hand. Mondolino's grip was surprisingly firm. "Now," Soames said, "in regard to your own security, I was surprised to see the villa so lightly guarded. Is there only one man on the gate?"

"One man on the gate and my valet. He is dependable. His name is Constanza. Perhaps you have heard of him?"

"Testu Constanza? He is still alive?"

Mondolino chuckled. "He is alive and he is almost as old as I am. I'll tell you something, Anglais. I'd rather have him protecting me than any of the young ones. He has eyes at the back of his head."

"I understand," Soames said, smiling, "but I would like to put one of my men in your garden if you don't object."

"As you wish. I'm sure your *patron* would approve. It would be a symbol of our cooperation."

Ahmed Taroud had decided to take four men and a driver with him for the attack on the villa. After two days and nights observing the villa they were sure there were no more than three men on guard. Traffic in and out of the main gate had been rare. They'd logged daily visits of Campagna and Perret, the arrival and departure of food delivery trucks and Soames's presence but they were unable to identify him. The arrival of Soames's man complete with small suitcase was duly noted as a probable reinforcement since he had not reappeared. Mondolino's Cadillac had come through the gates three times, twice with only the driver and once with Mondolino and Campagna sitting in the backseat.

The plan was to go over the wall at a chosen spot on a flanking street well hidden by the heavy foliage of a large oak tree. They'd use a collapsible ladder and a mattress to cover the glass shards. Taroud and one of his men would be armed with silenced .22 caliber pistols. The others would be carrying Heckler & Kochs. Moukli had warned them not to use the automatic weapons unless it was absolutely necessary. He'd stressed the importance of silence and surprise. Moukli had completed the diagram of the villa's interior. During his attendance at Mondolino's meetings he'd managed to use the second-floor toilet and he'd made a point of locating the old man's bedroom.

Taroud put aside his glass of sweet mint tea and wiped the excess oil off his pistol. Moukli was smoking a joint of hashish, watching the swirls of smoke climb toward the ceiling. Two men were playing cards on the stone floor and the others were talking in low voices in a far corner. They had two hours to wait.

"It should not be difficult," Moukli remarked. "Remember, it is Mondolino we want. The others are unimportant."

"Understood," Taroud replied.

"Our real work will begin tomorrow," Moukli said. "With Mondolino and Haro gone, his organization will collapse. Campagna might try to hold things together but he has lost his touch. He is afraid of dying and too fond of stylish clothes. We'll have no trouble finding more people. Once the word gets out we'll be swamped with recruits. The fence sitters will jump in our direction."

Taroud said nothing. When Moukli was on hashish he liked to hear himself talk.

"You're not going to warn Mondolino?" Mattei asked, loading his Magnum.

"No," Bastide replied. "Bellot hopes to stop them before they get into the grounds. If we tell Mondolino, his boys will man the walls and pop off at anything that moves."

Mattei looked skeptical. "It's a big risk," he said. "Aynard wouldn't approve."

"Aynard is peacefully counting his stitches. Let's not worry about him."

"Did you tell Commissaire Bigeard?"

"Bellot did. Bigeard said 'good luck' and went back to weighing his latest haul of schnouff."

"Too bad Lenoir lost that *type* on the bus."

"Lenoir would lose his mother at her own birthday party."

"Don't be too hard on him," Mattei said. "He's improving."

"He is? I'm glad you told me." They left the office and started down the stairs.

"What's our role tonight?" Mattei asked.

"Strictly backup. It's an anti-gang party and we're the late arrivals."

"This way," Mattei said, leading Bastide across the street to the hulk of his Mercedes.

"You didn't get an official car?" Bastide asked.

"Lenoir has ours and the anti-gang squad has stripped the garage. They must have all their people out there."

"Have you had your brakes repaired?" Bastide asked apprehensively.

"They're fine. Just a little squeak now and then."

"God protect me," Bastide grumbled. "I should have a high-risk bonus for riding with you."

The light from a full, orange moon filtered through the trees of Mondolino's property and cast long shadows on the surrounding streets. There was a soft breeze from the sea. Joe Bellot sat quietly next to his driver. They had parked far from the nearest street lamp. Each car door was slightly open to permit a quick, silent exit. One of the detectives in the rear seat was clipping his nails.

"Put that damn thing away!" Bellot snapped. The detective folded the clipper and dropped it into his pocket.

Bellot had placed his men to cover all approaches to the villa. Moukli's men would have to climb the wall. On the off chance that they might have the combination to the electrically controlled gate, Bellot had two men close to the main entrance.

"Run another check," he said.

The driver lifted his walkie-talkie and began calling for a report from each stake-out. Bellot lit a cigarette, bending low under the dash to hide the flash from his lighter. He smoked with the glowing cigarette tip concealed in the palm of his hand. It was 2:18 a.m.

"Any time now," he said.

Mattei took a circuitous route to reach their allotted position. They were to cover a stretch of wall at the right rear of the property. The brakes of the Mercedes squeaked like dying mice as they rolled to a stop.

"*Merde,*" Bastide complained. "You might as well blow a bugle to announce our arrival!"

"I'll take it in next week," Mattei promised.

Bastide leaned forward, peering into the darkness, trying to locate Bellot's men.

"They're well hidden," Mattei said.

"I hope," Bastide replied, extending the aerial of his hand radio. "*Chat noir, chat noir,*" he called. "This is *merle.* Over."

"Blackbird, this is black cat," Bellot responded.

"We're in position," Bastide told him. "Any action?"

"Nothing. Calm as a tomb."

"Understood . . . out." Bastide put the radio on his lap, leaving the channel open.

"I'm hungry," Mattei said. "I only had a *paté* sandwich for dinner."

"That's more than I managed," Bastide said. He was thinking about Dinh Le Thong. He was trying to find a way of repaying Thong for all the help he'd provided over the last few years. Thong had taken risks to assist him. Being on the DST payroll assured some protection but Bastide was concerned for his safety. Police informers had relatively short life spans in Marseille. His thoughts shifted to Janine. He wondered what she was doing. He pictured her in some luxury hotel sharing a room with Théo Gautier, trying to sleep despite the old man's snoring. He imagined her with her eyes open, thinking of him.

"Blackbird," the radio spluttered, "we've got visitors."

"Let's go," Bastide murmured. They got out of the car and moved into the shadows. A vehicle had turned into the far end of the street, its dim parking lights like two distant cat's eyes. Bastide put his hand on Mattei's shoulder.

"Swing it around," he said, indicating the Mercedes. "Block the street."

Mattei hurried back to his car, backed it up and brought it around in a wide turn. There was a sudden flash of bright lights ahead of them and some shouting. They could hear running and scuffling. Someone shouted, "Police!"

"Come on," Bastide shouted to Mattei, drawing his revolver, heading toward the lights. A man was running toward them. "Stop!" Mattei ordered. The shadowy form leapt into the foliage to their left. They sprinted after him and stopped where the man had disappeared. Bastide stepped off the sidewalk into a wooded area full of waist-high brush, his Magnum ready, Mattei providing cover. Bastide stopped to listen but heard nothing. Two of Bellot's men pounded up, breathless.

"We'll get the son of a bitch, Inspector," one of them said before plunging into the bushes.

"Cowboys!" Mattei muttered.

Bastide holstered his piece. "Let's go find Bellot," he suggested.

Five men were lying face down on the street, their hands cuffed behind their backs. Bastide shielded his eyes from the bright headlights, seeking Bellot. He found him at the open back door of the van.

"Jackpot!" Bellot said, smiling. "Take a look at this."

There were three Heckler & Koch 94's and a .22 caliber pistol with silencer lying on the bed of the van. An anti-gang detective came around the side of the van and threw a 9mm Browning automatic in with the other weapons. "One of them had that in his belt," he told Bellot.

"Who got away?" Bastide asked.

"I don't know," Bellot said, "but he won't get far. I've sent two cars around to head him off."

"No Moukli?" Mattei asked.

"No," Bellot told him. "The big chief stays far from the battlefield but I think some of these prima donnas will sing soon enough."

Bastide slapped Bellot on the back. "Good work," he said, "I think we can scratch the Moukli gang. After this, whoever's left will find urgent business elsewhere."

"I hope you're right," Bellot replied, "but until we've found Moukli . . ."

"We will," Bastide told him. "Let's go, Babar, they don't need us. *Ciao,* Bellot. I'll help you tomorrow with the songbirds." Bastide indicated the handcuffed men.

"*Cinq sur cinq,* Roger. Until tomorrow."

Powerful flashlights were searching the wooded area as they walked back to Mattei's car.

"Perhaps we should stay for awhile?" Mattei asked.

Bastide shook his head. "No, let them earn their money. Come on back to my apartment. I've got some *pistou* I can heat up for us. Just what we need."

Bastide chuckled as they climbed into the Mercedes.

"You're amused?" Mattei asked.

"I was just thinking of Mondolino," Bastide explained. "He certainly heard all the commotion. The old bastard must be dying of curiosity."

Mattei smiled at the thought. "He's probably calling his people out of bed for a detailed report."

Bastide leaned back against the seat, lighting a cigar. "This could be the end of our gang war," he said.

Taroud lay perfectly still in the drainage pipe. He could hear the police thrashing through the nearby undergrowth and see their flashing lights. At one point he'd frozen as one of the searchers stood on the pipe directly over him before moving on. If only they don't bring dogs, he thought. There wasn't much time left before daylight. He knew he'd have to make a move. They were sure to bring uniformed police to continue the search at dawn. He shivered and shifted his position to avoid the water running through the pipe. He shut his eyes for several seconds trying to remember where he was in relation to the main streets and a possible route of escape. He would have to move to his left toward a lightly populated area where there were few villas and many gardens. He could wait there to blend into the morning work rush.

"Disaster," he said quietly, reliving the surprise and shock of the police ambush. Not a shot fired and he was the only one still free. He remembered the two *flics* appearing before him, their faces lit by the headlights. "Bastide," he muttered, as if the name was a curse.

Commissaire Norbet Bigeard had a square face, a thin monastic beard and large, soft eyes that looked out on the world's vices with infinite sadness. He lived and breathed his work as chief of the narcotics section. He considered his temporary replacement of Commissaire Aynard as a troubling inconvenience. Now that he'd congratulated Bellot and Bastide on their night's work, he couldn't wait to get them out of his office.

"We'll go after Moukli now," Bellot said, "but I think his gang is finished."

"Good," Bigeard replied. "Can we then say that the expected 'war' will not occur?"

Bellot hesitated and Bastide filled the gap. "I think we should wait another forty-eight hours," Bastide suggested. "It's too early to be sure. He's still dangerous."

Bigeard looked pained. "There are a pack of journalists downstairs waiting to talk with you. We can't tell them to come back in forty-eight hours. They've got to write their stories now. If you don't see them they'll fill the gaps with fantasy." Bigeard looked at his watch. "It's now ten-twenty. I suggest you sit down together and work out what you want to say. I'll pass the word that you're willing to meet with them at eleven. All right?"

Bastide and Bellot agreed with a marked lack of enthusiasm.

"Our press officer will help you get ready," Bigeard said. "He can advise you on policy questions and step in if things get rough. Be careful what you say about Mondolino. We don't want his lawyers on our backs."

They met the media at the far end of the ground floor canteen. Bastide and Bellot sat at a table with the press officer between them.

He did a good job of fielding questions and stepping in to deflect what he considered oversensitive lines of inquiry. The representative of Marseille's Communist daily tried to link the arrest of the North Africans to racial prejudice. A honey-voiced writer from the right wing newspaper fed them leading questions in the hope their answers would allow him to speak of a "police triumph." Bastide and Bellot measured their responses carefully, making it clear that the events of the night before, while positive, were part of an ongoing investigation. The phrase "gang war" was used often, despite the press officer's attempts to downgrade what had happened to a simple "clash." An attractive woman TV reporter concentrated on Antoine Mondolino's role as a probable target. The press officer loosed a flood of words to say nothing in response. The woman persisted, addressing a follow-up question directly at Bastide.

"Go ask Monsieur Mondolino!" Bastide snapped.

The press officer was obviously shocked by the show of irritation. When it was over Bastide went to the canteen bar for an espresso. Lanzi followed him. The chubby journalist habitually saved his most important questions till after a news conference.

"*Mon cher* Bastide," he said, his blue eyes like jellyfish behind the thick lenses of his spectacles, "is it not true that your success last night was due, in part, to excellent intelligence?"

Bastide dropped a cube of sugar into his coffee and said nothing.

"You see," Lanzi continued, "I'm thinking of doing my piece on the importance of police informers in this city. Those other hacks are rushing off to write about 'gang wars' and racial affronts. I always dig deeper. I like to give my readers . . ."

Bastide emptied his espresso cup in one gulp. "No comment," Bastide said, putting some change on the bar.

"But you can help," Lanzi argued. "I want my facts to be accurate."

Bastide guffawed as he walked toward the door. "Don't change now," he told Lanzi, "no one would recognize your style."

Bastide took the stairs up to Bellot's office two at a time. The press conference had wasted precious minutes. If Moukli had any brains at all he'd be leaving Marseille. Bastide wanted Bellot to send a bulletin alerting the police at the airport and docks, as well as the Gendarmerie posts on the *autoroutes*.

Robert, l'Anglais, Soames had been thinking along the same lines with the same urgency. The events at the villa had driven Antoine Mondolino into a rage. Moukli's attempt on his life and the fact that the police had intervened without warning him of the threat had been a double blow to his ego, an affront to his honor. The old man was now in bed under sedation with a doctor in attendance.

The word had gone out. Everyone in the Mondolino organization was looking for Moukli. All their contacts knew a heavy price was on his head. Mondolino's gunmen were doubling their efforts in the Arab quarter, questioning narcotics dealers, barmen and pimps. Before Mondolino succumbed to the tranquilizer, he'd insisted that Soames work in tandem with Testu Constanza. Mondolino had been willing to let his elderly bodyguard leave the villa. Moukli's death had become more important than his own safety. Soames would have preferred to work alone or with a younger man but Mondolino had been adamant. When Constanza had climbed into the Volkswagen beside him, Soames had suggested a quick trip to the rue d'Aix to see what information their men had gathered.

Constanza had shaken his head. "We go to the docks," he'd declared. "The ferry for Algiers leaves at noon. If I were Moukli I'd feel the need for some sea air."

Soames turned off the Quai de la Joliette into the dock area and pulled to a stop not far from the ticket office. The white-hulled ferry was moored nearby, smoke sifting from its funnel, cargo being lowered into its hold. Truck drivers were lined up outside the barn-like customs shed while their manifests were checked. Algerian families were waiting to board. They were divided in two groups, the men talking and gesticulating, the women and children sitting patiently on their baggage.

"Look," Soames said.

Two husky CRS troopers armed with MAS submachine guns were patrolling the dock. Constanza shrugged and watched them as they passed.

"They are of no importance," he told Soames, "but *they* are." Constanza gestured over his shoulder with his thumb. Soames looked in the rearview mirror. Two plainclothesmen were leaning against a car parked near the entrance to the docks.

Constanza smiled. "We are looking for the same man," he said. "Moukli should be honored at all this attention."

"It's not good," Soames replied. "We can't do anything with so many cops around."

"I agree," Constanza said. "I'll be back in a moment."

He got out of the car before Soames could ask him where he was going and walked slowly over the cobblestones to the ticket office. Soames relaxed and lit a Gauloise. He was used to being his own boss. He resented Constanza's attitude. Mondolino's bodyguard was treating him like a beginner. He watched one of the plainclothes detectives who had gone to talk with a customs officer. A busload of passengers arrived from the downtown terminal. They unloaded their baggage and moved toward the entry gate, tickets in hand. According to Mondolino's description, Moukli was a tall, flashily dressed Algerian in a light suit. He paid no special attention to the bent old man carrying a cheap plastic suitcase, guided through the customs control by his half blind son. Soames decided they were wasting their time. Moukli was probably on his way to Lyon by now in a rented car or well hidden in the Panier. He made up his mind that they'd leave when Constanza returned. He didn't have long to wait. Constanza climbed back into the car with considerable effort.

"What were you doing?" Soames asked.

"I bought a ticket to Algiers," Constanza told him. "A single outside cabin. It was very expensive."

"I don't understand," Soames said, exasperated. "There is no reason."

"But yes," Constanza replied calmly. "Moukli and Taroud have just passed through customs. Didn't you see them? The old man and his son? Very clever . . . but not clever enough. I shall say goodby now," Constanza said. "I like to get settled before the sailing."

"But you have no bag. Are you armed?"

Constanza turned back the sleeve of his shirt to reveal the knife strapped haft down on his left forearm.

"That is purely for self-protection," he said. "Once in Algiers I'll find some old friends who'll be glad to occupy themselves with Moukli. I must go now."

Constanza shut the door behind him. He lingered a moment, his gnarled hands on the window. "Tell Monsieur Mondolino his hunch was right," he instructed Soames. "I expect to be back in a few days. Watch yourself in Marseille. It can be a dangerous city."

CHAPTER 8

Bastide was waiting for Janine on a café terrace in the Vallon des Auffes. The sun was prickling his skin with its strength and he had a cool *pastis* in his hand. The water of the small fishing port was lapping at the stone quai, the gulls were wheeling overhead and the tall arched bridge at the harbor entrance threw cool shadows over the moored, double-ended fishing craft. The Vallon had remained a village within Marseille, despite the high rises on the nearby hills. It was his village. His father's boat had been moored there and they'd crested the waves together at dawn to drop their baited lines in the choppy waters off the Corniche. He was still known as "Antoine's son" in the café. It was one of the few places in the city he could relax. He sipped his *pastis,* sighed and closed his eyes. Someone was blocking the sun. He blinked and sat upright. Janine was smiling at him, one hand on her hip.

"Is this how our civil servants protect us," she asked, "sleeping in the sun while the gangs run the city?"

He jumped up, took her in his arms and kissed her.

"*Doucement!*" she warned, gasping for breath.

He laughed and helped her sit down. Her stay in the Greek Isles had obviously agreed with her. He shook his head in wonder. "Janine," he told her, "you're magnificent."

"*Merci,*" she acknowledged the compliment. "It was the scuba diving and a diet of grilled fish and underdone lamb."

A barman from the café appeared with an ice bucket, a bottle of champagne and two chilled glasses.

"What's this?" she asked.

"A celebration," he explained. "Your homecoming party."

She looked out toward the sea, frowning. The barman opened the champagne, filled their glasses and left.

"I'm sorry about our last conversation," she said. "I know you were under pressure. I shouldn't have hung up."

"It was my fault," he told her. "It's nice to have someone worry about me."

"*Tchin, tchin,*" he said raising his glass. "To our basic incompatibility."

She laughed and they drank their toast. "You are a bastard," she said. "But I really was worried. I moped around after calling you. Even the incorrigible Greeks lost interest in me. I was glad to leave."

"How's Gautier?" he asked.

"He's fine but aging fast. He picked up a bug on Milos and spent two days nursing his tummy. He didn't want me to come back but I insisted."

"You timed it right," Bastide said, savoring the champagne. "Our *war* is over."

"Thank God! Tell me about it."

He reached out to run his hand along her cheek and touched her full lips with one finger. "Must I? I'd just prefer to look at you."

"No," she said softly, "you must tell me what's happened."

"The troublemaker was Moukli, an Algerian who worked for Mondolino. He went too far. He's gone now and I don't think he'll come back. Mondolino and Grondona have agreed to a peace . . . of sorts. That's it."

"But . . . ?"

Bastide held up his hand. "No," he said, "that's enough. I came here to relax. Tell me more about your trip."

She gave him a detailed description of the leased yacht, the crew and the cruise. She described the islands with their high white cliffs, sparkling villages and terraced restaurants. He joked with her about the handsome young Greeks she'd captivated and she countered by asking him about how he'd spent his leisure hours. He hadn't felt so content in weeks. It was enough for him to observe her gestures, her lashes and the tempting line of her figure.

"Where will we eat?" she finally asked.

"What?" he responded lost in an erotic reverie.

"You weren't listening!" she said, accusingly.

"Oh, but I was," he told her, pouring more champagne. "Let's make it easy tonight. What do you say to Chez FonFon?"

She glanced over her shoulder at the dun-colored facade of the restaurant across the narrow street. "Perfect," she replied. "FonFon will be perfect."

The red sun was dropping into the sea through a wavering heat haze when they crossed the street to the restaurant. The legendary FonFon met them at the door, his face round and tanned. He greeted them like royalty and proffered a choice table by the window. They inspected the large wicker tray of fresh-caught fish, examining a silvery *dorade,* the sleek *loup de mer* and the coral *rouget.* They decided on *soupe de poisson* as a first course followed by two grilled *langoustines.* Bastide ordered a bottle of white wine from the Bodin vineyard in Cassis.

"How is Babar?" Janine asked.

"He's fine. He actually lost some weight. We've been very busy."

"All those killings," she said, "it must have been terrible."

Bastide nodded. "It was not enjoyable," he admitted. "I'm glad it's over."

"You look tired," Janine told him. "Will you be able to take some time off?"

"I might. I've got to go see my mother in Arles. Perhaps I can take a few days there. She needs help with repairs at the *mas.* The old place is disintegrating."

"I'd like to meet your mother . . . some day," Janine said.

"You'd like each other," Bastide replied with the uneasy feeling they'd covered the same ground before. His mother had known about them from the very beginning thanks to the gossip from her old friends in Marseille. She also knew about Janine's past as Gautier's mistress. Someday, Bastide told himself, I'll take Janine with me to Arles.

The rich soup arrived steaming in its tureen and they began to eat. The sun disappeared and the lights of the port blinked on, shimmering on the calm surface of the dark water. Bastide felt completely relaxed. The events of the past month faded from his mind. He forgot about Moukli, Grondona and Mondolino, the killing grounds of le Panier, Mazargues, the Brasserie and the Agadir.

Much later, when they'd finished the tender langoustines and were sitting with their coffee and Armagnac, Bastide opened his light summer jacket to reach into an inner pocket for a Havana. Janine watched him with the contented look of a well-fed feline, a slight smile on her face. The smile faded as she leaned toward him.

"Roger," she said, "you're not carrying your *pétard!*"

"No," he admitted. "I'm sick of weapons. I thought I'd leave it home tonight. I'm developing calluses on my hip from the damn thing. I don't need it when I'm playing the role of lover." His joking didn't dissipate her concern.

"It's not very smart," she told him seriously. "You have too many enemies."

Bastide shrugged. *"Basta!"* he said. "You're beginning to sound like Mattei. Drink up and we'll go home for a nightcap. I've moved the mattress out onto the balcony. We can make love under the stars."

Janine lifted her snifter. "To the man who always plans ahead," she said.

Testu Constanza had taken a single room on a upper floor at the Hotel Aletti. From his open window he could look out on the port and the Bay of Algiers. It was only 9 a.m. but the city was already simmering under a merciless sun. There wasn't a breath of wind. The palms were motionless against a bright blue sky. He lifted his cup and drank the strong black coffee, watching the dilapidated tank truck spraying water on the dusty streets.

Constanza had been back to Algiers only one since the war and he found himself enjoying his second visit. Outwardly, the city didn't reflect the profound political and economic changes since independence. It appeared a little shabbier, a bit more rundown, but its basic beauty was still intact. With such a location, he reflected, how could it be otherwise.

The trip over had been uneventful, the weather perfect. Moukli and Taroud had spent most of the voyage in their cabin but he'd seen them at dinner from a vantage point on deck. He hadn't risked entering the dining room himself. Moukli would have recognized him. When the ferry had docked he'd watched them go ashore and drive off toward the Casbah in a cab. He'd carried out his business that evening on the busy terrace of the Hôtel Saint-Georges, high above the city. He and his contact had drunk Dutch beer and chewed small green olives while they planned Moukli's demise.

The Mondolino representative in Algiers was a middle-aged, stick-thin Kabyle with two metal front teeth . . . the legacy of free treatment at a Soviet-run dental clinic. Constanza had met him during his previous visit. He found him efficient but overcautious. The man had a well-founded fear of the Algerian police and planned his actions carefully to avoid police involvement. They'd reached agreement by dinner time and Constanza had gone off alone to eat at an Italian restaurant near the Aletti.

Constanza had a boring wait ahead of him. He'd already purchased an airline ticket for the morning flight to Marseille. He would have to wait by the telephone for confirmation that all had gone as planned. He finished his coffee and went to the *armoire* to get a pack of cards from his jacket. He put on his spectacles, sat down at the coffee table and began to deal himself a hand of solitaire.

Bastide and Bellot climbed the wide stone stairway to the Hôtel Dieu. The ancient hospital building was high above the Vieux Port with a magnificent view of the city and Notre-Dame de la Garde. Commissaire Aynard had insisted on a briefing before they turned in their written report. They reached the top of the stairs, passed the parked ambulances, and entered the hospital, taking the elevator to the second floor.

Aynard received them sitting up in bed in a high-ceilinged private room. He looked pale, older and surprisingly helpless. Bastide felt an unaccustomed twinge of sympathy . . . until Aynard opened his mouth.

"You should have been here yesterday," he said dryly. "What delayed you?"

"We had to speak with the judge on the Moukli case," Bastide explained. "It took all day. He's a difficult man."

Aynard accepted the explanation with bad grace, shifting gingerly on his pillow and glaring at them.

"The Préfet seems pleased," he said, begrudgingly. "I suppose you have done a good job."

The admission, coming from Aynard, was like an unreserved commendation. "But," he continued, "I understand Moukli got away?"

"He can't be located," Bellot said. "The search continues."

"There's a good chance he's left the country," Bastide added quickly before Aynard could comment.

"*Mon cher* Bastide," Aynard said, "the case is not over till we find him. It might be premature to declare the war ended. Moukli could find new recruits or new allies. If he returns . . ."

"If he returns," Bellot said, "we'll grab him."

The Commissaire shifted again, to ease the dull pain in his abdomen. "Just make sure your report reflects this uncertainty," he told them. "And remember, prepare yourselves for the official hearing on the Agadir affair. Some people might think you were too quick on the trigger."

Bastide and Bellot stopped in a small café near the hospital for an espresso. "What do you make of him?" Bellot asked. "Is the man human?"

"They may have implanted more ulcers instead of removing what he had," Bastide replied.

"It's unbelievable," Bellot said. "I didn't expect a medal but he gave the impression that we've made a mess of things. I don't think I like our Commissaire."

"You've just joined ninety-five percent of the force," Bastide told him, finishing his coffee. "I've got to go back to simple homicide work. It's the unfinished business with Barberi. I'm sure he was the trigger man in the Russo shooting."

They walked out onto the street. "Well," Bellot said, "I'm still trying to squeeze something out of Haro but he's a sphinx. Today, I'm off to Nice for a talk with my man Mourand. I want to set up a discreet surveillance of Grondona. He could still be tempted to go after Mondolino now that the old man's in a weakened condition."

"If you want a good Niçois meal try the restaurant Barale. They serve ravioli you won't find anywhere else."

"Always thinking of your stomach," Bellot chided.

"Why not," Bastide replied. They shook hands and Bellot walked to his car.

Bastide decided to take his time getting back to the Hôtel de Police. Barberi could wait. It was too nice a day to hurry.

Robert Soames was shaving in his small room at the rear of the Mondolino villa. He found himself in a difficult situation. He'd promised Mondolino to deal with Inspector Bastide but Grondona wanted him back in Nice. He'd been able to put off his departure, arguing that Barberi would need someone to help organize his defense and watch over the lawyers if the case came to trial. Grondona had grudgingly granted Soames his wish. But Soames knew Grondona might change his mind. Considering the backlog in the courts it could be months before Barberi stood in front of a judge.

Soames had thought that Mondolino might change his mind but the old man seemed to have a deep fixation on Bastide. Haro's arrest had affected Mondolino deeply and he'd added that to Bastide's offenses. He wanted the *flic* dead. He finished shaving, washed the soap from his face and patted on some astringent lotion.

Soames was determined to do the job. The money was too good to lose. If Grondona found out he'd never forgive him. It wasn't simply that Grondona wouldn't tolerate a cop killer in his organization, he'd view the hit for Mondolino as a gross act of disloyalty and a punishable offense. Soames slipped a clean shirt over his muscular torso and tucked it into his trousers. He spent a minute in front of the mirror combing his thick dark hair. Satisfied with his appearance, Soames lifted an Air France flight bag from the floor and put it on the bed. He tossed a sheet of newspaper on the covers, unzipped the bag and removed a heavy automatic pistol and began to strip it. It was an Israeli Desert Eagle, a .357 Magnum with an eight-inch barrel. It was a reliable arm with a lot of hitting power and negligible muzzle-flip. He broke the gun down in seconds and had begun to clean it when he reached a decision. After the Bastide job he would not go back to Nice. He had good contacts in London who could always find him a job far from France. Grondona would not take his unauthorized departure lightly. A self-imposed exile in Africa or the Far East would be the only sensible thing to do.

Bachir Moukli drove along the Jetée du Nord and parked the borrowed Volvo at the water's edge near the Algiers Yacht Club. A fresh breeze was blowing from the bay. He breathed in the salt air as he got out of the car. A low lying gray patrol boat was moored nearby at the naval docks, its motor purring like some giant cat. The lights of the Casbah glittered and winked above the port. Moukli had invested a considerable amount of money in a new wardrobe. Clothing was expensive in Algiers and the general quality was low but he'd found a light, well-cut Spanish suit and some Italian silk shirts. It was all part of an effort to convince his colleagues that he was still in business. He knew word had probably reached them of his debacle in Marseille but he had to convince them it was a temporary setback. He would blame it all on an anti-Algerian vendetta mounted by the Grondona and Mondolino gangs with police connivance. The important thing was to rebuild his organization with the help of some of the old Algerian gang leaders now living in Algiers. He would have to appear unshaken and sure of himself. He'd left Ahmed Taroud in a small apartment deep in the Casbah. Taroud had spread the word that Moukli was seeking new recruits. He was already interviewing applicants eager to try their skill and luck in Marseille. Moukli straightened his tie and climbed the winding stairs to the Yacht Club restaurant.

His hosts greeted him with effusive embraces. They were both well-dressed, plump men with gray hair, very much at home in their surroundings. Moukli accepted an *apéritif* at their insistence but only sipped it to be polite. He hadn't touched alcohol or hashish since leaving Marseille. He wanted his mind clear for the evening's business.

Their table was well isolated from the other diners at the far end of the room. The pleasantries, questions about their individual families and a discussion of Algerian politics carried them through their first course of grilled *rougets.* They got down to business when the main course of lamb was served and the waiter had retired. What, he was asked, had happened in Marseille?

It was the opening Moukli had been waiting for. He wove a complicated narrative of treachery and betrayal, carefully avoiding the fact that he had plotted the overthrow of Mondolino. He sought an emotional response by underlining the racial attitudes of Mondolino and Grondona. He named the compatriots who had been killed and accused the police of supporting the gangs.

His hosts sliced their lamb, filled their mouths with meat and rice, and drank from full glasses of red Mascara. They looked up from time to time, watching him as he used his hands to make a point, their eyes expressionless and unreadable.

"Eat, my friend, eat," one of them urged. "We have all night to talk."

Moukli chewed a token mouthful, drank some Vittel water and continued. He appealed to their business sense, inflating the profits that could be taken from the Marseille rackets and exaggerating Mondolino's lack of control and vulnerability.

"Why do you believe you could succeed now," he was asked, "when your first attempt was a failure?"

"They don't expect me to return," he explained. "The element of surprise would be great."

"And the police?"

"It would be finished before they could intervene," Moukli said with conviction.

One of his hosts left the table for a visit to the rest room. As he passed the *maître d'hôtel* at the top of the stairs he nodded surreptitiously.

"Come," the other man was telling Moukli, "you've hardly touched your dinner. Enough talk for tonight. We shall continue tomorrow. We find what you say of great interest. Now we shall have the *tarte au citron*, a house speciality, and some coffee. I hope you will be able to come to lunch on the weekend at my beach house at Zeralda. I want you to meet my family."

"Thank you," Moukli replied, "that would be enjoyable."

Later, they said goodby on the quai and Moukli watched the two men drive off before he climbed into the Volvo. He was slightly encouraged but still cautious. They were obviously interested but far from convinced. He turned the key. There was a sterile click from the ignition. He tried again. Nothing. He cursed, climbed from the car and walked to the hood. The double-edged blade of the carefully balanced throwing knife struck him between the shoulder blades with extreme force. It sounded like a hatchet hitting a hollow tree. Moukli fell forward on his hands and knees, blinking his eyes in shock and horror. He felt a heavy weight pressing down on him. He tried to resist the pressure but his arms gave way and he fell forward on his face. Someone lifted him by the belt and dragged him forward. He saw the dancing reflections of the Yacht Club lights as he fell six feet into the oily water of the harbor.

Moukli's two hosts drove up a wide, deserted avenue to the Hydra sector of Algeria. A full moon lit the facade of the old colonial buildings and clouds of insects were swarming around the street lights.

"The man was a fool," the driver said. "He destroyed years of work in one month."

"We will have to make a friendly approach to Mondolino," his companion sighed. "If not, none of our people will be safe in Marseille. At least Constanza can confirm how we helped with Moukli."

"He was a fool," the driver repeated. "Never trust men who wear white suits."

Bastide had gone to the Palais de Justice to plead for Barberi's continued incarceration.

The handsome young juge d'instruction shook his head. "We can't hold Barberi any longer," he said. "We just don't have a case. I've stalled Maître Casanove for twenty-four hours but he is impatient. He wants his client released."

"I'm sure Barberi did the job on Russo," Bastide said. "Soloman is about to crack. Give me another twenty-four hours."

"Impossible," the judge told him. "If you had some decent witnesses we might have done something. Russo's woman was hopeless. She's even denied he made the flower market hit in Nice. She says you threatened her. No, Inspector, we've got to let Barberi and his playmates walk."

Bastide made a despairing gesture. He glanced around the judge's office, taking in the shelves of bound volumes, the legal diplomas, the certificates and the autographed, framed photographs of the judge with local officials and his fellow jurists.

"Can't we hold him on a technicality?" Bastide asked.

"No," the judge said firmly, rolling an expensive gold-tipped pen between his hands, "it is out of the question. I would be the happiest man in the world if you could walk in here with something solid. I'd love to put that bastard inside and throw away the key. Now, if you don't mind, I have a trial tomorrow and I've got a lot of preparation ahead of me."

Bastide stood up and walked to the door.

"Oh, Inspector," the judge called after him, "congratulations on the Moukli business. You saved us all a lot of work."

"Thanks," Bastide said drily, shutting the tall door after him. *"Fils à papa,"* he grumbled to himself realizing the judge was still in short pants when he was fighting in the *djebels* of Algeria.

Mattei was leaning against a stone column absorbed in a copy of *Lui* magazine.

"Come on," Bastide said, "I want to get the stale smell of justice out of my nostrils."

"What did he say?" Mattei asked, slipping his magazine into a coat pocket.

"He said no."

"I expected he would," Mattei commented. "You can't blame him. The law is the law."

"Very profound, Babar. You'll be studying for a law degree next."

They walked in silence to their illegally parked, unmarked car. It had been ticketed. Mattei folded the ticket and threw it on top of the dashboard. They drove around the Vieux Port and up the hill to the Hôtel de Police. As they climbed the stairs to their office Bastide raised his head, sniffing at an unfamiliar odor.

"What the hell?" he murmured. He pushed open the door and stopped dumbfounded. "*Ça alors!*" he exclaimed.

The desks and floor were covered with a paint-stained canvas drop cloth. A painter at the top of a ladder was wielding a roller. Another was crouched in the corner stirring a large bucket of gray paint. They greeted Bastide and Mattei and went back to their work.

"I don't believe it," Bastide said, examining the completed portion of the ceiling. "Someone is actually painting our office!"

"Finally," Mattei said, reaching under a canvas to retrieve a notebook and a packet of cigarettes. "Now where do we go? We can't work here."

"Let's use Bellot's office," Bastide suggested. "He's still over in Nice. In fact, I want to call him."

"You can have your office back tomorrow morning," one of the painters told them. "We'll leave the windows open tonight so it'll dry out."

"Perfect," Bastide replied, shutting the door behind them.

"Gray," Mattei complained as they went down the stairs. "It'll look like a damn prison."

"We are witnessing a miracle," Bastide replied. "Don't spoil it."

One of Bellot's men vacated Bellot's desk so Bastide could use the telephone. He was a young detective with long, unkempt hair and a two-day growth of beard. He was wearing a checked cap and a soiled cardigan. He took a seat at another desk, removed a small, undercover derringer from his pocket and shook two cartridges onto the blotter. He sensed Mattei's eye on him.

"How's your weight problem?" the detective asked. "Still crunching carrots?"

"Do you really have to look so scruffy?" Mattei asked, ignoring the question. "Most of the gangsters I know can afford to dress well. They must see you coming miles away."

Bastide finally located Bellot at the Préfecture in Nice. They talked for about ten minutes. When Bastide put down the phone he sat in silence for several minutes, smoothing his mustache.

"What's up?" Mattei asked.

"Grondona's behaving himself," Bastide finally replied. "All quiet on the Nice front. But there is something curious. Soames, l'Anglais, hasn't returned to the fold. Bellot and Mourand think he's still in Marseille."

"So?"

"So . . . why would Grondona let his top guy stay here? Does Mondolino know about it? If he does, what are Mondolino and Grondona up to? If he doesn't . . . ?"

"Maybe he's found a *gonzesse,*" the detective volunteered. "He's probably borrowed one of Mondolino's broads for a little spring plowing."

"Hey," Mattei growled. "Who pressed your button? Don't you have something important to do?"

"Hey, yourself," the detective countered, "this is *our* office."

"That's enough, both of you!" Bastide warned. "Do you have a dossier on Soames?" he asked.

The detective pointed toward an open bar-lock cabinet. "Under S," he said, glaring at Mattei. Bastide got up, pulled out a drawer and rifled through the files till he found Soames's folder. He went back to the desk and began to examine it. He took a long look at the mug shots. Soames had the face of a heavy. His eyes were full of malice. From the look of his neck and shoulders, Bastide guessed he'd spent a lot of time pumping iron. Soames's list of convictions was small. They'd all been for comparatively minor offenses, including carrying concealed weapons and breaking a longshoreman's leg with a tire iron. He'd never spent more than eight months in jail. The most interesting section of the dossier dealt with Soames's suspected crimes. During Grondona's takeover of the Roll On-Roll Off monopoly, Soames had been implicated in the murder of a ship's captain. They'd found the body fouled on an anchor line and showing signs of torture. A light-fingered *croupier* from one of Grondona's casinos had been left hanging on a hook in a meat locker and the headless body of one of Soames's former girl friends had been picked up in the Baie des Anges by the crew of a passing yacht. Bastide vaguely remembered the murder of the *croupier* but Nice homicide had handled the cases. He'd been too busy in Marseille to follow them closely. He finished reading the Soames dossier, closed it and pushed it aside. He rubbed his tired eyes. The detective was probably right. Soames was probably taking his *repos de guerrier* with a Marseille prostitute before returning to Nice. Despite his wonderful night with Janine, Bastide realized he was still on edge.

"Babar," he said, "let's get out of here."

"Where are we going," Mattei asked, puzzled.

"You'll see," Bastide replied. He turned to the detective. "Thanks for your help," he said.

"Just take your bear with you," the detective replied, sarcastically.

Mattei started out of his chair but Bastide stopped him. He walked toward the detective, smiling. The detective, misreading his intentions, returned the smile. Bastide's right arm shot out and his hand closed on the detective's throat, his thumb pressing on his Adam's apple.

"We don't like comedians," Bastide growled, as the detective struggled to keep his balance. "You'd better learn to respect your elders." A solid push sent Bellot's man and his chair crashing to the floor.

"*Allons!*" Bastide waved Mattei toward the door and they left the office.

"You were a bit hard on him, Roger," Mattei chuckled.

"You and I are going to have a few drinks," Bastide said, putting his hand on Mattei's shoulder. "I haven't got the last few weeks out of my system. Will you promise to drive me home?"

Mattei checked his watch. "It's only six-thirty," he said. "You want to start drinking now?"

"Why not? It means we'll get home earlier. Collar Lenoir and tell him to cover for us. I'll meet you outside."

They parked on the Cours d'Estienne d'Orves and dropped into le

Péano for their first drink. Bastide ordered a whiskey and water and Mattei asked for a *cannette* of beer. Mattei eyed Bastide uneasily as he downed half of his glass.

"Give me your *pétard,*" Mattei whispered when the barman had moved away. "If you're determined to get cooked, it's better to be unarmed."

"I'm not carrying it," Bastide told him. "Relax, we're technically off duty."

Two drinks later they left the Péano for le Phoenix on the rue Sainte. The owner and the three prostitutes working the bar recognized them as cops. They received a cold reception but Bastide's exuberant behavior soon reassured them and the *patron* offered them a second round. Mattei refused politely and suggested it was time to eat. Bastide brushed the suggestion aside and insisted on buying drinks for the girls. Encouraged by this unexpected largess a practiced hustler moved two stools closer and concentrated her voluptuous charm on Bastide. Mattei told her to keep her distance.

The warmth of the whiskey had infused Bastide with goodwill. He smiled at everyone, admired the display of flowers behind the bar and complimented the *patron* on the quality of his Scotch. Now the *patron* was uneasy. He wasn't used to sympathetic policemen. He waited for their next move with foreboding and greeted their departure with genuine relief.

A heavy portion of spaghetti carbonara at Chez Antoine dissipated some of the whiskey's effect but Bastide insisted on a full bottle of house red despite Mattei's suggestion that a half bottle would be enough. When they'd finished their dinner Bastide led Mattei to le Son des Guitares, a Corsican bar noted for its impromptu music and singing. Mattei was quickly recognized by some of his countrymen. His presence put an understandable damper on the proceedings. Two more whiskies had reactivated Bastide's enthusiasm and he insisted on stopping by Chez Maurice before going home. The affable Maurice greeted them at the door of his cave-like *bistro,* twirling his Guard's mustache, and poured Bastide a double dram of pure malt before grabbing his guitar to sing a raucous song about the lonesome lives of policemen's wives.

It was almost 2 a.m. when they returned to their car. Mattei had called headquarters from each stop and he checked again on the car radio before driving Bastide to his apartment. Mattei helped Bastide up the steep stairs to his door and made them both some black coffee. He left when Bastide had fallen into bed and begun to snore.

Soames picked up Bastide's trail the next morning. He'd simply used the telephone book to find his address. He'd parked the rented Volkswagen near the apartment. When Mattei had stopped to pick up Bastide at 8:30 a.m., he'd followed them to the Hôtel de Police. He was not yet sure where he'd make his hit. Mondolino wanted complete secrecy. It was important to have everything foolproof when you were doing a job alone. When Mattei's Mercedes disappeared into the parking lot under the Hôtel de Police, Soames drove on to the Boulevard des Dames. There was no need to show himself unnecessarily in an area alive with policemen. He pulled over, locked his car and went into the café Nord. The Desert Eagle rode easily in its nylon-covered, foam shoulder holster. Soames sat at a table, wrote Mattei's license number in a small notebook and ordered a Perrier. He folded his arms and sat back against the plastic-covered banquette to think. There was no use shadowing Bastide during his working day. It would not be wise to drop the *flic* while he was on duty. Ideally his target should be alone and there should be no witnesses. He ticked off the best scenarios in his mind. The apartment was a natural. It would provide privacy and isolation but he'd have to choose another weapon. His .357 Magnum would sound like an artillery piece in an enclosed space and bring every resident onto the stairway. When his Perrier arrived he crushed a lemon wedge over the glass with his powerful fingers and wondered just how often Bastide traveled alone. Mondolino had briefed him about Mattei and Lenoir. He'd also told him about Bastide's mistress, Janine Bourdet. He knew they didn't live in the same apartment but he had no way of knowing how often they were together. If he had the time he'd watch Bastide over a period of days to develop a definite movement pattern. But his time was limited. If Bastide had no idea he was marked for execution the job would be comparatively simple. Mondolino had told him the Inspector considered himself a gourmet. It would be interesting and perhaps useful to see which restaurants he favored. He left the cafe, drove to the Place de la Major and parked the Volkswagen so he could see the garage exit of the Hôtel de Police.

"You'll get no sympathy from me," Mattei said, putting the styrofoam cup of black coffee on the desk.

Bastide didn't look up. He sat with his head in his hands.

"Your *gueule de bois* is a fitting punishment," Mattei lectured. "Do you realize how much you put away last night? How much you mixed? It's a wonder you're ambulant!"

"My hangover is my business," Bastide mumbled, reaching for his coffee.

"Just tell me why?"

"Speak softly," Bastide pleaded. "There's no need to shout."

Mattei opened the wall locker, removed Bastide's holstered Manurhin revolver and pushed it across the desk. "Here," he said. "It's dangerous to play the bleeding heart in this business. From now on you carry your piece, even when you go to the *pissoir*."

Bastide nodded and pointed toward some papers that had been left on his desk earlier that morning. "What's all that?" he asked.

"A false alarm," Mattei told him. "Some eager *gendarme* in Carpentras collared an Algerian with a vague resemblance to Moukli. He turned out to be a vineyard worker known locally as a serious family man. Lenoir called to order his release this morning."

The door banged open and Bellot stormed into the office. "What the hell's going on!" he demanded.

Bastide shut his eyes and clutched his forehead. "It's not necessary to shout," he groaned.

"No one pushes my people around," Bellot shouted, still fuming. "You assaulted one of my men in *my* office. I don't permit such things!"

"Take it easy, Joe," Mattei said, calmly. "Can't you see our friend is suffering?"

"The hell with that," Bellot continued. "I want an explanation."

"Look, Joe," Bastide replied, opening his bloodshot eyes, "I'm sorry. It was a misunderstanding."

"Your man was acting the fool," Mattei explained. "He's a wise ass. He had it coming to him."

"Just the same . . ." Bellot was calming down. He peered at Bastide and a slow smile spread across his face. "My God," he said, "he *is* in bad shape! What was he celebrating?"

"I'm not sure," Mattei replied. "But he wouldn't go home till he was well cooked."

"When you two are through examining my corpse," Bastide said, "perhaps we can go to work?"

Bellot sat on the edge of the desk. "Have you heard anything about Soames? He still hasn't shown up in Nice. I'm not sure that even Grondona knows where he is."

"Maybe he ran off with Moukli," Mattei suggested. "They'd make a good couple."

"Let's not worry about Soames," Bastide said. "Aynard won't be satisfied till we find Moukli. Surely we must have some leads on the son of a bitch?"

"We've combed the Arab quarter," Bellot replied. "We found the cellar where he was holed up, a packet of mint tea, some dirty glasses and a strong smell of hashish, but nothing else. Everyone in the area has had their lips stitched."

"I'll shake Halimi's cage," Mattei said. "He is late on his reporting schedule."

Bastide stood up with care. He fixed the holstered Manurhin on his belt and finished his coffee. "One thing is certain," he told them. "I need some fresh air. Let's see if we can find Halimi now."

Forty minutes later they spotted Halimi walking along the rue du Bon Pasteur. Mattei saw him first and pointed. "There he is," he said. "I'll pull over."

Bastide scribbled a note, folded the piece of paper and took a map of Marseille from between the front seats. He was out of the car before it stopped. He caught up with Halimi and pretended to be asking directions, pointing to the map. Despite his surprise, Halimi played the game. He bent over the map, feigning interest, while Bastide slipped him the note. Then Bastide thanked him and walked back to the car.

"So?" Mattei asked.

"I told him to meet us at the Anse Catalans in half an hour," Bastide explained. "If we're lucky there'll be some well-built young things playing volleyball on the beach."

"You're improving," Mattei laughed. "Last night wasn't fatal after all."

Soames had observed the playacting with Halimi. He wasn't sure what it meant but when Mattei turned back toward the port he stayed three cars behind them.

The sidewalk railing above the small beach at the Anse Catalans was already dotted with idle male onlookers. The volleyball game was a mixed affair but most of the players were women, including a heavily endowed blond with a miniscule bikini. Each time she leapt into the air or ran for the ball her breasts escaped from the narrow strip of her halter. Bastide remained in the car. Mattei settled down to wait. A small dark girl, a pocket Venus, caught his eye immediately. Mattei decided she had more sex appeal in her little finger than the bobbling blond could ever muster. She reminded him of his wife when they'd first met. He squinted into the sun and lost himself in dreams of conquest and pleasure.

Halimi shambled up to Mattei and stood beside him. "What's so urgent?" he asked without looking in Mattei's direction.

"What do you have on Moukli?" Mattei asked.

"I was on my way to call you," Halimi said. "I . . ."

"Get to the point!"

"Asnir, the driver, has heard some bad news. Moukli is no more."

"What?"

"It appears to be true. He spoke with his uncle in Algiers last night. Moukli and Taroud, the Moroccan, slipped out of France on the ferry. Moukli was planning to make contact with some old friends in Algiers. He did . . . and he is dead."

"Tell me more," Mattei demanded, his eyes fixed on the svelte brunette as she fell to her knees in the soft sand.

"Moukli's body was found in the harbor. The police have called it a drowning but I think some money has changed hands. There was a deep knife wound in his back."

"And Taroud?"

"I know nothing of Taroud."

Mattei glanced sideways at Halimi's pudgy face. "Good work," he murmured. "I suppose you've run through the *fric* I gave you?"

"What do you suppose has kept Asnir so talkative?"

"You'd lie to your grandmother," Mattei said with a sardonic smile.

"Impossible," Halimi replied. "She's been dead for sixteen years."

"I'm leaving," Mattei told him. "Enjoy the volleyball."

Mattei reported on his conversation with Halimi as they drove back to the Hôtel de Police. Bastide was pleased. He almost forgot his hangover.

"We'll have to get on to the Ministry and ask them to send a cable to our Embassy in Algiers," Bastide said. "Their security officer should be able to squeeze an official confirmation of Moukli's death out of the Algerian police. How he died is unimportant. Once we have the confirmation we can close the case."

"And perhaps Aynard will calm down."

"It's possible, but I don't think that bag of raw nerves will ever relax."

Bastide sat in his apartment staring at the telephone. He was stripped to the waist and he'd opened all the windows of the apartment to create a cross current of air. The case had been officially closed that morning, once the confirmation of Moukli's death had come through. Bastide was hovering on the edge of an important decision. He scratched the hair on his chest, trying to think. He left the telephone and went into the kitchen to pour himself a *pastis.* He knew he was stalling and it irritated him. He went back and stood over the telephone, jiggling the ice cubes in his glass.

"Enough," he said suddenly, picked up the receiver and dialed Janine's number.

"What's the matter?" she demanded immediately.

"Why does there have to be something the matter?" he replied. "I called to ask you something."

"What is that?"

"Would you like to come with me to Arles tomorrow?"

"To meet your mother?" Her surprise was obvious.

"It won't be to attend a bullfight."

"I'd love to."

"Can you pick me up at nine? Is that too early? I would like to get there before lunch."

"That's fine. How long will we be staying?"

"I have two days off," he told her. "We'll come back Saturday morning. Hold on, why don't you come here and spend the night? That will make it easier."

"Very well, I'll see you about seven."

"Good. Till later."

He replaced the receiver and drank some *pastis.* There was no turning back now. He saw it as a form of commitment to Janine but he was already wondering if it had been a wise move. How would the two women get along? Would his mother be difficult? Old age had made her more outspoken and set her ideas in concrete. He could only hope that her hospitality would dominate any antagonism she might feel toward Janine. He sincerely hoped so. He knew Janine wouldn't tolerate aspersions to her past or disapproval of their relationship. He sighed and returned to the kitchen. Whatever happened he knew he'd be in the middle.

"*Imbécile,*" he told himself, "you've done it now!"

CHAPTER 9

Bastide's mother stood in the mottled shade of her small orchard looking up at the cherry trees. Their tiny fruit had already turned dark and she was certain there'd be an early crop. The ground was dry under a bright sun. Cicadas were buzzing and clicking in the nearby pines and honey bees were working the scattered lavender bushes. Madame Bastide moved on to the pear trees, her ancient retriever following behind, his drooping tail wagging for no apparent reason. The Inspector's mother was a well-preserved seventy. Although she moved slowly, her carriage was erect and her weathered face bore the traces of her former beauty. Her white hair was gathered in a tight bun under a wide-brimmed straw hat. She was wearing the light, flowered dress that Bastide had given her for her last birthday.

Reassured that the pears had escaped the birds for another day, she turned toward her garden to cut some roses for the dining room table. Clipping the stems of a pink bloom she reviewed the preparations for her son's visit. Her lunch was ready except for some last minute touches. Cream was to be added to *potage purée d'artichauts* and the *canard aux olives* was simmering over a low flame. A fresh salad of *frisé* was cooling in the sink and she'd prepared a crusty, glazed *tarte aux pommes* for dessert. Two bottles of Gigondas had been opened and set to breathe on the sideboard. She had also planned their dinner. A light meal of cold roast beef and a mustardy potato salad.

She sniffed at the fragrant roses. A yellow jacket buzzed angrily around her head. She waved it away and walked over the flagstones toward the house. She wondered what this Janine would look like. One of her old friends from the Vallon des Auffes had described her as "an attractive woman." That meant nothing to her. Madame Bastide was sure of one thing. They would not sleep together under *her* roof. She'd made a special effort to clean and ready the extra bedroom for the guest. She was also determined to be the perfect hostess. It was not often her son introduced her to one of his women. She wanted to make the best of it, even if Mademoiselle Bourdet had been a rich man's mistress. She entered the coolness of the thick-walled farmhouse and arranged the roses in a *faïence* jug. She glanced up at the wall clock over the fireplace. Roger would be arriving in an hour.

L'Anglais was under considerable pressure. Mondolino was impatient. He'd accused Soames of stalling. Soames had explained that Bastide was seldom alone. He'd also described the rendezvous he'd observed at the Anse Catalans. This had only infuriated Mondolino.

"If I wanted a spy, I'd hire a good one," he'd blustered. "I'm paying you for a hit. If you can't deliver I'll find someone who can!"

Soames frowned, recalling the awkward moment. He craned his neck to make sure the cream-colored Peugeot had not turned off the main highway. He'd watched Bastide and the woman leave Bastide's apartment earlier that morning and followed them out of Marseille to Salon. He'd slowed when they'd turned off the autoroute onto the Route Nationale for Arles, not wanting to get too close. They had both been carrying light suitcases when they'd left the apartment. He assumed Bastide was off duty and would be away from Marseille for at least one night. It could make things easier. The rural Gendarmerie moved a bit slower than their city colleagues. This could provide him with precious time.

He rolled down his window but the hot, dry air of the Plaine de la Crau offered little relief from the heat. He speculated on Bastide's destination. Perhaps they were going to one of the expensive hotels at Les Baux. Soames wished he knew more about Bastide. It made things easier when you could predict a target's movements. The Peugeot slowed before swinging out to pass a long freezer truck. Soames pressed down on the accelerator to close the distance. If he lost Bastide now he could forget Marseille and his money.

"Let's go to lunch tomorrow at Baumanière," Bastide suggested.

"What?" Janine replied, removing her dark glasses. "I thought you just wanted to relax at the *mas.*"

"It would be a special treat for my mother," he explained.

"It's fine with me," Janine said. "I haven't been there for years."

They approached Arles and the road narrowed. Janine took a small mirror from her purse and applied some lipstick. She was wearing a white halter dress of raw silk and two gold chain necklaces with matching loop earrings. Her short black hair glistened in the sunlight. Bastide reached over and put his hand on her bare shoulder.

"My mother will be impressed," he told her, smiling.

"Why do you say that?" she asked. "What is she expecting to see?"

"Relax," he told her. "She's not an ogre."

"I know," she said, "but I'm too old to be presented for approval. I feel like a twenty year old about to meet her fiancé's family."

"Just be yourself," he said. "If you have an awkward moment, mention cooking, roses, the church or me. That will keep her busy for a good fifteen minutes."

They entered Arles and drove along the Boulevard des Lices toward the Rhône. The open tents and striped parasols of a country fair were set up in the main square. They could hear accordion music from the carousel. The streets were filled with children. A band of camera-laden tourists were debarking from their bus for a visit to the old church of Saint-Trophime. Red-and-yellow wall posters announced the weekend *corrida,* the café terraces were full and there was a tempting odor of grilled meat and herbs from the busy restaurants. Bastide swung up onto the Pont de Trinquetaille and they crossed the Grand Rhône, its wide flow dark in the center and brown with silt near the shore.

"Ah," Bastide sighed, enjoying the cool wind off the water, "it's good to be alive, with you, and away from the office."

"Well put," she said. "You deserve some time to yourself."

"You're right," he replied. "When I'm working and under pressure I forget what normal living must be."

"Let's not talk about your work for the next forty-eight hours."

"Agreed," he promised. "If I do, give me a good kick."

Antoine Mondolino was sitting on a wicker chair in the middle of his rose garden. He was wearing sports clothes, a white linen cap and dark glasses. His cane was between his knees and he was drinking mineral water from a stemmed glass. Paul Campagna sat beside him. He unbuttoned his shirt collar and loosened his tie as a concession to the heat.

"I'm pleased the way things have worked out," Mondolino said, putting his glass down on the small table at his side. "It was good that Moukli died in Algiers. Do we have further reports on his people?"

"Scattered to the winds," Campagna replied. "I think most of them have gone north, to Lyon and Paris."

"When l'Anglais does his job," Mondolino said, "things should be back to normal." He watched for Campagna's reaction and smiled. "You still don't approve?"

"I've explained my position," Campagna explained. "At best, it's a needless provocation. If there's trouble . . ." he shrugged his shoulders.

Campagna was sincerely worried. The last few weeks had brought disturbing changes in Mondolino's character. His insistence on the Bastide hit had been only one of the symptoms. The old man seemed to have lost interest in the day-to-day operation of his organization. His previously sacrosanct daily schedule had disintegrated. He'd slept late, spent an hour at a time staring out the window at his garden and he'd delegated certain decisions to Campagna that he'd normally have handled himself. He seemed to have suspended his interest in everything but Soames's mission. Campagna's prime concern was what would happen once Bastide was out of the way. He was not sure what agreement Mondolino had made with Soames. Grondona was expecting Soames back in Nice but if he learned what had happened he'd have a tactical advantage over Mondolino; a standing threat to use as he saw fit.

"Paulo," Mondolino said, "you are worried about l'Anglais, aren't you?"

Campagna, surprised, had to nod, admitting his concern. The old man may be acting strange, he thought, but he hasn't lost his perception.

"I did not choose him on a whim," Mondolino explained, resting his chin on the crook of his cane. "I am sure he has already made plans to leave France, once he is paid. He is not a brilliant person but he is certainly not stupid enough to return to Nice. Grondona doesn't like his people working for someone else. He'd feed him to the fishes if he found out. But don't worry. At this point there are only three persons involved: l'Anglais, you and myself. Soon, there'll be only the two of us."

Campagna turned toward Mondolino frowning. "I've asked Testu Constanza to see to it," Mondolino explained. "Testu asks no questions. He needs no explanations. We shall make it look like an act of unofficial police vengeance. That will keep them busy."

The sound of church bells carried to them from the small chapel perched on a nearby hill. Campagna said nothing. He was glad the old man was thinking ahead but this time he seemed to have omitted the possibility of something going wrong.

"Allez," Mondolino said putting his weight on his cane. "The sun is too hot and it is time for lunch."

Bastide took some ice from the refrigerator and sighed with relief. There had been a certain amount of stiffness at the start but the two women seemed to be compatible. His mother had made a point of addressing Janine as mademoiselle until Janine had insisted she use her first name. He knew Janine's obvious enthusiasm for the *mas* and its furnishings had impressed his mother. They were now on a tour of the old farmhouse and he was enjoying a few brief moments alone. The aged retriever had stayed with him, fixing him with its adoring rheumy eyes, waiting for him to take the Rossi 12 gauge out of its rack for a rabbit hunt.

He could hear them upstairs, their voices rising and falling as they moved from room to room. He walked into the kitchen, glass in hand and lifted the lid of a dented copper pot to inhale the unctuous perfume of the bubbling *canard aux olives*. He picked up a spoon and savored the sauce. It brought instant memories of childhood. He looked out on the orchard, noting the encroaching weeds and wild brambles. There was a burst of laughter and they both appeared at the head of the stairs.

"I have seen some of your secrets," Janine declared, waving a photo. "Was this your first love?"

He examined the print. It was a group shot taken at his old lycée. He recognized himself but he couldn't remember the girl. He'd had his arm around her waist.

"Nathalie Forge," his mother said, smiling. "Don't you remember her? Her father sold fine olive oil."

"Ah yes, Nathalie," he acknowledged. "She had heavy legs."

"How ungallant," Janine chided him. "From this photo I'd say she had more attractive attributes."

"Roger always liked his women with flesh on their bones," his mother said.

"Then nothing has changed," he replied. "Can I fix you two an *apéritif?*"

They moved into the sitting room where he poured a glass of port for his mother, a Noilly Prat and lemon for Janine and a *pastis* for himself. There were plates of crisp, puff paste *amuse-gueules* filled with anchovies and toasted almonds on the coffee table.

"Take off your jacket, Roger," his mother suggested. "It's stiffling in here."

He served their drinks, excused himself and went upstairs. He'd almost removed his jacket when they'd arrived until he'd remembered the Manurhin revolver on his hip. He'd always spared his mother any exposure to the more lethal side of his profession. Today's visit was no exception. He went into his room, removed the holstered Magnum and put it in the top drawer of the *commode.*

Soames parked his rented car and stood for a moment looking at the small road leading to what appeared to be an old *mas.* He could see patches of its tiled roof through a stand of bamboo. A long, descending stretch of the Route Departmentale had given him a view of the Peugeot turning off onto the side road in a cloud of dust. Soames unzipped his light jacket and readjusted the Desert Eagle in its shoulder holster, insuring the butt was free and the safety strap loosened.

He examined the overhead wires and located the telephone line. He examined the roadway, found it empty and climbed quickly up the telephone pole to the junction box. He cut the line with a folding Opinel knife and slid down the pole to the ground. He wiped some perspiration from his forehead and disappeared into the bushes.

It was much cooler out of the sun. A heavy growth of pine trees had shed their needles on the sandy soil, providing a soft carpet that muffled the sound of his movements. He made a long swing to his left, away from the *mas,* stopping periodically to listen. He knew it would be a question of compromise between speed and caution. He wanted to finish the job and leave as soon as possible. He also wanted to *bousiller* Bastide when he was alone. He could not afford witnesses and for practical reasons he had no desire to kill anyone else. This, he recognized, would be his biggest problem. There would be the woman . . . plus whoever else might be at the *mas.*

He stopped by a small creek and splashed some cool water on his face. The cicadas were reaching their midday crescendo, white butterflies darted close to the stream's surface and not one car had passed on the road he'd just left. He leapt over the creek and turned in the general direction of the *mas,* well away from the small approach road.

Joe Bellot caught Mattei outside the Hôtel de Police on his way to lunch. "Ho, Babar!" he shouted, running to catch up with the Corsican.

"What's up?" Mattei asked.

"Where's Bastide?" Bellot asked.

"Visiting his mother in Arles. Why?"

"There's something I don't like," Bellot told him. "Soames still hasn't returned to Nice. One of our informers there has passed the word that Grondona is very upset about it."

"So?" Mattei shrugged. "That's natural. After all, l'Anglais is Grondona's top gun. Maybe he's taking the cure."

"It's just strange," Bellot said, rubbing his chin. "You don't suppose Mondolino and Grondona are going to start chopping at each other again now that Moukli's out of the way?"

"Bonne mère!" Mattei exclaimed. "Why look for trouble when it isn't there? The war is over, the city is quiet, we have an easy weekend ahead of us and my wife will put my *zizi* in a sausage slicer if I'm late for lunch."

"Will Bastide be calling in?"

"I doubt it. He left orders not to be disturbed unless Aynard fell down the stairs and broke his neck."

"Well," Bellot said seriously, "tell him I want to talk to him about Soames as soon as he gets back."

"Done," Mattei replied. *"Au revoir!"*

Mattei nursed the engine of his Mercedes into life and kept it rumbling with a full throttle. He drove through the tunnel under the Vieux Port, up past the Foreign Legion recruiting station at the Fort Saint-Nicolas and parked near his apartment on the rue Decazes. He pulled a shopping bag full of cheese, bread and lettuce from the backseat and locked the car. He nodded a greeting to a fellow tenant as he entered the hallway and walked to the elevator. Someone was standing in the shadow of the stairs.

"Halimi!" Mattei hissed, "what the hell are you doing here?"

"I am sorry," Halimi whispered, stepping back under the stairwell. "I know this is not wise but it is a matter of importance."

"Spit it out," Mattei ordered.

"It may mean nothing," Halimi said, "but . . ."

"Just tell me!" Mattei snapped, losing patience.

"Someone who supplies me with information has noted the same car parked near the Hôtel de Police twice. A rental Volkswagen."

"You came here to tell me that?"

"If you would allow me to continue. The car in itself is unimportant. But my friend, who has a sharp eye, noted something disturbing. The driver of this car arrived each morning shortly after your friend Bastide drove into the police parking lot and he definitely saw him drive off when Bastide left . . . obviously following the Inspector."

"How does he know Bastide?"

"He works across the street from the Hôtel de Police. He watches the coming and goings. He knows the faces. He exchanges greetings with many policemen. Bastide is well known and easy to recognize."

"I don't know this *mec*," Mattei said.

Halimi's shrug implied that Mattei was not very observant.

"Did he recognize the driver?"

"No, but he described him. A burly fellow with abundant dark hair, about thirty, wearing a light windbreaker jacket. He did not get close enough to give further details. As the driver was seated, he does not know how tall he was."

Mattei frowned. The vague description could fit Soames. He remembered what Bellot had just told him.

"Here," Mattei said, pushing the shopping bag at Halimi, "deliver this to my wife. Fourth floor left. Tell her I'm out on a case and won't be home for lunch. That's all. Don't tell her anything else. Don't answer any questions. Just leave."

Mattei hurried out the door. Halimi sighed and pressed the elevator button. He broke the tip off one of the *baguettes* and began to chew on it as the small, wrought-iron cage rattled down to the ground floor.

Janine was enjoying herself. She watched Bastide over the rim of her glass, her eyes sparkling with contained humor. Under the effects of her *apéritif* and the Gigondas his mother had regaled them with tales of Monsieur Fontet's continued unwelcome attentions. She swore her aged neighbor was a satyr and told them he'd recently purchased some high-powered binoculars to spy on her. She'd also attempted to feel out Janine on religion without much success. Bastide had hurriedly changed the subject but he was now the target of a new inquisition. His mother's approach was obvious and innocent but Janine was amused as Bastide squirmed under his mother's unsubtle interrogation.

"But you've been an inspector for years," Madame Bastide reasoned. "Surely, it is time for a promotion. All the great work you've done. Do you have enemies among your superiors?"

"But no, *Maman,*" Bastide replied, cutting the last sliver of meat off a duck leg. "There are just so many positions. They must be vacated before one can move up the ladder. It takes time."

"Too much time, if you ask me," she said gravely. "Don't you agree, Janine?"

"Roger tells me little about his work," Janine said.

"That's more than he tells me," his mother complained. "I think . . ."

"Maman, the duck was delicious," Bastide said quickly. "You haven't lost your touch."

"Why should I? Here, let me take your plates and get the salad."

"No," Janine said, "let me. You two sit and relax."

She gathered their plates and went into the kitchen.

"I believe she is a nice person," his mother said. "A bit distant, but nice. I can see she has a sense of humor."

"She does," Bastide agreed. "I like her very much."

"Just *like?*" his mother said, narrowing her eyes.

"You sound like a trial judge," he told her chuckling. "I should have brought my lawyer."

"She is well made," his mother continued. "I am sure she'd give you healthy children."

"Oh là là," he protested, putting up his hand, "you'll stop at nothing to fill these chairs with grandchildren!"

She looked down at the tablecloth, her fingers playing with the napkin. When she looked up again her eyes were filled with tears. "I don't have much time left," she said softly.

He put his hand on hers, feeling an unaccustomed and painful tenderness.

Soames separated the tangle of wild berry bushes with one hand and examined the rear of the *mas.* He saw a flicker of movement through what appeared to be the kitchen window. It looked as if someone was working over a sink but the sun was in his eyes. He moved to the shade of some cyprus trees, and hid behind an old, unused henhouse. He'd noted the Peugeot was the only car parked in front of the *mas.* There was a good chance that Bastide and the woman were alone inside. It was now almost 2:30 p.m. Soames decided to give himself two hours. If, during that time, he didn't learn who was in the *mas,* or Bastide didn't show himself, he'd have to go in after him. He left the henhouse and moved back about thirty feet to the thick bamboo growing at the edge of a dry irrigation ditch. The location provided cover but he could still see the *mas.* He sat down on the edge of the ditch, took a handkerchief from his pocket and cleaned the lenses of his dark glasses. He wouldn't be able to watch the Peugeot but he should hear the engine if someone were to use the car. He calculated that he could sprint to the entry road to intercept whoever it might be before they left the property. Soames put his glasses back on, removed the Desert Eagle from its holster and wiped the fine film of dust off the handgrip and butt.

Bastide blew a cloud of cigar smoke toward the fireplace and smiled down at the retriever. The old dog had put its heavy head on Bastide's knee and was looking up at him expectantly.

"Have you ever seen a dog smile?" Bastide asked Janine, putting down his coffee cup.

"I suppose I have," she replied, stretching and lying back among the cushions on the divan.

"Just look at this one. He's been smiling ever since we got here.

Now, he wants to go for a walk and he won't give me a minute's peace until we do."

"What's his name?"

"Dauphin," Bastide replied. "Good old Dauphin. He was a great gun dog with a soft mouth and the courage of a lion. Now, it's all sleep and dreams." He rubbed Dauphin's neck and the heavy tail tapped on the coffee table.

"Do you think your mother is asleep?" Janine asked.

"Yes. She takes her siesta every day at this time. She sleeps for one hour and comes down refreshed and thinking about preparing the next meal."

"Next meal! I couldn't eat another thing today."

"That's what you think," Bastide said. "By dusk you'll have an appetite. It's the air here. It's not like the city. You'll see."

"Come over here and kiss me," Janine told him.

Bastide pushed Dauphin out of the way, walked across the room and bent over her. He leaned closer and they kissed. When they separated she looked into his eyes.

"Your mother made it clear that she'd arranged a separate bedroom for me," she said smiling.

"I guessed as much," Bastide replied. "She has old-fashioned ideas."

"I suppose it won't hurt us," Janine said.

"We'll make up for it when we get back to Marseille," Bastide promised. "Now let's not keep Dauphin waiting. Let's go for that walk and work off the effects of our lunch."

"It's too hot, Roger. Can't we just doze here for awhile? It's so peaceful."

"If you insist," he agreed. "I'll give you half an hour. Then I'll show you where we used to swim when I was a kid. There's a finger of the Rhône that winds close to the rear of our property. It's shaded by acacias and full of crayfish."

"I can't wait," Janine murmured and shut her eyes.

Mattei tried to keep his Mercedes at its maximum speed and made a special effort to ignore the ominous, repetitive clicking from its overworked engine. Lenoir sat next to him, one hand braced on the dashboard, the other clasping his seat belt as they swung out to pass heavy trucks and slow moving sedans.

"You need air in your tires," the young detective said, wiping some perspiration from his forehead. "You've got a slight shimmy."

"It's nothing," Mattei told him, his eyes on the road and a heavy hand on the horn to force a small Fiat into the slow lane.

"Do you really think Bastide's in danger?" Lenoir asked.

"No, I just wanted to show you how fast this antique could go," Mattei replied, giving Lenoir a quick glance of disapproval.

"But Soames would be mad to go after a *flic,*" Lenoir reasoned. "Particularly now that the heat is off. It doesn't make sense."

"It does if the price is right."

"Then it's not a personal vendetta?"

"Professionals like Soames can't afford personal vendettas," Mattei explained. "If he's after Bastide it's on someone's orders."

"I can't see why Grondona would take such a risk."

"Who said anything about Grondona?"

"Soames is his man. He's not working for anyone else . . . is he?"

"I don't know. That's what we've got to find out."

Mattei slowed as they bumped into a dusty stretch of highway. Yellow signs indicated road work ahead and black arrows warned of single lane traffic. A workman with a red flag waved them down. They had to stop, waiting for oncoming traffic. Mattei pounded slowly on the wheel, reciting a litany of muffled curses. When the road was finally clear he gunned the engine and sped forward leaving the signalman in a cloud of yellow dust. They had just settled into a steady speed with no traffic ahead when they heard the police klaxons. Mattei raised his eyes to the rearview mirror. Two white-helmeted *motards* of the Gendarmerie were in hot pursuit and closing fast.

"It's not possible," Mattei groaned while Lenoir craned his neck to look over his shoulder.

"You'd better slow down," Lenoir said, "before one of them ruptures himself."

Mattei took his foot off the accelerator and they glided to a stop on the shoulder of the highway. One *motard* pulled in ahead of them, the other stopped behind. They took their time dismounting and steadying their cycles before approaching the Mercedes. The first *motard* approached the driver's window and touched his helmet.

"Messieurs," he said, "get out, if you will."

Mattei poked his open wallet at the *motard,* displaying his police identity card. "Mattei," he growled impatiently, "Police Judiciare. This is sous-inspecteur Lenoir. We're on an urgent case."

The *motard* raised his tinted glasses to read the identity card. "I see," he said uncertainly and gestured for his partner to join them. He passed Mattei's wallet to the other *motard* who read it and peered into the car. "You're not using an official vehicle?" he asked.

"No," Mattei snapped. "we're from homicide. An inspector is in danger and if we're not back on the road in three minutes I'll have your balls in a nutcracker . . . all four of them! Understood?"

"Sorry, Inspector," the *motard* said, handing back the wallet. "Do you need an escort?"

"Get out of the way," Mattei ordered, slamming the Mercedes in gear. "If there are any more of you on the road between here and Arles, radio ahead and tell them to leave us alone."

The afternoon heat and the buzzing of the cicadas was soporific. Soames was having a hard time keeping his eyes open. There had been no movement from the *mas* and he had already planned his move. First, he'd puncture the Peugeot's tires to make sure no one could escape. Then he'd enter through the back door. He doubted it was locked during the day. People in the country were lax about such things. If it was, he'd have to check the windows. If that didn't work he'd go to the front door posing as a lost motorist seeking directions. That method would increase the risk but he didn't have any other choice. He shifted his position, waved away a persistent mosquito and watched a file of ants struggling up the side of the irrigation ditch laden with white eggs.

The sound of a door being opened brought him fully alert. He rose silently behind the screen of dry bamboo and slid the Desert Eagle Magnum from its holster. The dog came out first. Soames frowned. He hadn't counted on a dog. Then there was the woman. Bastide appeared last. The inspector paused on the threshold and shouted something over his shoulder. So there was at least one other person to worry about. He cocked his pistol and locked the thumb safety. An upward flick of his thumb would release it.

Bastide called Janine to his side and gestured toward a lumpy patch of bare ground. "This was my vegetable garden," he told her. "I produced some prize radishes one year. There were carrots, green beans, beets and onions. I was quite a gardener. That peach tree over there was planted when I was ten. Look at it now. Here, let's sample the fruit." Bastide walked to the tree and picked two down-covered, red-streaked yellow peaches. He wiped them on his sleeve and handed one to Janine.

Soames watched, gauging the distance. He could drop them from where he stood but he couldn't take any chances. It had to be perfect. He moved closer to the henhouse, keeping his eye on the dog. It was obviously old and slow moving but it was an added complication. Bastide and the woman were standing under a tree with their backs turned to him. The wall of the henhouse would provide him with a good hand brace for his weapon. It was too bad about the woman but she should have stayed inside.

Tired of waiting for his master and impatient to start on the promised walk, Dauphin shuffled away from the peach tree and paused, waiting for Bastide and Janine to follow. He raised his black snout, sniffing the air. Soames reached the henhouse and knelt beside it. He brushed away a spider web, braced his heavy pistol against the sagging wall in a double-handed grip and brought the rear and front sights together on Bastide's back.

An aggressive growl issued from Dauphin's chest as he began to lumber toward the henhouse. His teeth were bared and he moved surprisingly fast for such an old dog. Bastide, surprised, turned and called Dauphin but the retriever ignored the summons. Soames cursed and shifted the sights onto the dog. The animal was only fifteen feet away when he squeezed the trigger. The Magnum's blast flushed some pigeons out of the bushes. The heavy slug lifted Dauphin into the air and threw him backward onto the ground, flecks of his blood darkening the dry soil.

Soames stepped out from behind the henhouse, the Magnum leveled at Bastide and Janine. "Walk toward me," he told them in a flat, calm voice. "Hands behind your heads."

They obeyed in stunned silence. Bastide's mind raced. He was sure he was facing Soames. The gunman was fulfilling a contract. There was no other explanation. He knew they were facing immediate death. He'd never felt so helpless in his life. They walked past Soames and he fell in behind them. He'd decided to finish it behind the screen of bamboo, in the irrigation ditch. Then he'd find whoever was in the house and plant them with the *flic* and his woman.

"I don't know who you are," Bastide lied, as they approached the bamboo-screened ditch, "but you're making a mistake."

"Keep walking," the gunman responded.

"I'm a police inspector," Bastide continued. "You don't want to kill a *flic.*"

"Climb up on the edge of the ditch," Soames ordered, "both of you."

"Whoever hired you wouldn't want you to hurt this woman," Bastide said. "She has nothing to do with the police."

"Kneel down," Soames told them, moving closer.

Bastide had made up his mind. He'd try to rush their captor. It was their only chance. He'd shout to Janine to run. She might be able to escape. Anything was better than an execution. He was halfway to his knees, muscles tensed, one hand reaching out for the ground to give him some purchase for a sudden desperate rush. The blast of the shotgun made him gasp. He swung around to see Soames going down and his mother standing behind him with the smoking Rossi held tight against her cheek.

"Stay where you are, *salaud!*" she shouted. "That was only one barrel!"

Soames was on his knees, the Desert Eagle still in his right hand. Bastide rushed him as he was trying to lift it, stamped his right forearm into the dirt and wrenched the gun from his fingers. He jammed the barrel under Soame's right ear and pushed him flat.

"Lay still, you bastard," he panted. "It would be a pleasure to kill you."

His mother came forward cautiously. "Is he hurt badly?" she asked. "I aimed at his legs."

Bastide examined the bloody, holed trousers. "He won't be running any races," he said. "Maman, give the shotgun to Janine and get me some rope." She did as she was told.

Janine stood whitefaced, awkwardly holding the shotgun. "I think I'm going to be sick," she murmured.

"It's not the moment," Bastide told her, "but if you have to . . . take your finger off the trigger and point that thing at the ground."

She turned her back and vomited, her body jerking in spasms.

When his mother returned with a long, stout piece of rope he tied Soames's feet and hands together behind his back and passed a coil around his neck.

"There," Bastide said, standing up, "he won't be going anywhere in a hurry." He examined the Magnum in his hand, put the safety on and slid it under his belt. He went to Janine, retrieved the shotgun and handed it to his mother. He put his arm around Janine's shoulder.

"Is it over?" he asked.

She nodded, wiping her mouth with a handkerchief.

"Good," he said. "Can you make some telephone calls for me?"

"Yes," she replied, clearing her throat.

"Call the Gendarmerie in Arles. Tell them to send some men over here to pick up a wounded prisoner. Then try to get Mattei, explain what happened and ask him to come. If you can't get Mattei try Inspector Bellot of anti-gang. I'd do it but I don't want to leave him."

"He was going to kill both of you," Bastide's mother said softly when Janine had gone into the house. The shotgun was shaking in her trembling hands.

"Put the gun away, Maman," he told her. "We won't need it now."

"Roger," Janine called from the kitchen door, "the line is dead."

"Naturally," Bastide murmured, frowning down at Soames. "You'll have to take your car into Arles."

Soames muttered something but Bastide couldn't hear him. "What's that?" Bastide asked.

"I'm losing blood," Soames said, trying to look over his shoulder at his shot-peppered legs.

"So you are," Bastide replied, "but not enough to worry about."

He crouched down beside Soames to search him. He found a wallet in his back pocket and examined the papers.

"I knew it," Bastide murmured, "Grondona's going to have a lot of explaining to do. Your life won't be worth a *centime*, Soames, once your playmates know you've muffed it."

"Roger!" Mattei shouted, pounding around the corner of the *mas* like a freight train, Lenoir at his heels. "We just got here. We stopped Janine as she was pulling out. What the hell happened?"

"An unwelcome visitor," Bastide told him, indicating Soames. "The bastard tried to kill us."

"He's been following you in Marseille," Mattei said.

"How did you get here so quickly?" Bastide asked.

"We had a tip."

Bastide sighed. "If it wasn't for my mother you'd have found us in that ditch over there."

"*Putain!*" Mattei said, impressed by Soames's wounds. "Shotgun?"

Bastide nodded. "He's lucky it was loaded for birds."

"Where did you get that cannon?" Mattei asked, pointing to the pistol in Bastide's belt.

"It was his," Bastide explained.

"Where's your piece?" Mattei demanded.

"Upstairs in a drawer."

"It's not possible!" Mattei said, shaking his head.

"Look, no lectures!" Bastide snapped. "I'm not in the mood. Lenoir, watch this scum. Babar, contact the Gendarmerie on your radio and get them out here. Then we'll all have a stiff drink and take Soames back to Marseille. I intend to squeeze that son of a bitch till he's dry."

It was almost 3 a.m. when Mattei returned from the holding cell to report on Soames. Bastide had finished five pages of handwritten notes on the incident at the *mas* for his formal report. He took a cigar from his mouth when Mattei walked into the office.

"Well?" Bastide asked.

"Zero," Mattei replied, dropping into his desk chair. "L'Anglais is definitely not talkative. He is following the 'I am only a poor, uninformed soldier' routine. It took me an hour to have him admit he worked for Grondona."

"Who's with him now?"

"Lenoir's perfecting his interrogation technique."

"That ought to confuse him," Bastide commented.

"I think Soames needs a little scare," Mattei suggested.

"No rough stuff. This is too important to hand anyone a legal complaint."

"At this rate we won't know who ordered you planted till next Christmas."

"I'll try to reason with him," Bastide said, crushing his cigar in an ashtray. "The man is no fool. He might respond."

"Good luck," Mattei said, yawning. "I'm going home for a few hours sleep. I'll be back at eight."

The individual holding cell was at the rear of the Hôtel de Police on the basement level. It was separated from the large tank by twenty yards of dank, concrete corridor. The tank was filled with nightly pickups. The vagrants, drunks, prostitutes and pickpockets were sitted in various states of discomfort, their one blanket pulled over their heads to avoid the bright overhead light. Bastide walked past the tank, nodded at a uniformed policeman on duty in the corridor and pointed ahead to Soames's cell. The policeman preceded Bastide to the door and opened it with a large key. Soames was lying on the small, steel spring bed in a corner of the cell. His bandaged legs were raised on a hard pillow and he'd wrapped a blanket around his shoulders.

"Get me a chair," Bastide told the policeman. When the chair arrived he turned it around and straddled it, resting both arms on the back. Soames blinked at him warily from under his mussed hair.

"Soames," Bastide began, "I'm going to talk and I suggest you listen. I won't be offering you a cigarette, or asking how your leg feels or if there is anyone on the outside you'd like to contact. I've given up acting the sympathetic *flic.* A very short time ago you tried to kill me and someone I care about. You tried to turn us both into maggot meat. It shouldn't be hard for you to understand that you aren't one of my favorite people. I really don't care what happens to you now. I'm only interested in knowing who ordered the hit. The sooner you tell us that, the sooner we can work out your future."

"I . . ." Soames started to respond.

"Ta gueule!" Bastide shouted. "I'm not finished. You're probably thinking that a few years behind bars might be an acceptable price to pay while the stir you created fades away. Well, let me disillusion you. I'm all for putting you out on the street again as soon as possible."

Soames raised himself on one elbow. "I see no reason for keeping you under lock and key as long as you insist on playing the deaf-mute," Bastide continued. "Knowing this city I think it would be much more profitable for us to let you go—under instructions not to leave Marseille—and keep a close watch on you. Not to protect you, but to see how soon someone else takes a personal interest in you. It would be sort of a hare and hounds proposition . . . with you as the hare. Just think what your friends would think. They'd have a lot of unanswered questions. Why was he released so quickly? Did he sing? What did he tell the police? Is he a plant? You'd have to move a lot. It's hard to hide from your friends."

"You're bluffing," Soames said. "Trying to hit a cop is good for at least five years. You can't let me go. The courts wouldn't allow it."

"You're stupid," Bastide responded calmly. "I'm the cop you tried to kill, remember? My testimony is crucial. We work as a team here. Once we agree on something we don't have second thoughts. Look at it from our point of view. Once on the outside, you'll draw the peöple we're looking for . . . like flies to shit. It'll be a lot easier than spending public funds for a long drawn-out hearing and wasting the time of busy policemen and judges. If anything happens to you in the process . . . well, that would certainly be all right with me."

"You don't scare me, Bastide," Soames said, pushing himself into a sitting position. "You're spouting fairy tales."

Bastide stood up, lifted the chair and put it outside the cell. He turned to look down on Soames. "Think about it," Bastide told him. "I might be able to get you out of here tomorrow." Bastide stepped out of the cell and swung the heavy, barred door shut. The policeman came back to lock the cell.

"One other thought," Bastide said before leaving. "You probably won't be alone long. We might be moving you into a four-man cell soon. You're enough of a pro to know that prison isn't the safest place in the world when your old friends want to get to you. Sleep well."

A blinding ray of sunshine brightened the office. Bastide, Mattei and Lenoir, bleary-eyed and silent, were drinking coffee at their desks. Bastide had spent an hour the night before preparing the stage for their playacting. Soames's personal effects were on Bastide's desk: wallet, a cheap cricket lighter, the dark glasses, his belt and shoelaces, a small book of addresses that Bastide had photostated and Soames's spotted windbreaker.

"The coffee gets worse," Mattei said. "They must be using the old grounds." His complaint hung in the air, unchallenged. Bastide checked his watch, put his cup aside and glanced at the door.

"He should be here any minute," he told them. "Let me do the talking."

"If Aynard knew what we were doing he'd have us back on the beat within hours," Mattei volunteered. "Do you think it will work?"

"We'll know soon enough. Listen, I think they're coming."

Someone tapped on the door and Bastide told them to come in. Soames entered awkwardly on his crutches, assisted over the threshold by a uniformed policeman. He blinked in the bright light. He'd grown a dark stubble during his overnight incarceration.

"Lenoir," Bastide said, "a chair for our visitor."

Lenoir gave up his desk chair to Soames and took the prisoner's crutches.

"Everything's worked out for the best," Bastide told Soames. "We're going to let you walk. Your effects are all here. You better check them to be sure nothing's missing."

Soames looked at each detective in turn. "I don't understand," he said. "What does this mean?"

"It means you're free to go," Bastide said flatly. "Check your effects and sign this release form. Inspector Mattei will give you a paper that tells you what you can and cannot do. Among other things, you are not permitted to leave Marseille and you will be prepared to assist us at any time in our on-going investigations."

Soames drew in on himself, like a slug under salt. "This is not possible," he murmured. "You can't release me! I . . . I demand legal counsel."

"To keep yourself in jail?" Bastide asked, feigning astonishment. "Come now, we're giving you a chance few gunmen ever get. If you insist, of course, we could contact Grondona or even Mondolino to see if they could supply one of their lawyers. It would be a new experience for them . . . arguing the case of someone who prefers les Baumettes to freedom. *Allez*, let's get this over with. We have other things to do."

Soames stared at Bastide. Bastide returned his gaze without flinching until Soames looked away.

"*Ça va*," Soames finally said. "I want to talk to you . . . alone."

Bastide nodded to Mattei and Lenoir. They left the office, taking Soames's escort with them. The door clicked shut. Bastide folded his hands and raised his head, waiting.

"I'll want protection," Soames said, his voice almost a whisper, "and a transfer far from here."

"I think we can arrange that," Bastide said. "Come on, empty your sack!"

"It was Mondolino," Soames told him. "The old man wanted your skin."

"Who else was involved?" Bastide asked.

"It was a personal thing," Soames said, "between the two of us."

Bastide stood up and exhaled audibly. He walked to the window, unwrapped a cigar and lit it. "Now, I'll tell you what you're going to do," he said, enunciating each word carefully. "You're going to repeat what you told me in front of witnesses and a stenographer. Then we're going to see a juge d'instruction to get the legal process under way. When the time comes you'll appear in court and repeat all the details you're about to give us."

"You promise me protection?" Soames asked.

"I wouldn't want to lose you now," Bastide told him. "You're too important . . . for the moment. Fate is a strange thing, Soames. Not too many hours ago you were trying to kill me and now I'm your protector."

Bastide, Mattei and Lenoir got out of a police sedan in front of Mondolino's villa. Bellot and one of his men were in the car behind them. A fresh *mistral* was bending the tall trees and whipping dust swirls off the unplanted soil near the sidewalk.

"Remember," Bastide said as they walked to the gate, "this is my collar."

"I put a car behind, just in case," Bellot said.

Bastide pressed the bell and waited to speak into the intercom.

"Who is it?" Paul Campagna's voice demanded.

"Inspector Bastide. It's a matter of urgency. It has to do with Monsieur Mondolino's safety."

There was a long pause, then a click. The gate swung open. They hurried over the gravel drive, past the rose garden and up the stairs. Paul Campagna was waiting at the door.

"What is this?" he asked obviously disconcerted by their numbers.

"Take us to Mondolino, quickly," Bastide said, "or stand aside."

"But . . ." Campagna began. Bastide pushed past him into the villa. Testu Constanza appeared in the hall, blocking the way to Mondolino's study.

"Take him," Bastide told Mattei. Constanza found himself face against the wall, the barrel of Mattei's Manurhin digging into his ribs. Bastide pushed open the door and stepped into the study. Mondolino looked up in surprise from an armchair by the window. His yellow-tinged white hair seemed to glow in the afternoon light and his small eyes narrowed as the detectives entered his private domain.

"They refused to tell me what this is all about," Campagna shouted from the doorway.

Mondolino shrugged as if the intrusion was a small inconvenience. "What does the young inspector want," he asked, scratching his cheek with the crook of his cane.

"Antoine Mondolino," Bastide said, "you are under arrest on charges of attempted murder, the hiring of a paid assassin to cause bodily harm to a senior officer of the Police Judiciare and a number of other offenses, including ordering the murder of one Bachir Moukli in Algiers. You'll find all the charges listed here." Bastide threw the warrant onto Mondolino's lap. The old man looked at the paper for a moment before brushing it off his knees onto the floor. Campagna came forward slowly, picked up the warrant and began to read it. His face was flushed and his hand unsteady.

"You will come with us now," Bastide snapped.

"I go nowhere," Mondolino replied. "Paulo, contact Perret and get my lawyers over here . . ."

"Oh no," Bastide interrupted, "not this time. No special privileges, Mondolino. You can see your lawyers when they visit you in jail. Campagna, you've got five minutes to pack a bag for him or he goes as is."

Campagna left the study accompanied by one of Bellot's men. Bastide felt Mondolino's eyes on him.

"*Alors, vieux,*" he said, "do I look like a ghost? I'm sure if you'd done the job yourself I'd have stopped breathing long ago. Things aren't like they used to be, are they?"

"I won't go," Mondolino rasped, his face a mask of hate.

"Get him out of here," Bastide ordered.

Bellot and Mattei moved forward, dodged a blow from Mondolino's cane, lifted the old man from his chair and carried him out of the study.

"Stay here," Bastide told Lenoir. "I don't want anything touched in the villa, particularly Mondolino's files." He reached the front door in time to see Mattei and Bellot easing Mondolino into a car. He was still yelling in protest but his voice had weakened. Campagna came down the stairway with a small suitcase in his hand.

"Come along," Bastide said, crooking his finger, "we have some questions to ask you too."

Commissaire Aynard's office was crowded. Several bottles of champagne, glasses and some dishes of salted nuts were placed on the white cloth spread over his conference table. Bastide stood between the Commissaire and a portly representative from the Préfecture. Mattei and Bellot were among the group of detectives and uniformed officers. Aynard shot his cuffs, adjusted his spectacles and cleared his throat.

"If you please," he said signaling for silence. "I have a pleasant duty to perform today. We in the police seldom have time for celebrations but when we do, they are particularly significant. We are here to honor an outstanding colleague, someone who is known and respected by all of us." Aynard paused to smile in Bastide's direction. Bastide was uncomfortable and hot. The hypocrisy of Aynard's performance irritated him.

"He probably rehearsed all this in front of a mirror," Mattei whispered to Bellot.

"I'm speaking of Inspector Bastide," Aynard continued, "who was instrumental in ending what could have been the worst gang war this city has seen for years."

A brief round of applause filled the room.

"It has often been said that our work goes unnoticed and unrewarded. This is, of course, untrue . . ."

"*Merde,*" Mattei mumbled.

"Today I have the privilege of announcing the promotion of our friend Roger Bastide to Inspecteur Principal."

"Bravo!" Bellot said loudly, drawing a searing glare from Aynard.

"Inspecteur Principal Bastide," Aynard concluded, "on behalf of the Minister of the Interior, I present you with the papers attesting to your new rank and my own best wishes on this happy day."

A police photographer recorded the presentation, camera clicking and strobe light flashing.

"Now," Aynard announced, "if you would all come to the buffet, we will drink a toast to our guest of honor."

Bastide moved through the crush to receive the congratulations of his friends. Mattei gave him a bear hug, grinning broadly.

"It was long overdue," Mattei murmured as corks popped and the wine was poured.

Aynard raised a token glass, proposed the toast and the volume of conversation rose.

Bastide put his arm on Bellot's shoulder. "You deserve to share the credit," he said.

"Next time," Bellot replied, winking. "I think they can only afford one promotion a year."

Mattei appeared beside them, frowning at his glass.

"*Vin mousseux,*" he grumbled. "The cheap bastard didn't even spring for champagne!"

Bastide and Mattei drove to La Mère Pascal after the promotion celebration. Janine and Marie Mattei were waiting for them. Dominique popped a bottle of Bollinger as they pushed open the door and Jean, the aged waiter, shuffled forward to shake Bastide's hand. Dominique came around from behind her bar to plant two generous kisses on Bastide's cheeks before filling their glasses. She poured champagne for a young couple sitting at one of the tables and asked them to join in her toast.

"To one of the few *poulets* in Marseille who is consistently *sympathique!*" she announced with a flourish. After they'd drunk to Bastide, Dominique led them to a specially prepared table.

"I only hope your new rank doesn't mean La Mère Pascal will be below your status from now on," she said as they took their seats.

"No fear of that," Bastide replied.

"Good," Dominique said, reassured. "If you hadn't said that I was prepared to serve you frozen peas and a hamburger. As it is, I have condemned you to drink champagne throughout your meal. Now, I must get back to my kitchen."

Janine leaned across the table to squeeze Bastide's hand. "Congratulations, Monsieur l'Inspecteur Principal," she murmured. "I'm proud of you."

"To us," he replied, raising his glass.

"What are we eating on this special occasion?" Madame Mattei asked, sitting on the edge of her chair like a plump pigeon.

"Dominique has prepared a special menu," Janine told her.

The two hour meal began with *médaillons à la creme d'oursins.* The delicious and delicate *médaillons,* made with a purée of fresh sea urchins and beaten egg flavored with cayenne, were served on small slices of crusty pastry. The second offering, canneloni in individual dishes napped with a sauce *coulis* under a snowfall of melting, grated cheese came to the table hot and bubbling.

Later, Dominique reappeared to help Jean serve the main course of grilled quail nested on a bed of toast, moistened with their own juices and accompanied by a molded pyramid of rice spiced by a touch of saffron.

The champagne corks popped, Jean did his best to keep their glasses filled, and the conversation was loud and punctuated with laughter. Bastide proposed a toast to Bellot. Mattei did the same for Lenoir. Mattei's wife ate with an enthusiasm that threatened the stitching of her gown. With the salad and cheese board out of the way, Dominique produced a thick earthenware bowl of her rich chocolate *mousse,* insisting that they each take a hefty serving. She returned with a bottle of aged Armagnac when Jean filled their *demitasse* cups with strong coffee. Bastide insisted that Mattei accept one of his Havanas and the two men eased back in their chairs, contentedly drawing on their cigars, snifters of Armagnac in their hands.

"Look at you," Marie Mattei said to her husband. "Your eyes are almost shut."

"Did you ever hear the one about Napoleon and the mother superior?" Mattei asked.

"Oh no," his wife laughed, shaking her head. "When he starts to tell Corsican jokes it's time to go home."

"I think you could use some sleep too," Janine told Bastide.

"The women are suddenly in charge," Bastide said grinning. "But they're right. First we must compliment the chef."

He got up and walked unsteadily into the kitchen. Janine and Marie Mattei exchanged knowing looks. Bastide returned with Dominique who was duly praised and applauded. Bastide fumbled for his wallet but Dominique pushed it back into his pocket.

"We'll take care of all that tomorrow," she told him. "In any case, the champagne was offered by the house."

They said their goodnights outside. Mattei's wife took the driver's seat of the Mercedes despite Babar's halfhearted protests. Bastide and Janine waved them off and began walking back to Bastide's apartment. He put his arm around her and pulled her close.

The streets were almost empty, the humming street lamps threw patterns of amber light on the pavement and a stray cat blinked at them from the shadows. Far off, in the direction of the rue Paradis, they could hear the repetitive hee-haw of a klaxon as a police vehicle sped toward the Canebière.

About the author

Howard R. Simpson, a former U.S. Foreign Service Officer, is now a consultant on international terrorism and a newspaper columnist. One of his last Foreign Service assignments was as American Consul General, Marseille. He now lives in the Republic of Ireland. A GATHERING OF GUNMEN is his fourth novel for The Crime Club, following *Junior Year Abroad.*